Love Waits

A Novel by

Maureen E. Broderick

D1523794

Baxter Books
Connecticut, USA
1999

LCCN 98-072570

ISBN 0-9664483-5-9

*Book design, composition and cover composition
    by Hermann Beck, Printtable, Inc., Stamford, CT
Cover design by Corinne Thieme, Stamford, CT
Printed and bound by BookCrafters, Chelsea, MI*

For
My Family
Patrick, Deirdre and
Valerie

For
My Parents
William and Elinor

For
Tana

December 18, 1998

To Missy,

Maybe you'll recognize the backstage characters I've thrown together into my characters.

Maureen E. Broderick

About The Author

A novel will come to you as in a dream. "The words of one of my favorite professors, Sr Ann Cyril, SND. I, of course, took her literally and indeed dreamed of my characters Bret, Maddie and Monika, names and all. The end result, **Love Waits**, my first novel."

Maureen E. Broderick's "checkered career" has encompassed wife, mother of two daughters, fashion model, receptionist, office manager, church organist and vocal soloist, music teacher, theater box-office manager, and wardrobe supervisor/dresser. Born in Weymouth, Massachusetts, raised and educated in Boston (BA English, Emmanuel College) she currently calls Connecticut home.

Love Waits

I

I've got time, Maddie convinced herself as she steadily inched toward the backstage door. Once through, she braced her back against its forward motion, making sure no noise would disturb the almost breathless silence surrounding the dialogue emanating from the stage.

Go for it! She ran down the hallway, across the sixty foot lobby, up the business office staircase, two steps at a time, and sprinted across the balcony that spanned the width of the lobby before reaching her office door.

Panting, she skidded to a stop at her desk, snatched up a manila envelope addressed MADDIE CHASE, PRODUCTION MANAGER, GENESIUS PLAYHOUSE, SOLVANG, CALIFORNIA. "Lord," she gasped, "this forty-something body is in worse shape than I thought!"

In her haste she knocked over the framed picture of her daughter that occupied the corner of her desk. "Whitney, love, I'm sorry. Here you go, back to your place of honor." She returned it lovingly, taking a second to align it properly.

A gunshot echoed through the building, setting her off like a starter's pistol. *Oh, God, they picked up the pace! I'm not going to make it!*

As she frantically ran towards the staircase, the house was plunged into darkness. Nervous murmurs of surprise rippled through the audience as the actors moved with well-rehearsed assurance to their proper change locations backstage.

Maddie's sneakers dug ridges into the lobby carpet as she frantically raced toward her post.

"Where the hell —"

"Over here," Maddie whispered to the searching actor. Her late arrival left her far off-center to his marking and he handed off his coat to the empty space where she should have been standing. As she moved to her right to prevent its fall to the dusty floor, his hand reached out for his change, a robe and scarf. Confusion turned to delight when he realized he'd taken possession of a handful of Maddie's sweatshirt and her left breast.

She backed away and thrust the clothes at his chest, causing him to relinquish his hold. He turned toward the stage whispering, "Oh boy, do I love my work!"

Even though the incident lasted no more than seven seconds, it was too long for Maddie. She leaned against the nearest wall, berating herself. *No problem, you said, Maddie...prop girl sick tonight...Do it yourself, Maddie...You've run wardrobe departments, been a dresser, run props...You can read a cue sheet...You're in great shape...Right! Superman, able to trouble-shoot the production, help wardrobe as well as props...You idiot! There's back-up crew ready and waiting...and Kevin Martin is too important a star to offer him less than his due...unless, of course, you substitute with choice parts of your anatomy! Oh, Lord!*

Tall, dark, handsome TV idol Kevin Martin was toiling through his second show in a year and a half at the Genesius, keeping his stage techniques honed.

Kevin's likable TV persona, Mark Dayton, Palm Springs detective with Cary Grant charm, had endeared him to his devoted following. He was Dayton, not Kevin Martin, to millions of viewers, his versatility lost to them in the restrictions of the single character.

Movies and television introduced actors like Kevin to memory gymnastics through out-of-sequence shooting and almost split-second dialogue changes. It was easy to become reliant on retakes to save a scene but difficult to maintain concentration during mind-numbing spasms of intense, draining, "under the gun," last minute or "come-in-under-budget" filming.

Kevin, a victim of what Ben Cameron, a directing genius equally at home in Hollywood or on Broadway, called the "sublimation of the classical heritage," had received a personal invitation to perform at the theater, named for the patron saint of performers.

Lovingly called the Genny, the theater was the brain child of Ben, founded as a stage craft sanctuary for film-weary actors. *How could any well-trained actor feel fulfilled when only half of his abilities are called upon day after day?*

One week after his sixty-fifth birthday, Ben's years of planning and preparation became reality. He opened his own theater, a complex he'd been quietly building for many years, the place he intended to spend his "golden years" polishing and preserving the rusting stage skills of personally selected screen actors.

Ten years before, only Ben saw the logic in purchasing a sprawling ranch, far off the beaten track between Los Angeles and Santa Barbara. Its isolated locale fulfilled his need to provide a workspace free from intrusion and distraction, essential for the well-known actors he intended to welcome there.

Implementing his hand-picked method in hiring personnel for every department of his theater, he populated his domain with people who believed in his concept.

The year of Ben's purchase coincided with Maddie's landing a receptionist job in a Broadway production office. It wasn't long before her innate love for theater emboldened her to delve into learning the ropes, working days at the office and spending evenings in arts management courses or observing backstage in theaters in which they had productions. For the first time in ages, Maddie felt she was doing the right thing for herself.

Networking in the business became her social life. She realized very soon that what you know is far less important then who are your relations or acquaintances.

Her company usually consulted Ben Cameron first when a plum came along, and when he arrived in New York for a production conference the year after she was hired, the seeds of her future took root.

Thrilled to see his "niece-in-law" again, he took an immediate interest in her plans for the future. She revealed to him her special love for his passion in life, the art of acting.

He sensed her hunger to learn and took an active interest in her courses, often expanding on their scope. Maddie was a willing and able student and impressed him with her capacity to struggle through his challenges and her ability to overcome them.

He insisted to her bosses that she work behind the scenes with him, and thanks to him, her resumé could include her work on three Broadway shows in seven years.

He knew, from the first moment his theater blueprints lay before him, whom he wanted managing his productions. By the time he approached Maddie about The Genny, she was actively seeking a reason to justify a move to the West Coast. Her daughter had signed a movie contract six months earlier, closed her successful one-woman show, and moved to Hollywood. Maddie had the Yellow Pages open to "Movers" before Ben had finished his sales pitch.

Applause! Cheers! Maddie shook her head, surprised she'd spent so much time lost in thought. She pulled off her headset, mercifully free of problem calls from Ben or the stage manager since her mad dash. In less than a minute, post-show backstage activity swirled around her.

With any luck, she wouldn't see Kevin right away. She

knew how unprofessional she'd been and didn't need him to tell her.

Lord, I'm forgetting that envelope! It fell somewhere around here when I reached for that damn coat. She spotted a yellow lump lying near the entrance to the chorus dressing room.

Kevin, standing in the doorway, watched her approach.

Focused solely on the envelope and hoping it wouldn't be kicked around anymore by passing actors and crew, Maddie was blind to him.

"Trying to distract Kevin in a major way? You have no idea how many times I almost blurted out 'breast' for any word starting with a B," he scolded with a smile. "What would Ben have thought?"

Maddie, startled, opened her mouth to speak but thought better of it, seeing cast and crew in the area pause. They sensed something in the air, that the best show of the night was about to begin. "I'm sorry, Kevin. I was trying to do too many things besides filling in and didn't..."

"You're sorry? I'm not! I'm elated!" he proclaimed, raising his voice. "None of you, fellow thespians, can appreciate how very passionate I've become about this hands-on kind of theater."

Maddie shook her head, laughed, and looked toward the assemblage. "At one time or another, everyone here has grabbed the wrong thing in the dark. I've been groped before. Haven't all of you?" She found smiling agreement from one and all.

Kevin slipped his arm around her waist, saying provocatively, "Come, my little tantalizer, to my dressing room, my personal research lab. I feel a desperate need to confirm my findings." He smiled impishly as his eyes drifted slowly towards her bust.

She jabbed her elbow into his side, covering her discomfort with a smile for their audience.

He responded by tightening his hold, turning her towards him and kissing her long and hard on the mouth. A voice rose from the back of the group, singing "He Touched Me" and the others joined in.

Kevin released her slowly, stooped to pick up the envelope at his feet, and placed it in her hand. She clutched it to her chest as she stood silently, embarrassed, confused. He hugged her again as cast and crew laughed and cheered.

"You're beautiful, intelligent, have a great sense of humor, you've got it all," he said for all to hear but continued in almost a whisper, "Now tell me, why so tense? You're as tight as a violin string! You need to relax, unwind. I know you're all work and no play; bet you haven't had a vacation in years. Let Dr. Kevin cure all your ills. I know just the place to do it too, my beach-house at Malibu. Think of it, you, me, the Pacific lulling us to sleep after long, passionate hours of every kind of...."

"Oh, please, you take my breath away," Maddie quipped, trying to hide her confusion with a bantering tone. In the half minute it took him to lead her by the hand he wouldn't release through the chorus's room to his dressing room, she regained some control.

Once at his door, Maddie said, "Now that we've provided the post-show entertainment for the troops, let's get back to reality." She pulled her hand gently out of his. "I'm more of a handful than you think - and I don't mean 36D. Suggesting Malibu to a middle-aged woman could be very dangerous. What if I took you seriously? Kevin, I was a college sophomore when you were born. Your fans would think you'd taken leave of your senses!"

Maddie backed slowly but surely toward the stage door as she spoke. If Kevin harbored any plans to pursue his ideas, she was determined to talk him out of it.

A tormented reprise of the night's events haunted Maddie's drive back to Los Angeles.

The envelope lay on the front seat beside her, still unopened. She glanced at it out of the corner of her eye. *No doubt you're full of nothing but work for me. Looks like somebody* has a swollen importance gland—hand-delivery, private courier. Well, lah-dee-dah!

Can't be that important. I know Ben would tell me if something big was coming down the line. Come to think of it, I didn't see Ben after the show. Hope everything's all right. Maybe he heard about Don Juan Kevin and me. I'll call him when I get home. No, with my luck I'll call at exactly the time that night owl finally dozes off. How does he exist on so little sleep?

Traffic on the freeway lightened a bit as she approached her exit and her concentration focused on maneuvering her car into the right lane. California driving was still stressful for her even after eighteen months. She'd become resigned to never adjusting to it. To her, New York traffic had been chaotic, but California's was just plain crazy!

Thank God, I made it off that road in one piece! The ride seems longer every night! Fifteen more minutes to home...and bed. Oh, that sounds so good.

Her breast still felt the pressure of Kevin's hand and her mouth his kiss as she unlocked the back door. She tried drowning the sensations in a hot shower and a tall glass of lemonade. Liquid applied internally and externally didn't deaden the feelings, merely dulled them.

An hour later, as she dozed off, a little voice deep inside whispered, "You left the envelope on the front seat, dummy."

"Fine, and it can stay there," she mumbled, turning over. In thirty seconds her eyes were open, and she gave in, got up, put on a robe, and ran out to the garage.

"Mom, what in Heaven's name are you doing? It's two in the morning and you're outside running around in your robe!"

Maddie held up the envelope as she ran up the back steps to the door. "The world's most important package, and it comes with a curse." As she spoke she regarded her daughter Whitney, tall and slim, her figure enhanced even her shapeless terry cloth robe.

"Sorry I woke you," Maddie apologized, hugging her. They crossed the spacious kitchen together. Whitney stopped to fill a kettle with water for tea as Maddie continued on to the breakfast nook.

The two women sat at the round oak table, the envelope, spotlighted by the overhead Tiffany-like lamp, centered between them.

"Well, Mom, since that thing is the author of my ruined sleep, I want to know what's so "URGENT" about it. Just whose 'DO NOT BEND - PHOTOGRAPHS' deserves all this special attention?"

Maddie regarded the envelope skeptically. "This thing had better be worth what I went through because of it!" She recapped the fiasco at the theater and the resulting after-show scenario.

"Wow! We both had a crazy day," Whitney exclaimed, sitting back and crossing her legs. "Wait until you hear this one! I've told you what a couch case Dave Dumas, the star of my ridiculous opus, is."

Maddie stared in rapt attention at Whitney but didn't respond.

"He hit a new high - or would it be a low?—today. It turns out that one of his many problems is a terror of maneuvering on a narrow surface, like a board, at any elevation, even a couple of inches. Our scene involved us escaping from one roof to another - yup, you guessed it - on a board laid across the open space. On screen it looks like we're ten stories up but in the studio it was actually no more than six inches off the floor."

Maddie continued to stare, and Whitney rambled on. "Get this, he took one look at the board and turned pale. When Fred— you remember my director, Fred Roman, good ol' Frettin' Freddie—called 'Action,' Dave broke into a cold sweat. They had to hold shooting and fix his make-up three times because of this. Finally, he asked for a stand-in. The answer was no; the scene is staged in such a way that it would be very obvious if there were two different Davids making the crossing."

"When Fred began muttering and pacing in circles he grabbed at his last resort."

Whitney, with her mother's eyes riveted on her, pulled out all the stops. "David asked for a wire, you know, a harness, like trapeze artists use! By this time the crew and I were bursting a seam trying not to laugh out loud. Poor Fred, desperate to get something done that day, would agree to just about anything by that time to get this simple scene shot. Harness and all, we go into it, and you'll never believe what happened."

Maddie blinked but didn't respond.

"This was how it was supposed to look." Whitney stood, inched her way forward on an imaginary board, took a few wider steps, and dropped to all fours. "It's at this point that the camera swings down, creating the illusion of our eye-view of the ground below. Dave was supposed to crouch and crawl right behind me but, God only knows how, he fouled up the line and ended up hanging inches over the board and me, looking for all the world like a Macy's Thanksgiving Day Parade balloon." She burst out laughing.

Maddie's expression didn't change.

Whitney crawled the few steps to her mother, rose to her knees and looked intently at Maddie's profile. Just as Whitney thought, her mother hadn't heard one word she'd said. She stood and resumed her seat, returning to her relaxed, cross-legged position. "So they decided I would do the scene by myself. We left him hanging there, went out to the nearest ten story buildings, laid a narrow plank between two of the roofs and ..." Whitney checked for any reaction from Maddie. None.

"I walked out without a hesitation. Boy, did it bend in the middle." Once again, she checked for a reaction.

"They set both ends of the plank on fire. It split under my feet, and I fell headlong into a watery pit of ravenous piranhas, which just happened to be in the alleyway, under a cardboard box..."

Maddie stirred. "A pit of what?"

"Ravenous piranhas, each tooth honed to a fine, razor-sharp edge."

Maddie's eyes opened wide, "Razors? Teeth?"

Whitney looked at her fingernails as she said, "It's all on film, every gory bite. The director was most impressed that I would do all that for his film."

Maddie gasped, "'Gory bite?' What are you talking about?"

"Your guess is as good as mine! You were off in another galaxy while I was telling you a very funny studio story. I can take a hint. You just don't care anymore."

Maddie ran her fingers through her hair, trying to center her mind. "You know I care! I'm interested, more than interested, in anything to do with you."

"I was only kidding, Mom. You rarely zone out like that. What's eating at...whoa! Whom did I accuse of not listening? Did you say you kissed *the* Kevin Martin?"

Maddie, suddenly confronted, tried to put some distance between herself and her daughter's newly-aroused curiosity by getting up and heading for the china cabinet.

"Yes, but let's get it right. He was the kisser; I was just the kissee. I'll save you the bother of asking how it was. It was a kiss, that's all."

Whitney watched her mother, so concentrated on setting out cups, saucers, and spoons. Maddie continued to avoid facing her, returning to the oak hutch for a tin of tea biscuits.

" 'It was a kiss, that's all,'" Whitney mimicked, studying her mother as she approached the table. "He's adorable! I wouldn't mind a chance to, shall we say, get close to him."

"Oh, please! He's too young for you, " Maddie stated emphatically, sitting down hard and placing the box on the table with a bang.

"Too young? Mom, we're almost perfect for each other; he's twenty-eight and I'm twenty-five. What do you mean too young?"

"Mentally, emotionally, all that unessential stuff. He's physically twenty-eight but a lot of the rest is playing catch-up. Another one of those who thinks you'll drop dead if he deigns to look at you. You need a more mature man."

The kettle whistled. Whitney went to the stove and poured the boiling water into an Irish Belleek china teapot in which she'd placed their favorite blended tea. As she carried it to the table to steep, she reproved, "How did I suddenly get into this part of the discussion? Stop trying to side-track me. Well, tell me, how did you feel when he kissed you?"

Maddie fixed her daughter with a serious look and retorted, "I felt like a high school teacher with a precocious student. Shocked, not thrilled."

Whitney was disturbed at her mother's reaction. "Mom, come on. All men aren't takers like Dad or Vic. You were open and giving to each of them and all you got out of it was battered and bruised and ended up acting as if you could never do or be enough. I, to this day, don't understand why you thought you were inferior to them. I hope by now you've learned to treasure what you have to offer."

"My daughter, the psychologist," Maddie said, briefly meeting Whitney's eyes before looking away again.

Ignoring the interruption, Whitney went on, "Actually, maybe Kevin isn't all that wrong. An affair isn't such a bad idea. It might do you some good. Hmmm, Malibu. Alone with a handsome man for a few weeks. You'd both know from the start it was going nowhere, but it'd be fun while it lasted and good therapy for you."

As she spoke, Whitney recalled her father, standing apart, as if above it all, she thought, disinterested, unsupportive of anything Maddie attempted at home or work. And then there was Vic, the rebound focus of Maddie's long-suppressed passions. Vic, who proved to be far more in love with himself and his quest to see his name in lights than in anyone or anything else. Whitney was surprised by her glimpse into the still-present, devastating, negative effects of those two.

Concern for her mother's frame of mind and afraid of pushing her too hard, Whitney felt it wise to change the subject. "Are you going to open this?" She patted the surface of the envelope. "What the..? That's definitely not a videotape. Not cassettes either."

Maddie dropped her hand onto it, hitting more than feeling it. "What is that? Oh, I don't want to know! I wouldn't be surprised if it were a bomb."

Whitney poured the tea and slid a steaming cup in front of her mother. "Why so serious? Something we can talk about?"

Maddie shifted in her chair and stared at her cup as Whitney studied the cookie box contents, stalling, working at trying to appear casual.

"Whit, I found out tonight that a vow I made to myself after Vic disappeared, to set up barriers to prevent being hurt again, is working."

Whitney wanted to look away from her mother but found she couldn't.

Maddie continued, "There's a shield around every part of me capable of feeling. I ran into it tonight, when Kevin kissed me. Not one fiber in my body reacted, no rush, no thrill, just...nothing. No reaction. None at all." Her voice drifted off to almost a whisper on the last few words.

Whitney slowly raised her cup and took a sip of tea, wishing it were a good shot of Scotch.

Maddie's voice intruded, "Boy, am I ever protected! It was like hitting a thick, spongy wall. It was shocking. It shook me...I mean, finding for the first time it's there and that it's so...so strong...impenetrable." She raised her cup towards her lips, pausing short of her mouth, a worried expression flitting across her face.

Whitney caught the look, and in the ensuing silence, studied Maddie. For years she'd admired her mother for getting her life together after her father died. Stress and negative emotions, her father seemed to thrive on them. Mom kept getting quieter, as if she were retreating, trying to cope. Now she'd make Whitney think she could take on anything that came her way, anything except a man, that is.

In less than half a cup of tea, just a few sentences, Whitney's illusions disintegrated under the realization that Maddie's greatest success had been in maintaining such a good front. Her mother's self-deprecating humor disguising her reality.

Maddie's eyes met Whitney's and she hastily looked toward the stove, away from the silent scrutiny. "Did you leave the burner on?"

"No, I didn't, and don't change the subject. Please."

Maddie spoke, still turned away, "I had no idea I'd succeeded so well."

Whitney sipped her tea and thought, *Forty-six...looks maybe late thirties...nice figure...attractive. Easy to see why Kevin would be interested.*

"Whit," Maddie continued thoughtfully, "when Kevin put his arms around me, I actually felt a jolt of fear." She turned back to Whitney. "My body went rigid! Inwardly, I was screaming, 'Stop it! I don't want any of this!' I kept reminding myself not to feel anything, and then—it struck me—I actually wasn't. I wasn't reacting. Nothing was happening inside me...nothing."

Whitney discovered that what had sounded like Maddie boasting about her vow was actually a fear of her own creation. "Mom, maybe he's just the wrong man. I'll bet, given the right mood and the right guy, you'd feel things you don't suspect still lurk inside of you."

Maddie stared at the envelope. "Don't waste your money! It's a no-win bet because I won't let it happen. Believe me, it's better for everyone this way!"

Whitney's concern for the woman she loved so dearly was rising. "Mom, you have so much love in you. It's meant to be given, not hoarded. I know there's a nice man out there looking for you. He'll show you how beautiful life really can be. How can he find you if you stay locked up, hiding inside of yourself?"

"My dear Whitney, I'd be invisible if I could. I need a man like a snake needs shoes. Mr. Love-of-My-Life can stay out there, under whatever rock he calls home, because I am never, never going to be hurt again. All those years of pain are going to be out-distanced by as many years as I have left of loving no one but *moi et toi*!" Maddie announced as she removed a half dozen butter cookies from the tin.

"Start eating like that," Whitney observed, noting the calories stacked next to her mother's teacup, "and there'll be a lot more of *toi* to love."

Maddie ceremoniously placed a cookie in her mouth and savored it, a Mona Lisa smile on her face. She swallowed it with a sip of tea, noting, "Who cares! Women watch their figures to attract or keep a man. Imagine! I've been trying to stay thin like I was still in that race. Ha! Thank you, Kevin Martin, you've shown me the error of my ways," and she bit into another cookie.

Whitney decided not to argue. Instead, she refilled their cups and approached the subject from a different angle. "Are you telling me you have absolutely no interest in men? Come on, you can't tell me there's no one who can turn you on. Let's take the movies, for example. There's not a man on the screen who can get to you?"

Maddie laughed. "Okay, okay, Whit, you're absolutely right! My secret passions will now parade before you in all their glory! You want names? Paul Newman, Robert Redford. Larger than life, handsome as all get out and so very, very unattainable, so completely safe. My imagination can bring them to me anytime I choose. But, do you know what's especially nice? They never disappoint me and I can tune them out at will. I even get to do what I've never done in reality, walk away!"

Whitney swallowed hard. Anger, regrets! She felt as if she'd opened Pandora's box! She grabbed for the nearest safe subject, "I can't stand to look at that package for one more second. If you're not going to open it then I am, right now!"

Maddie pushed it toward her. "Be my guest. It's not going to effect the world scene if I don't do the honors."

Whitney ripped the end of the envelope, and the mysterious lump, an eight-millimeter reel of film, slid onto the table. Maddie picked it up, exclaiming, "Whit, I haven't seen one of these in years! My father covered all the events of my first twenty-one years in home movies. Those old reels looked just like this."

As Maddie spoke Whitney removed and studied the paper contents. "Oh, this is unbelievable!"

Maddie, lost in her reminiscence, vaguely heard what Whitney had said. "Did I ever show you those films? There are dancing recitals and birthday parties...Oh, excuse me, what did you say?"

Whitney hugged the papers and picture, not letting her mother get a glimpse at them. She smiled despite herself, repeating her comment.

Maddie put her hand out, "What are you going on about? Let me see."

Shaking her head, Whitney hugged them tighter.

"All right, then," Maddie said, "we're regressing to your preteen pranks? It's the old twenty questions bit, right?"

"Why not?" Whitney answered, releasing one arm to grab a cookie from the box and pop it into her mouth.

"Oh my goodness! You're so intense you're forgetting how the camera will show that cookie tomorrow."

Whitney chewed, swallowed and shrugged her shoulders. "One cookie? Maybe. I won't eat anymore, though, because I just found out they're nowhere near as delicious as what I'm holding."

"You know, Miss Whit, you can be a real pain in the you-know-what sometimes! Okay, this has to be from an agent or an actor wanting to submit to the rigors of the Genny. Question Number One: male or female?"

"Male. Oh, without any question, male, definitely male, all male, totally male! Oh, what a male!"

"Sure, Whit, nobody's that great! I know who's accepted Ben's invitations for the next year. Let me see. Steve Varney? Couldn't be. His stuff is in my file. David Lassiter, maybe? No, come to think of it, I spoke to his publicist earlier this week, and she's giving it to me at our lunch meeting next week. Those are the only two 'names' he's slated for the next ten months. Neither of them strikes me as being 'definitely, all male' once you get past the anatomy. Could someone be sending ahead?" Maddie stared seriously at her silent, grinning daughter, "Either he's got one huge opinion of his own importance and a backer with deep pockets, or he is so exalted that a personal courier is an everyday thing with him."

"Concentrate on the latter," Whitney said. "Here comes the most interesting piece of information. He's coming to your little establishment in a month."

"In a month? That's crazy! We're slated for an *Othello* in two months, and there's nobody of any fame and glory appearing. Ben's calling it our salute to the uncelebrated stars who make it easier for the super novas to collect their Oscars and Emmys."

"If this guy is small-time, I'll walk naked down Rodeo Drive at high noon," Whitney stated emphatically.

"Good God, Whitney! Who the hell is it?" Maddie pleaded.

Whitney relished the moment as she slowly lowered the packet to the table, glossy picture up. "Tsk, tsk, Mother, watch your language! You've always told me not to swear."

Maddie tried to cover a gasp with a cough when she saw Bret Atkins' smile beaming up at her.

If there were such a monarchy, he would be the reigning king of movies. A continually successful longevity earned him a status shared by few in the business.

The gasp did not escape Whitney's notice and she privately begged God to let this develop into a major problem for

Maddie's "men, who needs 'em?" philosophy.

Atkins was the actor Whitney had in mind when she questioned Maddie about her cinema loves. She was glad she hadn't said, "What about Atkins?" when Maddie left him out. She'd been an avid fan of his for as long as Whitney could remember.

She knew Maddie's' protection, her wall, would be given the hardest test when this man crossed her path, and she chuckled remembering her mother's remark about the envelope being cursed. *You bet it is, Mom, cursed with the ultimate test for you.*

"What's so funny! This is a disaster!" Maddie fretted. "How am I supposed to do anything for this production when I don't even know who's in it? Ben never runs things this way! What in Heaven's name is going on here?"

Whitney pulled the enclosed letter from under Atkins' picture, advising, "Read this before you have a fit!"

Maddie stared at Whitney as she took the paper from her. She slowly shifted her gaze and read,

> I'm sorry for this last minute appearance on the scene. I've refused a picture which I'd expected to do (long, boring story, both the script and the refusal), so now I have free time for something I've only been able to think about since Ben opened his theater.
>
> Reliable sources have told me your next production is to be *Othello*. Thought maybe Ben should see what my feel is for the Master, so I've enclosed an old (from the 'Seventies) film shot of my last night in live theater. The city was New York and the character, Marc Anthony.
>
> If he thinks I'm not right for the *Othello*, I'll wait for another opening in my schedule to work with him.
>
> Thank you in advance for dealing with

any extras this will entail. Once again, I am sorry for the short notice.

Everything being favorable, I look forward to meeting you on September 1.

Bret Atkins.

If I tried to set the perfect tone for that letter, Whitney marveled, *I wouldn't have done that well. He sounds too good to be true, forty-something, tall, not-too-dark, handsome, famous...and humble? Maybe his "humble" is as much an act as Mom's brave face. Whatever, thank you Lord! Her heart will do a tap dance whenever he appears around a corner. Even if he doesn't speak to her, just the sight of him will weaken her defenses. In the next two months she'll be forced to realize she's still very much a feeling woman.*

I've seen the expression on her face at his movies, lost on another plane—devouring him with her eyes. By the time the Othello is finished and he fades off into his world, she'll see a truer picture of herself and her feelings.

The tea party suddenly fell apart as Maddie stood, eyed Atkins' picture on the table, said good night, and walked out of the kitchen, leaving Whitney to clean up.

First sign of a crack! She'd never leave so much as a glass on the table if she was in control. How long did that take, all of twenty seconds?

Whitney carried the dishes to the sink and rinsed them, thinking, *For her, Kevin Martin packed about as much power as a fire-cracker. But Bret Atkins? Here comes the H-Bomb! Diversion (Bret) plus distraction (palpitations) equals destruction (one ugly wall)! Oh please, God, from my mouth to Your ear.*

She loaded the dishes into the dishwasher, wiped off the table, and headed for the doorway, singing the last line of the song she'd been humming, "And the walls came a-tumblin' down!"

II

*T*here was a rumor afloat that Ben Cameron lived in the Genny. Almost true. A cottage tucked away at the west end of the property had served as his residence since the opening of the theater. Only a short ride in his dark green golf cart separated him from the weathered-shingled five story, octagonal theater building. Easy access made it possible for him to prowl about at any time of the day or night.

Sun-up usually found him at his desk, pouring over the work Maddie had placed there for his scrutiny and signature the previous evening. There never seemed to be any lessening of the paper onslaught generated by actors, managers, agents, technicians, unions, costume and scenery designers, and on and on.

Mornings and afternoons, six days a week, he conducted workshop/rehearsals, and by sunset, he could be found lurking somewhere backstage, checking on that night's performance readiness.

A favorite midnight haunt was the control booth. Swivel chair tilted back, feet up on the desk, he reviewed his notes for cast and crew from the night's performance.

From the ninth through the eleventh week every three

months, the theater was dark. A diverse group of scenery people and technical and cleaning personnel descended on the place. Designers poured over scenic drawings; maintenance performed needed repairs; cleaners buffed and polished. Right on time, every time, all stood ready for the next cast.

Ben forced Maddie to stay away at least three days of those off-weeks, telling her, "You need your rest. You're not as young as you used to be, you know!" But, if he was sure Maddie was out of earshot, his answer to anyone who remarked about his own extended hours was, "As you get older, you need less sleep." In truth, the long work days generated by a producing theater seemed to energize and revitalize him.

The rigorous travel and work schedule of the past had kept him trim. His physique had changed little over the years and appeared it never would; he still didn't sit long enough for a calorie to turn to fat.

It was at Harvard he'd became conscious of his average height, having roomed with a 6 foot 8 inch basketball player for four years. Whenever they'd double-dated, he was shorter than his roomie's date. He found particular pleasure that his 5 feet 11 inches "towered" over Maddie's 5 feet 9.

She, in turn, had spent most of her adult life wishing herself 4 inches shorter. "Lurking deep inside me is a petite little thing just screaming to get out!," she told anyone who coveted her height. "Please, cut me down to size!"

As the sun climbed above the horizon, Ben reached for the phone but then thought better of it. *I know she's got the packet from Atkins. I saw Kevin hand it to her. Oh, good Lord, she'd die if she knew I'd seen that episode backstage. She looked like she was either going to faint or belt him one. Even so, I can't imagine why she didn't swoop through that door last night, accusing me of playing a joke on her, not believing she's going to be working with Atkins.*

He ran his fingers through his thick shock of silver gray hair, a well-known Cameron gesture, invariably stemming from impatience. *I know she worships this guy. It all happened so fast with him. Even I was surprised.*

Again he reached for the phone. "Oh, hello, Whitney. Is Maddie all right? She isn't sick, is she? I didn't hear from her. I was absolutely sure I would."

Whitney sat on the edge of her bed. "5:15. Why does the phone ring at 5:15 only on the mornings I'm racing to get to the lot by 6:00? Mom's on her way, Ben. I can't believe you didn't tell her about Atkins!"

"I would have if she hadn't been out of my reach last night, playing prop girl backstage. I wasn't going to tell her something like that over the headset. Can you imagine her not reacting vocally? I myself got the surprise only minutes before her envelope arrived. I thought for sure she would have called."

Whitney laughed. "It didn't get opened until 2:30 this morning and, even then, I was the one who had to do it. Mom kept pushing it away from her, saying the thing was cursed. Her reaction? After a minor explosion, she just went to bed. Let me give you fair warning though, she's angry this morning." Whitney lowered her voice as if Maddie were home and could overhear. "Actually, this couldn't have come at a better time. She didn't have the greatest night. Something sent her into an emotional tailspin."

Ben didn't let on to Whitney he knew about Kevin. "I feel better knowing there's another explanation for her not calling besides souring from dealing with crotchety old me."

"Crotchety? Old?" Whitney repeated, looking at her watch. "Not anywhere near the right adjectives. You're an angel! Yikes, I've got to run."

As he hung up, there was a knock on his door. "Come in, Maddie."

"No great guess! At this hour, who else would it be?" she asked, unsmilingly.

He turned to the large picture window behind him and peered at the sky. "No storm clouds up there. Guess they're all in here. Sit down. You look like you're about to rain on my parade."

Dropping into one of the maroon leather chairs that faced Ben's massive, paper-strewn desk, she demanded in a controlled voice, "Not once, not ever, did you mention Bret Atkins' name. Even a tiny hint would have helped! Where are you coming from? What in heaven's name are you thinking? There's so much to do for someone like him. Do you care that I probably won't see my home again until this *Othello* is finished?"

Ben rose and leaned towards her across the desk, "Hold it! Come up for air! What is there to do for him that you didn't do for Kevin? Atkins, like everyone else around here, will be just another working stiff."

Maddie, disbelieving what she'd heard, stared up at him. "Just another working stiff? Are you nuts? He's Bret Atkins. He's...he's ...Bret Atkins!"

"And I'm Ben Cameron! Around a lot longer and got much more influence than he's ever had. What special things do you do for my daily appearance?" He tried to don an air of superiority, but a smile, playing at the corners of his mouth, ruined his act.

Maddie, distracted by his questions, didn't notice. "Well, I know all that... I mean about your being more important than he is! Well, you don't need special treatment. I mean....you're Uncle Ben, for heaven's sake! I've known you forever. He's Bret Atkins! Tell me this! Where's he going to live? At his home, wherever that is? If so, he'll need a chauffeur. No, he must have one of his own."

Ben interrupted. "Probably right. After all, 'he's Bret Atkins!'" He imitated her emphasis on the Atkins name.

Maddie scowled at him. "Ben, don't be cute! I'm serious! Will he stay in a hotel? If so, which of the nearby ones is the best. I've got to get the gears turning, security alerted and..."

Ben sat, tilting back in his over-sized leather chair, and stated simply, "He'll live here — in the dorm, like everyone else." He watched her shift from confusion to indignation.

"In the dorm?" she nearly shouted. "In 'The Slave Quarters'? Who's kidding who here? Whom here? Oh, nuts — whatever!" Maddie stood and began to pace, demanding, "In the dorm? That's totally unacceptable! He's a star, S-T-A-R. People like him *do not* live in dorms!"

Ben had rarely in the past gotten the best of Maddie in any discussion. She was too quick with a fast retort and seldom out of focus during an exchange. He was enjoying this moment immensely. "Didn't I say a few minutes ago something about everyone being equal here? Once Atkins crosses my lobby, all pomp and circumstance ceases. He is simply another actor, period. The members of our *Othello* cast will all be treated equally."

Maddie stared speechlessly at him. His tone of voice confirmed there'd be no question that he meant what he said.

His outward appearance belied his spine of steel. Ben, at age sixty-eight, and after spending thirty-eight of those years on the West Coast, had not yet abandoned his Ivy League look. A Harvard graduate in the '50s, he still favored the elegantly casual look of v-neck cashmere sweaters over open-necked shirts with slacks and loafers, a dress style so popular in Cambridge in his day that it almost reached uniform status. When his horn-rimmed glasses perched half-way down his nose, he looked professorial, especially when his pipe rested in the corner of his mouth.

Softening, he stated, "He's been around a long time, Maddie, cut off by his years at the top from the environment that nurtured him as an actor. He'll get the chance here to be one of the gang again. That alone could do him a world of good."

"You make him sound like Methuselah! He hasn't been around *that* long! He's only two years older than I am. Forty-eight isn't old!"

Ben was suddenly glad Maddie hadn't reacted as he'd anticipated. He was enjoying this exchange. "You're forty-six,

Maddie? No! You're kidding me! Forty-six! My Lord, how the years do fly. Why I remember when you were..."

"You know very well I'm forty-six!," she chided.

"So you are," Ben said with finality as if decreeing it. "Now, let me finish the thought I originally started. Atkins is a walking encyclopedia on film acting. Our cast is comprised of working feature players, each with at least five solid years experience in front of the cameras. Living in the same building, the opportunities for casual shop-talk will ensure their leaving here with more inside tricks from him about successful movie acting than they'll get about stage craft from me during rehearsals."

Maddie had stopped at the far end of the room and was staring at him. Indicating he'd like her to sit again he said, "Now back to your entrance into this scene. What are you going on about?"

Maddie repeated, "Ben, there are things to be done."

"What?"

"...things!"

Ben couldn't resist. "I can't imagine what these things are. What is so earth-shakingly important? Getting your roots dyed? Shopping for the right outfits? Having a manicure? Am I getting close?"

Maddie flared, "You? You trivializing my job? You of all people? Am I the only one here who appreciates just who Bret Atkins is? Are you smoking something funny in that pipe of yours?" She rose to leave, staring seriously at him. He came around the desk as fast as he could. "Whoa! This has gone too far! I found out about Atkins the same time that envelope was delivered and I called you from the booth only a minute after it arrived."

"Right! 'There's an envelope waiting in your office.' Really! For all I knew from your message, it could have been my winning entry from Publishers' Clearing House!"

Ben took her hand saying, "Oh, Maddie-mine," his pet-name since their reunion in New York, "I've wanted this guy here for ages, invited him before we even opened. Lucky for us I was still undecided as to who would play Othello. Now, I've got my answer." He squeezed her hand and she looked at him.

"I never meant for you to get so upset," he continued. "About what I said, you know, about what you have to do, I was only kidding. You know that, don't you?"

Maddie immediately backed off. "I'm sorry, Ben. I came in here ready to accuse you of all kinds of sins, including causing my car to die on the freeway this morning."

She walked back to his desk with him. "You thought I would come in here tripping the light fantastic, didn't you? What do I do instead? Get all huffed up. You and Whitney are saints to put up with me. I love you." She kissed him on the cheek before turning to leave.

"Now that we've settled everything," Maddie stated from the doorway, "I'm going to walk around this property until my head clears and my mind is focused."

"No thanks for inviting Atkins, even if I did it two years ago?" Ben queried.

"Thanks, I think. What a coup for you! I promise I'll remember to treat him just like any other working stiff." Maddie fortified herself with a deep breath, promising, "I'll remind myself of it if I feel I'm slipping into the fan category. I'll be fine. Really!" and tripped over her own foot as she turned to leave.

III

"**P**ut on your best bib and tucker! The Chases have a date tonight," Ben announced over the phone early one Sunday morning in mid-August.

"Is this the Cameron dating service?" Whitney quipped.

"Wanted to catch you before you left. Knew you girls would be setting off soon to torture those good church-going Catholics with your music..."

"It's our contribution to world salvation," Whitney countered. "We put them through hell on earth so they can march straight into heaven, martyrs for their faith. We're thinking of patenting our method."

Ben chuckled. "Why can't I ever get ahead of you?"

"Because I'm young and talented, and, if you ever do best me, I'll set my agent on you. Not a pretty prospect for you," Whitney joked, laughing with Ben.

"I'll keep this short and sweet. Megastudios is throwing a bash to publicize signing Atkins to a contract I hear is worth an arm and two legs. Thought it'd be a good chance for Maddie to meet him, you know, get her over her 'gees' and 'wows' before he arrives here."

Whitney laughed. "Think she'll need smelling salts?"

"Oh, Lord, I hope not! And you'll be there too, so all Hollywood can wonder who that gorgeous creature is on old man Cameron's left arm. Not a bad publicity factor for you, and a hell of a boost for my ego."

Whitney's heart beat faster. "Oh, yes, yes! But what about the gorgeous woman on your right arm? Mom isn't exactly chopped liver, you know."

"You, better than anyone, know I know that," Ben attested. "Maddie won't be on my arm though, she'll be clinging to it. I'm doing this because women, young and old, have told me Atkins has been almost — well — paralyzing the first time they've gotten close to him."

"Paralyzing? Oh, come on!"

"We'll see tonight. By the way, don't mention Atkins to your mother. Watching her reaction should be a great show!"

Six o'clock that evening, a silver limo pulled up to the white stucco bungalow shared by Maddie and Whitney in the hills above Malibu. The two women emerged from the house, Maddie wearing wine-colored chiffon, and Whitney in cream silk.

"I'll be the envy of every man there," Ben exclaimed, admiring his little harem.

Maddie headed straight for the limo, nodding to him while saying, "I never dreamt it would be impossible to get an appointment with a hairdresser in this city, especially on a Sunday! I feel completely thrown together and utterly a mess!"

"You look gorgeous," Ben admired. "You just might out-shine everyone else."

Whitney settled in and watched in amusement as her mother fretted over her "last-minute" rush, actually eight hours, and her home-done hair and manicure. Three times in one mile Maddie asked if her jewelry really complimented her outfit. "After all, I suppose just about everyone will be there, and I don't want to look like somebody's maid."

Ben chuckled, winking conspiratorially at Whitney.

As they arrived at the studio gates, Maddie reacted to the huge gathering of fans straining to see into each passing car. Disturbed by the crowd size, she leaned back hard against the seat. "So many people, all staring at us. It's scary! I can't even imagine how uncomfortable it must be to live with hordes of people watching your every move. I'd be a nervous wreck if this happened too often!"

Whitney observed, "But, Mom, they're friendly, happy. It looks like a huge party. I don't think I'd mind about a lifetime of this."

The chauffeur guided the car to the designated stopping area and the Chases and Ben emerged at the edge of the white-and-gold canopied entrance to Sound Stage Six, the oldest and most famous building on the lot, if not all of Hollywood. Standing on that spot since 1918, it had housed the filming of some of America's biggest and best-loved movies because through the years of mergers and sales, its ownership had been transferred to various studios.

Maddie had visited the huge, vaulted space only a few months previously when Ben invited her to accompany him to this major studio for one of his semi-annual temptations to abandon the Genny and do another movie. He'd given her an educational tour of the gigantic sound stage, almost empty then, between pictures. Ben drew word-pictures of its glorious history, back to Rudolph Valentino's day, bringing it to life for her.

Entering on party night, Maddie gasped at the vision she beheld. A forest of wisteria bushes, flowering trees, and sparkling fountains filled the building. White damask covered long buffet tables decorated with centerpieces of orchids, freesia, baby's breath, and ferns. Smaller variations adorned the individual dining tables.

An orchestra, hidden away, played as the rich, the famous, and the not-so-famous rubbed elbows. Stars and would-be-stars had wasted not a moment nor expense in preparation for the event. Some were giving their best personal performances in years for this very influential audience and a veritable host of photographers.

Ben was a magnet to all, and Maddie and Whitney felt they'd been introduced to most of 'moviedom' before a half hour had passed.

The evening dazzled Maddie, who tried not to stare when introduced to some of Hollywood's leading lights. Whitney basked in the glow of Ben's personal spotlight. This party offered him an innocuous way to introduce Whitney to the people she should know. He looked forward to eventually directing her in a movie, his only definite plan for another film, the one he'd consider taking a hiatus from his Genny to do. Whitney had all the obvious physical essentials Hollywood worshipped. She also possessed intelligence, talent, and a burning desire to make it.

Ben had said to Maddie only a week before, "She's a natural, a good intuitive actress, but all the beauty, talent, and brains in the world won't get you anywhere out here if you don't make the right connections. If I don't qualify as one of the most right, then I've wasted more than half my life in this business. She's spent enough time learning the ropes as a featured player. I want a good script and meaty role for her almost as much as she wants it herself."

There was no fanfare, no announcement but, nevertheless, a wave of spontaneous silence enveloped the room. Maddie looked questioningly at Ben and Whitney but they were staring fixedly at the entrance area.

Photographers rushed toward the main attraction of the night, shooting with incredible speed, creating a wall of bodies and an almost blinding glare.

Maddie, wishing she'd brought her glasses for a clearer look, said to Ben, "Who is that? I can't see! Who's causing such a commotion?"

"Keep looking. I'm more blind than you without my glasses," Ben commiserated, nudging Whitney, who turned away from them to hide her smile when he added, "I wonder who it could be!"

Maddie's attention riveted on the entrance. Finally, a break in the crowd created a line of vision for her. She gasped and turned to Ben, whispering, "It's...it's him!"

"Who's 'him'?" Ben asked leaning towards Maddie as if still unable to see.

Whitney forced down a rising laugh and affected a puzzled look equal to Ben's.

"Him!" Maddie whispered more strongly. "Him! Bret Atkins!"

Ben straightened up. "No, you're kidding! Is it really *him*?"

Oblivious to Ben's joking, Maddie continued, "Did you know *he* was going to be here tonight?"

"I guess I should have believed the rumor that 'everyone' was expected and warned you of even the slight possibility," Ben stated seriously. He turned to Whitney, "Did you know *he* would be here?"

Whitney kicked his shoe, saying under her breath, "Don't you dare drag me into this! She'll never let me off the hook if she so much as suspects I knew."

Maddie missed that repartee as she strained to see whether the "look"—the famous slow smile and penetrating eyes—that she and millions of other female moviegoers went weak-in-the-knees over, was a part of his off-screen persona. She was too far away to report on the eyes, but the smile was discernible.

She noted also that he was easily her height, if not more. Years ago she'd heard that Atkins was short, another Alan Ladd, and that the judicious camera angle trick shots that added many inches to Ladd were employed on Atkins' rumored 5 feet 7 inches. "If I decide my fantasy men are over 6 feet tall, I don't want reality intruding and cutting them off at the knees," Maddie had told Whitney recently, after seeing a picture of Atkins with some starlet who appeared at least four inches taller than he.

"Oh, my God, Ben," Maddie gasped, grabbing his arm, "He's headed straight toward us!"

Ben tried to free his captive right arm in order to shake hands but failed. "Bret, my boy, long time no see!"

Atkins, observing Ben's predicament, patted him on the shoulder, saying softly, "And in a little while, you may be glad to not see me again — for a long time." As he spoke he quickly surveyed Ben's companions.

"Bret, I'd like to introduce you to Whitney Chase." Ben raised his voice so all nearby eavesdroppers would hear her name. "You're meeting a future star, if I'm any judge at all. I was right about you, wasn't I! She's going far and fast."

They shook hands and Whitney stammered, "I'm so glad to meet you," blushing for the first time since high school.

"That's all, Whit?" Ben joked. "A woman of few words." She smiled and found she could not move her eyes from his face.

Ben leaned towards her, whispering, "Your mother is supposed to react like that, not you!"

Bret's eyes slowly but deliberately wandered from Whitney to Maddie and he moved his hand to her before Ben could speak. "Hi! I'm Bret Atkins, and you are?"

Maddie forced her right hand away from Ben's arm and placed it into Atkins'. Doing exactly what she knew she shouldn't, she let her eyes look into his and all power of speech failed her.

He glanced down quickly taking in the whole picture, from her V-neckline to matching shoes and back up again.

Oh, please don't look that closely! I'm thrown together! Maddie's mind pleaded during his scrutiny.

Ben tried to cover Maddie's silence. "You're too anxious to meet my harem, Bret. This is Maddie Chase."

Bret's eyes lit with recognition. "Oh, yes, I sent you that film. Ben, you had me believing she's a fat babushka-wearing grandmother. Your powers of description are waning, old man. Just look at her; she is beautiful!"

Ben couldn't resist. "Good Heavens, you're absolutely right! I really should get my eyes examined."

Atkins continued to hold her hand. Helpless to move and uncharacteristically mute, she thought, *I could talk if you'd just let go of my hand but, truth is, I'd be disappointed if you did.*

As if responding to her thought, Bret intensified their contact by enclosing her hand within both of his. He leaned towards her and whispered, "There's no way to have a conversation here. Let's be sure to make up for this at the theater next month."

He'd sensed rather than seen a group of studio executives zeroing in on him. Releasing her hand, he turned to Ben and Whitney, wished them all well, and was shuttled off to another group.

Maddie stood stock still, her now free hand still lifted in an empty handshake. Whitney moved in, lowered it to Maddie's side, and joked, "Earth to Mom. You can touch ground anytime now."

Ben closed the triangle and smiled at Maddie. She found her voice. "I can't believe it! Madelyn Chase couldn't think of a thing to say to Bret Atkins!"

Whitney observed, "Well, you could have at least told him your name. Couldn't you have told him that?"

Maddie put her arms around Ben and Whitney, "I really tried, but...I couldn't remember it!" They all laughed, but Maddie stopped suddenly. "He must think I'm the village idiot! I made a perfect fool of myself! I acted just like every ga-ga fan!"

"I'm certain he didn't even notice," Ben observed. "That man was too busy devouring you with his eyes. I look at home-made pineapple upside-down cake the way he looked at you — longingly, hungrily. Agree with me Whitney?"

Whitney softened Ben's observation. "Well, maybe not quite that much, but he was looking, that's for sure.

Ben's right about that."

Maddie heard the words but rejected the resulting thoughts. "No doubt it was part of the Atkins act, no more real than any scene ever filmed, Ben. And my reaction...I was meeting someone I've 'known' on the screen for years. Suddenly face-to-face with a man I've fantasized about much more than once. How embarrassing! Yes, that's it exactly. I was embarrassed. Well, I'll have to get over all that before he and I start working at the Genny next month, won't I?"

On the trip home, Maddie sat in a corner of the limo and stared out the window. Ben and Whitney exchanged questioning glances, regarded Maddie again and lapsed into talking shop as they returned to the Chases'.

At the limo door a still silent Maddie hugged Ben, kissed his cheek, turned and walked into the house.

Whitney watched her retreat, and as Ben joined her on the edge of the lawn, said, "She wasn't kidding about being ready for Atkins. She started the process before we left the studio, refortifying the Madelyn Chase Defense System, MCDS to you and me."

"Maddie's still bleeding, even after all these years! I never imagined. I should have pounded some sense into David's head when I had the chance," Ben thought aloud.

"Uncle Ben..." Whitney looked away. Fear spread through her, and she silently questioned the well-spring from which it arose.

"I know he was your father, Whitney, and I don't want to speak ill of the dead. Maddie's told me she hasn't given you much information on the Chase family, and I've put off telling you anything for years because, until now, I had no reason to bring it up. You need to hear this as much as I need to tell it to you."

She wished he'd say no more but her longing for family history that might supply answers to some haunting questions silenced her. She twisted the golden shoulder chain of her evening bag and looked into Ben's eyes.

"Please, no matter what I say, don't stop me," Ben started. "My father came up the hard way as a trader in stocks and bonds, from nowhere, from the bottom of the ladder to the top. He credited his success to his 'philosophy,' that by acting and thinking you are superior to others, you will be. Pretty highfalutin' for the offspring of a ditch-digger."

"I learned his lessons so well that by fifth grade I'd alienated every one of my friends. Retreating into my studies and feeding a voracious appetite for movies helped me decide at the ripe old age of twelve that by studying to the top of my classes and later doing quality work, I'd be successful and have more friends than I could count."

"My brother, Tom, your grandfather, on the other hand, became a life-long disciple of our father's teachings, placing himself on an extremely high pedestal. Truth be told, failure was his only superior skill. He lost every last cent of the Cameron money on his business disasters, dragging the family name down with him."

"What does a superior person do then? Why change his name, of course. He opted for Chase, a five letter 'money' name he said - like Astor, Cabot, Lodge - and set off to rebuild his fortune from any rich investor he could impress. I stuck with Cameron."

Whitney reached out for his hand. "Mom never told me any of this."

"How could she? Maddie's a victim. She can't look at anything to do with that family without stirring up anger at them for creating generations of emotional abusers and at herself for not seeing through your father's deceit, his 'I need you so much' act, before they were married."

"The mantle of superiority can be worn by only one in a household, only one king at a time in any realm. David had to compensate for years of degrading kowtowing to my brother. He established his own kingdom and ascended to the throne on his wedding day. His true colors showed after the honeymoon."

"No woman in the family had enjoyed equal status to her husband, and neither would Maddie. He needed her all right, as an obedient subject! How did he hold sway over Maddie? He turned her attributes into weapons; nothing she did was right or good enough for him. His forte though, was publicly belittling her intelligence, insulting her appearance, even degrading her sexuality. He rose to full power when her self-esteem collapsed."

"Before you ask, I'll tell you why she didn't leave: the 'until death do you part' of the Catholic wedding vows."

Whitney frowned. "I remember that she didn't speak unless spoken to when he was home."

Ben went on. "I liked Maddie the minute I met her, months before the wedding. Changes in her personality were showing two months after the big day. She was watching every word she said, becoming a carbon-copy of her husband when he lived under the same roof with his father."

"I confronted David right after you were born. He turned his back on me and never again acknowledged my existence. That's why you didn't meet me until ten years ago. Maddie's letters stopped after your first birthday. I continued to write for another year but didn't receive any answers. Twice, during those fifteen separated years, work took me to Broadway for months at a time but I didn't hear from her."

"Whitney, you've never known the Maddie I did when she was engaged. She was terrific, full of life and optimism. Your Aunt Louise, my Louise, fell in love with her immediately, wanted to take her home to be our daughter. God, how I regret we didn't! Thanks to your father, you never met your wonderful aunt while you were growing up, and after we found each other again, I was traveling alone to the East Coast. She'd developed a hatred for planes."

Whitney reached out and hugged Ben. Even after eight years as a widower, he still fought tears when he mentioned his Louise.

He patted her shoulder affectionately and they stood

apart again. "Even today, with all Maddie's successes, proof to the world and herself that David was wrong about her, she's still not the Maddie I knew. Oh, she seems happy and content if you didn't know her before her marriage. She fears her own feelings, and it still goes much deeper than you or I've imagined. Look at her tonight! We both felt it, right?"

Whitney nodded, and he continued, "Any other woman would be plotting to lure Atkins to her bed if he gave her even a third of that kind of attention. Not our Maddie! She's obviously attracted, so what's she doing? Mapping out battle plans to head him off at the pass. I've got no worries about her at work; she'll be in complete control on her own turf. As for Atkins? God help us all if he turns on the charm, or worse yet, if he's really interested in her!"

Whitney and he hugged again and she said, "You're absolutely right about Mom. I got my first clue only a few weeks ago, after Kevin..."

"Yes, I know about that incident," Ben interjected. "I'd be truly worried if Atkins' little surprise package was all it took to throw her into such a tizzy."

She took both his hands in hers and said earnestly, "Uncle Ben, I want to know the Maddie you did. You're surprised that time and our love and support haven't done more for her. We're obviously not the only prescription she needs. I think what should be added is a good, caring man."

Ben squeezed her hands and they walked toward the house. "You could well be right. Since Vic, she's death on actors, so I guess we can scratch Atkins as Prince Charming. Know a good yenta?"

Whitney found her mother's dress where Maddie had unzipped and stepped out of it as she entered her bedroom. It lay spread out like a wine stain on the pastel Oriental rug. Maddie, in half slip and strapless bra, was sprawled on her stomach across her bed, her face buried in a pillow.

"Mom, are you all right? Can you breathe?" Whitney asked as she lifted the dress and hung it on a hanger.

Maddie turned her head toward Whitney and coughed. "No, I guess I can't." She rolled over as Whitney sat down beside her. "Whit, I made a total ass of myself tonight. How can I face that man again?"

Whitney put her hand on her mother's shoulder, "I told you before, I don't think he even noticed. Women must react like that all the time. Look at me! I was stunned! He has to be used to it after all these years. Besides, he was far more concentrated on looking at you, I mean really looking, than on listening."

"That's silly, Whitney!" Maddie shot back. "He'd have to be blind as a bat to look at me when you're around. Face it, if he did zero in on me it's because I'll be working along with Ben on the *Othello*. Flatter the old broad, and she'll do back flips, be a worshiping slave. Old game."

Whitney thought to respond but Maddie went on. "He turns on the sunshine of his smile, and great icebergs melt. Did you see those women fawning and drooling over him as we were leaving? Well, not this one! Next time he pulls the flattery routine on me will be his last."

"Poor Bret," Whitney laughed. "Give the man a break, Mom. He just may be a nice guy."

"Fat chance!" Maddie responded seriously, taking Whitney's hand into hers as she sat up. "Actors! None of them are nice to the core. I've had my free home demonstration, and I heartily reject the product! Please, Whitney, don't even think of marrying an actor! As for Atkins eying me? Hah! Probably thinks I'm an easy lay."

"Mom," Whitney nearly shouted. "What are you saying! You don't talk like that, ever! Give this poor man at least an inch of goodwill. A soul as shallow as you picture would have to have messed up somewhere in all these years. I can't remember hearing or reading anything worse about him than the usual innuendoes, and they all seem to have been unsubstantiated. He's squeaky clean, and you're making him out to be Jack the Ripper."

"I've got years of experience, Whitney, bad experience. Men are men, handsome or ugly. The more involved with show business, the worse they are. I'll handle Mr. Atkins in my own way. He'll survive his stint at the Genny and be wonderful for his public. More importantly, though, I'll survive with no scars, no hurt. That you can put money on, my dear."

Whitney kissed her mother good night and left the room, knowing any further conversation would result in only a rehashing of Maddie's pain and convictions.

As she finished undressing and putting on a nightie, Maddie caught herself thinking, *I never thought he could look so good off-screen. I knew I was right! He's well over six feet tall! I barely come up to his eyes.*

Stop thinking about him, Maddie! Stop now, this instant!, she ordered herself vehemently as she walked into the bathroom. Covering her face with a cold washcloth, she mumbled into it, "Get on track, you blinking moron! He's a movie star you've fantasized all kinds of things about. So what? He's just a man. Super-actor himself."

She surveyed her face in the mirror above the sink and traced a finger over the thin furrow lines in her forehead. *Get real, Maddie! With Whitney there, who in God's name would seriously look at you twice. There's definitely an ulterior motive if he did.* She threw the washcloth and it hit the sink with a resounding slap as she turned, heading toward her bed.

Her mind wandered as she lay on her back and watched the full moon create shadows of swaying patio tree branches on her ceiling. *I wonder if an actress can actually remain unaffected during a love scene with him. I'd melt if he put his arms around me and more than likely die of ecstasy if his lips...*

Maddie nearly leapt from the bed, scolding herself. *Stop it! Stop it now! Get a grip! Take a cold shower!* She marched back to the bathroom, shutting the door with a bang.

Despite the long corridor which divided the house into two separate living areas, Whitney heard the slam. She put down the script she'd been studying and debated whether she should start keeping a notebook on the next few months. The *Maddie Faces Bret* saga at the Genny might turn out to be a great screenplay. It would absolutely be far more interesting than the one she was reading.

IV

"**M**arina! If you're still upstairs, will you come in here and tell me what you think of these?" An array of shirts, slacks, and jeans littered Bret Atkins' king-size bed; a suitcase sat open on the chair next to it.

"I'll never get dinner started if you keep calling me in here, Pavel," Marina cautioned as she walked into the bedroom and stood, almost at attention, near the foot of the bed. Her Russian accent added sternness to her tone, but the look in her eyes reflected nothing short of adoration.

"There's no rush to eat, Marushka." Bret looked at his housekeeper and held up two sport shirts, saying, "Do you like these? Think the colors are good on me?"

Marina, only half-regarding the shirts asked, "Fishing for compliments? Both of these colors are good on you and you know it. I have no experience as a wardrobe lady, and yet you've called me in here five times in the last fifteen minutes to check on shirt colors, styles, which jacket looks the best with what. Why is packing for two months at this 'gulag' so important to you? You don't fuss this much on Academy Award night. Actually, a wife would be better for this kind of job." She folded her arms and discomfited him with her steady stare.

"What do I need a wife for when I have you?" he quipped, pinching her cheek as he walked toward the dresser.

"It may be twelve years since your wife died, God be good to her." She crossed herself in the Orthodox manner. "But I don't think you forget what a wife can do for you. After all, Monika didn't come in a bowl of borscht."

"Don't start, Marina," he warned, but with a friendly tone in his voice. "I've told you over and over, I am perfectly happy with just two women under this roof. I don't want or need anyone else around here."

He handed her an armful of socks and underwear. "You can pack these," he suggested as he headed toward the bathroom. He heard her mumble something about a wife and duty in Russian and called out, "Which aftershave do you like the best? How about that new private blend with no name I wore to that studio bash?"

She stopped packing and turned in the direction of the voice. "I can't count how many times in two weeks you've mentioned that party." She mimicked him, "Will this go with that?" He came to the doorway, tightening the top of the aftershave bottle as Marina carried on. "Does that look good on me? What aftershave? I know what's up! I wasn't born...tomorrow!"

"Yesterday, Marina, not tomorrow. What are you staring at me for? I just want to make a good impression," he declared, taking the remains of the unpacked pile from Marina, placing it back on the bed.

"On who? Mr. Cameron? Your fellow actors? I don't think so."

Busying himself folding a shirt, he appeared to ignore

Marina's innuendo. She pushed on. "Silence speaks louder that a million words. It's a woman. All this preparation is for a woman. And you met her at that party! Oh, I think I know! She's going to be there, at the theater. *Da? Oh, eta ochen harasho!* Monika needs a mother."

"Oh, it's very good, is it?" he asked. "Monika is perfectly happy with you as her mother, and I've had it with any more involvements. My misfortune has been to meet women who would do anything and everything to get what they want — a role in a movie, furs, jewels. They make me sick! Nancy was the last good woman God put on this planet. I steer clear now, remember?"

Marina picked up the pile of underwear and dropped it in a heap in the middle of the suitcase, saying, "Da! I remember too a certain somebody crossing days off on the calendar since that studio night and humming during meals. Yes, you, humming! Definitely, it's a woman!" She turned on her heel and walked to the doorway but then stopped, glancing back at him.

He was half turned away from her, and she studied the famous profile of the man who had given her a desperately needed job thirteen years before, provided her and Boris Valenkov with a beautiful wedding six years ago, and who now needed her more than she'd ever needed him.

Bret Atkins, celluloid alias of stage actor Paul Davidoff, and a rising young artist, Nancy Byrnes, fell deeply in love, became completely entwined in each other, and married fifteen years ago.

Although working hard and rising fast, he made certain he attended her showings wherever they happened to be, even making a one-day round-trip flight from Rio to Washington, DC, on the ground in the US less than six hours and back in front of the cameras in Brazil two hours after landing.

In turn, she uncomplainingly gave him the space, support, and encouragement he needed to pursue his stage and ever-increasing screen work.

When, after two years, she discovered she was pregnant, Paul insisted someone be hired to do the housework and cooking. Nancy protested that the six-room condo in which they lived wasn't any challenge to her stamina, but he won.

A friend of Paul's mother had recently agreed to sponsor a Russian woman emigrating to the United States and was seeking employment for her.

Marina Marenkof, a forty-year-old teacher from Moscow, would accept any work to insure her future in America and prevent the possibility of being deported. All the way from the USSR, she worried about her hesitant English, fearful it would keep her from immediate employment.

To Marina's surprise and relief, she was interviewed by the Davidoffs two days after her arrival. Paul endeavored to put her at ease by conversing in his rudimentary Russian, a hold-over from childhood visits to his ex-Muscovite grand-parents.

She impressed them as an intelligent, well-mannered woman, and Nancy liked her immediately. That was enough for Paul, and he offered the housekeeper position with one stipulation, that she speak only English and not feel embar-rassed to ask for help whenever she got stuck for a word or phrase. Russian was allowed only if Paul initiated it and, after six months, she spoke surprisingly good English, complete with Nancy's Boston accent adding a special flavor to it.

In Marina's seventh month with them Nancy Atkins died in childbirth. No one, doctor or clergyman, could explain to Paul's satisfaction why her breathing had stopped and all resuscitation efforts had failed, why God took her from him. He was devastated but had little chance to mourn with an infant daughter to care for.

Marina tried to relieve him of the everyday chores of the baby-diaper changing, feeding, bathing. He hovered over her, studied every move as she handled the baby, and then imitat-ed her. As he became more proficient at these tasks, it often was a two-person race to reach the infant first when she summoned.

This proved a powerful experience for Marina, a chance to relive her happiest years. She'd lost her only child five years before in Russia, a daughter, then six, to pneumonia. The daily struggle to survive in the Communist state had forced her to seal off her feelings at that time. This new baby, a child with no mother, released floodgates of repressed emotion in Marina, a mother with no child. She was filled with the love and joy she'd despaired of ever feeling again.

Despite the gentle protests of both sets of grandparents and Marina, Paul stayed at home for months, refusing every screen offer, adamant in the conviction he had to be there for little Monika, the name Nancy and he had chosen if their child was a girl.

His fear that something horrible would happen if he wasn't physically present approached obsession. He'd allowed Nancy, helpless in labor, out of his sight at the hospital, and he'd lost her. He wouldn't permit the only tangible connection to his dead wife any further than a room away from him.

Early one spring morning Marina dressed nine-month old Monika in her finest and took off in Paul's Mercedes to visit his parents, the doting West Coast grandparents who lived 50 miles away.

When Paul awoke not only were his child and housekeeper missing but also his means of transportation. The note on the kitchen table read: "Will be home by five, Daddy. Marina and I are having a day out. She says you can use the day home alone to think about something besides me. Love, Monika."

On their return late that afternoon, Monika greeted Paul with such happy smiles he realized he had to be out of her sight for a while in order to get those wonderful extras. Gradually he relaxed and initiated his own absences from her. Two months later, he left to do a film being shot in Nevada.

As the years passed, Monika grew, and so did Paul's

career. He was away from home for prolonged stretches by that time so, when she was old enough to qualify, he placed her in an exclusive boarding school a few hours from home. Marina was heart-broken but understood the dangers a local school presented. Celebrities' children are natural targets for kidnapping or worse.

Bret felt her eyes on him and turned to face her scrutiny. "Marina, there must have been two hundred women there that night. It seemed as though they were all introduced twice. I can't remember who was who."

She chuckled. "Of course, sir."

"Well, I can't! I saw few faces because as usual I was confronted with mountains of cleavage, the overflow from pouring themselves into dresses at least two sizes too small. Actually, that's often far more interesting than their faces. Well, I have to amuse myself somehow at those gatherings!" he rationalized, placing the last shirt on the bed in the suitcase and closing it.

Marina countered, "I think there were 199 bulging dress tops which didn't get to you at all, but one woman was very different, and not because of her dress. You looked into her eyes and saw something that made you want to find out more. Now, I'll say no more on the subject because you'll just go on with those empty words that sound like a bad script instead of saying the truth." She marched into the hallway and proceeded down the staircase towards the kitchen.

"Mom, you haven't left yet?" Whitney called into the house from the back door. "She's usually long gone by this time," she muttered to herself.

Getting no answer, she walked through the kitchen and down the corridor to her mother's door. She'd looked forward to a day off from shooting and was determined to spend it doing no more than lying on the patio. "Everything okay, Mom?" she asked as she pushed the almost-closed door open.

"I'm sick of everything I own!" Maddie complained, turning in front of the mirror. "Oh, hi, Honey! I really need to go shopping. Everything here's so...dated!"

Whitney leaned against the door jamb, speculating, "If my calendar's right, it's September 1st, and Mr. Atkins swings into your orbit today." As she spoke she glanced at the large pile of dresses, skirts and tops thrown on the bed.

"Oh, those, " Maddie said, following her gaze. "They're for the church thrift shop." Maddie struggled out of a white dress as she spoke.

"You'll stock them for a month with that haul," Whitney quipped, looking at the bed again. She walked to Maddie's closet, taking out two dresses and a skirt. "Better decide on one of these. There's nothing else left in here."

Whitney offered the two dresses and Maddie chose, put on the pale blue shirt-dress, turned to look at herself from all angles in the mirror and asked, "What do you think? Make me look fat? How's the color? Do I looked washed out?"

"You look wonderful, Mom! He'll notice you even though you're not in the least bit concerned about that."

Maddie made as if to chase her out of the room and returned to the closet to make a shoe decision. Whitney heard boxes being moved from the shelf and shook her head, smiling broadly as she walked back through the kitchen and out the door to the patio. The already warm sun confirmed her decision to put on a halter and shorts when she got up.

"Tony, that looks like black-face," Maddie declared, examining the makeup the supplier had sent to the theater for Othello. Tony Cole had brought it to Maddie's office while the cast was being put through its first-day paces by Ben.

"Are you sure they know it's Shakespeare and not a minstrel show?" he questioned, smearing a streak of it on the back of his hand. "Yuck, it's even worse on!"

Tony, a veteran Broadway make-up artist, had begged

Ben to let him do this show. He'd worked with Bret twenty years before in New York and wanted to see close-up if it was nature and good genes or a very clever surgeon who had been that kind to him.

He'd worked two Cameron Broadway shows on which Maddie had assisted, and during the week preceding the first *Othello* rehearsal, they'd reminisced many times over coffee.

Maddie, on the phone to the supplier, was connected with the office with whom she usually dealt and put Tony on the line. She stood, offering him her chair as she handed him the receiver. Standing at the "thinking zone," her office's bay window, she listened as he explained color nuances and flesh tones.

Watching Tony, she noted how little he had changed over the years, except for his now long blond hair worn in a ponytail. Taller than he, she was sure she was at least 25 pounds heavier. Thin had always been an understatement with him, and when AIDS was identified, some decided that was the explanation for his almost gaunt appearance. Maddie had never doubted his explanation though, that he'd always metabolized faster than he ate.

"They're sending a messenger with what I requested, even though they don't believe me that it will be right. How could they understand what a stage Othello's needs are? Movie companies must be the bulk of their business."

They walked downstairs together and were passing through the lobby when Maddie heard Atkins' voice. She had arrived in the theater after him and had missed running into him throughout the day. She and Tony cracked open a door in the back of the house and stole a look.

Ben was in mid-sentence, "...and you shouldn't be reticent about questioning me as to why I'm asking for this or that. Your time here can be a learning experience from both sides of the footlights if we're open and honest in here."

He surveyed the cast seated on folding chairs and on the stage floor. His gaze stopped on Atkins. "We have in this group a person who needs no introduction to practically any-one in the civilized world. That in itself can cause problems for us. Your first order of business then is to descend on our star, get out all the "oohs" and "aahs" and be ready to buckle down to serious work tomorrow morning, ten o'clock. Go to it ladies and gentlemen, the stage is yours."

Ben exited to the wings leaving the group staring at a shocked Atkins. He heard Atkins say, "Look, I'm no different from any of you, just luckier, gotten some good breaks, some right place/right time miracles. I've looked forward to being here with you. Let's not use the name Bret Atkins for the next two months. It's more like a title than a name now anyway. Why don't you call me...let's see...how about Paul?"

He got up from the floor and the cast took the proffered opportunity to turn into fans. They'd studiously avoided it in the dorm since their arrival. By the time they'd finished, everyone seemed more relaxed.

Ben found Maddie in Dressing Room Number One talk-ing to Todd Philips, the costume designer. Tony was seated at the lit dressing table, fashioning a stylized black mask on his own face.

"Gracious, Tony, what is that stuff? Shoe polish?" Ben asked, inspecting the container of makeup.

"It's what they sent for our Othello. I don't think even Bret Atkins could look good in this stuff!" Tony declared as he smeared his blackened face with cold cream.

Maddie and Ben watched in fascination as the first Kleenex wiped across his check left most of the color on his face.

"Oh, nuts! I hope this doesn't need dermabrasion to get it off!" Tony wailed as he scooped a large glob of cream from the jar and massaged it vigorously onto his cheeks.

Maddie had come backstage for another reason besides make-up; she wanted to find out how "real" Bret Atkins was. Having worked in the past with actors in their mid-forties, she knew how much glue and whale-bone went into their fin-ished package.

As she wandered around the room, seemingly in final inspection of what was now the Atkins area, the makeup table, the closet, the shelves, she sought some sign of toupee glue, Poli-Grip, or an odd array of girdles and cinches which ensure a trim figure.

Failing to uncover any damning evidence, Maddie returned to her office only minutes before Atkins and his fellow actors exited through the lobby, laughing and sounding like a bunch of teenagers.

Why did I think having Atkins around here would make my job any different? I was still imprisoned in my office practically all day. I didn't see Ben for longer than five minutes at a time, let alone our star, Maddie thought as she exited through the same lobby fifteen minutes later.

That morning she'd put the top of her convertible down after clearing the freeway. Whitney wouldn't be the only one with a tan that night. Running late when she arrived, she didn't have time to put it up so the car had been left to sit open all day.

Holy crow, this seat is as hot as a griddle! Well, I'll put up the top and run the air conditioner for a few minutes before I head out.

Try as she might she couldn't get her car to start. *It can't be the battery; it's new. I just had a complete service done last week! What's the problem?*

She got out of the sun-baked car and searched her key case for the auto club card.

Someone approached from behind, and her New York City self-preservation instinct activated. Raising her ever-handy Mace spray to eye level, she turned quickly.

"Whoa! Don't!" Bret Atkins' voice startled her. "My room is right over there and I couldn't help hearing someone was in trouble. Thought maybe I could help."

Maddie exhaled in relief there was no danger and then gasped in surprise. She extracted the auto card from its slot, thinking, *Concentrate! Talk! Don't you dare make a fool of yourself!*

She could not feel the muscles in her face, but was reasonably sure she was smiling when she said, "Thank you so much for coming out, but unless you're a certified mechanic or a walking telephone, I don't think there's anything you can do."

He reached into his slacks pocket. "Your wish is my command!" and produced a cellular phone.

She laughed and it relaxed her, took the phone from his hand and dialed. "They won't be here for about two hours. Thanks." Handing it back, she added, "Guess I'll go to my office and get some more work done."

"Heavens," she suddenly exclaimed. "You must think I'm the rudest person on the planet! Please forgive me for not welcoming you earlier to our little torture chamber. You were already in the theater by the time I arrived. Ben is thrilled to have you here."

"Just Ben?" he asked, provocatively, she thought. *Don't start with me, Atkins.* Bypassing her thought but feeling more in control because of it, she said, "Well, of course I'm happy you are here. It will be wonderful seeing you on stage. You are one of the very few I've felt capable of doing it all, stage, film, TV...anything."

Atkins shifted his stance. He reacted irritably to her falling into the "fan" category. "Please stop. Let's get all this guff out of the way. Do you want an autograph? A picture, maybe?"

Maddie looked at him questioningly. "What on earth for? I have your signature on countless papers in my office, and if I want a picture I can take one from the files."

"Oh, I'm sorry. Please...," he apologized hastily, "I didn't mean to sound so...egotistical. After listening to an hour's praise from the cast, I've just about had it. When those actors compliment me, I see my own inadequacies. Some of them are much more talented than I. Oh, and thank you for your nice words." As he spoke he studied the ground.

They walked toward the theater and Maddie stole a glance at him, trying to confirm whether he was serious. She couldn't decide and filed the comment on his co-workers away in her memory for future reference. "One good thing has come out of all this, though," Maddie declared, changing the subject immediately. "I've proven I can speak. Didn't say one word to you that night we met at Megastudios."

Atkins stopped and watched her walk a few more steps. She realized he was no longer beside her and turned to him as he asked, "You didn't? I thought you were totally charming that night."

Maddie didn't know what to say and fished for her lobby door keys in her dress pocket.

Bret reacted, "Do you have to go back to work? Couldn't we have a cup of coffee or something?"

"I guess so." Maddie was curious as to what he wanted to talk about. "Sure, why not. There's always a pot on in the dorm kitchen." They crossed the parking lot in silence and entered by the back door.

She took a mug from the cabinet, poured his coffee, and watched him stir in a hefty amount of cream and two sugars. Her eyebrows went up.

Noting her surprise, he said, "No sweets, no fats, no eating pleasures. Those are the rules I have to live by as long as I'm in front of the cameras. I've counted on these two months of pounding the boards to fight off the extra calories I've promised myself."

He studied her as she moved between the refrigerator and sink counter. She was attractive in a classic way - Grace Kelly with dark hair. He liked her lack of heavy makeup and made a silent wager that the curves were hers, not a gift of medical science.

Maddie turned suddenly and caught his appraising look. He turned away fast, as if caught with his hand in the cookie jar.

Three cast members wandered in. Bret was disappointed he'd lost the opportunity to be alone with her. He hadn't gotten to say a serious word to her yet. He needed to find out why looking into her eyes that night, for only a moment, had such a jolting effect on him.

Before long, the group had expanded to such a size they'd outgrown the kitchen and were forced to move into the living room. Nevertheless, the impromptu party provided him with some interesting insights.

Someone mentioned Maddie's daughter, Whitney. He remembered meeting the beautiful young actress but had completely missed the connection in names. "Maddie's daughter!" A daughter who, he guessed was around twenty-five, forcing him to revise upwards his estimate of late thirties for Maddie.

He had little to say, preferring to be an observer. Maddie's regard for her actors showed in her natural ease with them, talking openly and laughing with them. This lack of artifice, which bridged the management barrier intrigued him. Intelligence and a sense of humor mirrored in her quick laugh and fast, witty retorts added yet another dimension. *I haven't seen all of that directed at me. She's still hung up on that damn Atkins thing! There are times when that guy is like a monkey on my back!*

An important question still remained unanswered for him. *If there's a daughter, there's a husband somewhere, but there's no ring on her left hand. Divorcee, widow, grass widow, single mother?*

His speculations were interrupted when the group, now involved in a game of Trivial Pursuit, exploded in laughter. Saying he had to make a phone call, he got up from the couch on which he had stretched out and waved to the assemblage as he left the room.

Maddie waved good-bye and mouthed a thank you as he left. Renewed laughter and comical remarks echoed through the room as he headed for his quarters on the next floor.

Why would I expect a special good-bye from her? I was treated the way I've asked to be, the same as anyone else in that room.

That's odd! I've just discovered something about myself. I don't like to think I'm special in any way but I seem to expect special treatment! Not as humble as you like to think, are you, Paul?

He threw himself onto the bed and punched Monika's number into the phone. "Hi, Puddin'. How're you settling in at school?"

"Okay, I guess. It always takes me a few days to get used to being here again. Hey, I've already asked my dorm mother if I can see you in your show. She said yes. Now it's up to you."

"You've just started classes, and already you're talking about gallivanting out? What happens to your homework that night? What is this educational system coming to?"

"To allowing me to see you perform, if you give your permission. You've promised me a couple of things, and I think you can give me one now."

Bret sat up. "Promise? What promise? Am I supposed to buy you something? What?"

Monika chuckled. "You're not listening! I said a couple of things, not one! I've heard that when you get old the memory is the first to go, but are your ears in trouble too? You really don't remember?"

Bret wracked his brain and said, "I can't think of what I said. Give me a clue."

She laughed. "You have to wake up those dying brain cells, Daddy. The first one I've already mentioned; you promised that when you were in a stage play you'd let me come to see you."

"That sounds like something I might have said, but I didn't think I'd be in the middle of nowhere when it happened. I can't leave here to go and get you."

Monika ventured, "Maybe she could do it for you."

"She? Who?"

"Gee Dad, one of your Oscars just shriveled up and died. That was the worst acting I've ever heard! She! Whoever it is you've been carrying on about for the last few weeks. I'll bet she's at that place with you. Maybe one of the actresses?"

Bret stood and began to pace. "Have you been talking to Marina? Filling your head with such silly ideas! I'll have to have a word with her!"

"Dad, don't blame Marina. I've got eyes and ears. You may think a twelve-year old is only an inch out of the cradle but I have news for you. I've known about the birds and the bees for years now and I know that a man without a woman isn't really living like a man should."

Bret was stunned. "What kind of people do you talk to? Telling a child things like that. I knew I was away too much! If I wasn't so involved here I'd leave right now and..."

"Don't be silly, Dad. You won't go anywhere because she's there, isn't she? Why do you get so bent out of shape when I mention her? Think I'll get jealous if you have a woman in your life? I'll be dating soon myself and..."

"You dating? Over my dead body!" he blustered.

"Don't go off the deep end, Daddy! There's still time to talk about it. I'm going to hold off until after Christmas," she joked, knowing he'd explode again and relishing her hold over him.

Monika shook the phone when silence greeted her goading. "Hello Dad? You still there?"

"I'm here. I think I should take you out of that place, that you'd be better off in a convent school. It sounds like one week back there and the sweet, innocent daughter I dropped off has become a...a..."

"Dad, even this place is better than a convent school! I'd rather be with you, but since I can't, this place has to do. Now all that would be different if I had a mother..."

"You do have one," he stated emphatically but backed away from the stern tone immediately. "She died, but she's still with you. No woman on this earth could take Nancy's place. Please don't..."

"I'm sorry, Dad. I won't say it again. Please don't feel bad."

He heard a whimper in her voice. "I'm sorry I snapped at you, Sweetheart. Don't think I haven't wanted to give you a normal home life with two parents but so far all I've met are...well, they're not worthy of meeting you. Your mom was so wonderful; she spoiled me for anyone else."

"See my side, Dad. You and I are separated for most of every year. I think you're wonderful for making it to all my recitals and honor days, even from Australia last year. I know it's because you love me when you do things like that, but I think it's unfair you have no one except a twelve-year old to love and make you happy. You're my hero, Dad. What am I? A daughter, that's all. Let's face it, I'm too short to be your hero and too young to be the kind of friend you can really talk to. When you hug me I feel safe and warm. I can never make you feel that way. So, you need a grown-up woman to make you feel all those things. I think Mom agrees with me."

Bret couldn't find words.

Monika added, "I love you more than anything, Dad, but believe it or not, I wouldn't have trouble sharing you. I know that if you love her, she's got to be kind of like my mom. I'd be too busy getting to know her to be bothered with all that jealousy stuff."

"Uh-huh," was all he could say through the lump in his throat.

She knew she'd touched a nerve and that it was time to sign off. As she walked back to her room, she whispered, "Thanks, Mom, I know you put those ideas in my head to shake him up. If I get to that theater, I can see her with him. What's even better, he can see her with me. Oh, yes, that would be nothing but good!"

V

*I*t had been a day of myriad small catastrophes for Maddie, more make-up problems just one among them, so she was running late with the work she needed to leave for Ben before she went home. She'd also missed the first rehearsal.

Not realizing so many hours had gone by, she was surprised by the voice of Bret Atkins, who was standing in her doorway, absentmindedly sipping from a paper coffee cup and surveying the books on her shelf. "Which one would you choose?" he asked. "You arrive in New York in the morning and you're leaving that night on the red-eye. Would you see a hit Broadway show, an opera, a ballet, or go to a concert?"

Her heart skipped a beat as she motioned him in while trying not to lose the mental math she was doing on the production cost sheets on her desk. She told herself, *Cool it! You redeemed yourself yesterday. Don't blow it today!*

Looking back quickly at the page, she jotted a sub-total in the margin and inquired whether he'd enjoyed his first session with Ben and the cast, a read-through of *Othello*.

She looked up, perplexed by his silence.

Now he was facing her, waiting for her response to his inquiry.

"Oh, you're not kidding? You really want to know?" Maddie asked in genuine surprise. She placed the papers in a folder and sat back. "Well, what's the show?"

"What show? Lord, I don't know," Bret said, moving into the room and to the far side of Maddie's desk. "How about whatever one you wish you could see right now."

"Hmmm...I have a list of those. Are you thinking of a special opera?"

"I'd guess you like Puccini. Let's say *La Boheme*."

Maddie smiled at his guess. "You're right about the Puccini, but I have to be lured there by a singer also. Who's the tenor?"

"Rudolpho, hm," he said, looking toward the window. "Let's see...who would you...this is hard. There are more than a few." He studied her for a few seconds and offered, "Guess all I can do is go with the one I'd like to hear, Placido Domingo."

Maddie stared back in surprise at his second right choice but shifted her glance quickly, fearing a repeat of her studio reaction when she looked into his eyes. "Very interesting choice, Mr. Atkins. How about the ballet?"

"Lord, woman, this was originally a simple question! Now I feel like I'm a contestant on The $64,000.00 Question! Let's see...what ballet. This one's almost impossible! Many, too many! I'll choose a few, *Coppelia, Don Quixote*...or how about *Spartacus* or *Romeo and Juliet*."

"Tchaikovsky or Prokofiev?" Maddie asked, before he'd finished his last word.

"For *Romeo and*...? Prokofiev," he answered without hesitation. "And save your breath. The concert is the New York Philharmonic. I wouldn't dare venture into repertoire but I will offer you a soloist."

"Who?"

"Give me a break!" he pleaded, sitting down wearily in the visitor's chair across the desk from Maddie. "How about a choice of instrument?"

"Good enough," Maddie replied with a smile.

He stared at her hands. The pencil Maddie had been holding slipped through her fingers and rolled across the desk toward him. She hoped he hadn't noticed the involuntary tremor his gaze had caused.

He stopped the pencil's forward motion with an index finger and stated, "Piano."

Maddie turned her chair to the window, afraid he'd see the surprise mirrored on her face. *What are the odds he'd pick all my individual favorites?*

"Well, what's your choice?" he persisted.

Maddie turned her head and smiled. "Since you placed the events in New York, I'll take three out of four."

He rolled the pencil back in her direction. "That's impossible! How can you do three in one day?"

"Easily, with stamina and nothing else to do," she replied, turning towards him and watching the rolling pencil disappear under the pile of papers nearest her.

"First, I'd make sure it was a Friday and go to the Phil's 11:00 morning concert to hear Beethoven's Fifth Piano Concerto, then cross the plaza to the Metropolitan Opera for the Matinee. Hearing Placido sing Rudolpho is pure heaven! Next, I'd grab a quick bite at a Lincoln Center restaurant. There should be enough time for me to sit by the fountain in the Lincoln Center Plaza and enjoy the passing scene before I jeté my way to *Romeo and Juliet,* danced to Prokofiev's score at the State Theater. One should always precede a ride to Kennedy Airport with a family feud, a murder and two suicides."

She fished the pencil out of its paper cave and laid it on top of the pile.

Bret shifted in his chair in amazement at the similarity in their tastes. He'd vowed the night before, after Monika's speech about "the woman," that he would find out all he could about Maddie, but felt that if he asked too many direct questions, she might clam-up or avoid him. He'd decided to try the Monika Method: the more innocuous the questions, the more natural the answers. *She'll probably think I'm some kind of a mental case but hey, I'm an actor! I'm supposed to be high-strung, eccentric,* he reasoned. "It was very interesting, very different, very inspiring. Why'd you leave out the Broadway show?"

Maddie blinked, trying to fathom his line of thought. "Does the first part of what you just said have any relation to the second?"

Bret took a sip of his now cold coffee and made a face. "Oh, that's awful!" He placed the cup on the desk, looking at it in disgust.

Maddie excused herself and left the room, leaving Bret wondering if he actually appeared as dumb as he felt. She returned carrying a fresh cup of hot coffee, liberally laced with cream and sugar, placed it on the desk in front of him, and returned to her seat.

He spoke as if she hadn't been absent for two minutes. "The first part answered your question, and the second was my question."

Maddie's mind reeled. What was he talking about? She felt like a complete fool. Why couldn't she follow his train of thought? She rubbed her hand nervously on the armrest of her chair and asked softly, "What was my question?"

He laughed. "Oh Lord, I'm sorry. My daughter tells me I do that, connect up unrelated questions and answers. I didn't realize I'd done it to you. You asked me if I liked today's rehearsal."

"I thought you hadn't heard me," Maddie replied as her phone rang. "Excuse me."

She turned towards the window, relieved for a break in the confusion. Tony informed her that the new make-up had arrived, and it was almost perfect. "Of course, we put it on Mr. Gorgeous, and it will take that extra step to perfection! By the way, you'd better give some tranquilizers or something to Beth, our Desdemona. She has just risen above euphoria, informed me she fell madly in love when he touched her. She's married, isn't she?"

Maddie forgetting Bret was just five feet away said, "Married or not, she's his wife for a couple of hours a day for the next two months. Who knows what can happen? Remember who we're talking about, Mr. Irresisti —" She stopped short and felt red, hot blood rush to her face. "Oh, not really ! I'll be right there! Is there no end! Not another mess!" She hung up and, without facing Atkins, excused herself and rushed out of the office.

Tony was still holding the receiver, wondering what had happened, when Maddie slammed open the backstage door. "I'm going to die right here, Tony! He was sitting in my office when you called!"

"Who?" Tony asked the flustered and distracted Maddie. He'd never seen her lose it like this within the walls of a theater when he'd worked with her in the past. He took her hand and squeezed it until she looked at him.

"Atkins! Who else?" Maddie groaned. "Oh, God, he surprised me so much by showing up in my office, I lost my concentration. Tony, I don't know how it sounded, sarcastic or... You don't think he might have heard it as...jealousy? I mean that's really stupid, but...maybe he believes all the garbage that's written about him."

Tony put his arm around her shoulders and walked her back towards the door. "Listen to Tony. If he's left your office when you go back, I think you can assume he's angry. He heard sarcasm. If he's still there waiting for you, there could be two good reasons. One, he heard it, thought it was funny, and will ignore it, talking on about something totally unrelated. Now follow me here, that could mean he wants to stay in the good graces of Ben's right hand, or..."

Maddie looked at him as they continued walking. "Or?"

"He's interested in you."

Maddie stopped, forcing Tony to do so too. "Don't be ridiculous! What could he possibly see in me?"

Tony looked at her from head to toe. "What I see, but for me it'll always be friends only; a dear and beautiful friend, I might add. Maybe he could use a dear and beautiful friend too, but, with him, that could change to lover in the twinkling of an eye."

Maddie blushed. "Don't be an idiot, Tony! Me?"

"You act your usual self with him and he'll be eating out of your hand in no time. In fact, he may be nibbling on other choice parts of your —"

Maddie rushed the last few steps to the door, leaving Tony behind. "Tony, stop it!"

"Then, of course, there's the possibility he heard jealousy," Tony continued. "At that rate, I give him ten seconds to make a move on you when you go back upstairs, and since you'd want to immediately eliminate Beth from any hope of competition, you'd be the most ardent lover he's probably ever had."

She opened the door, and without looking back, stated, "I am going to have you committed. You are definitely certifiable."

As the door swung closed, leaving him alone again, Tony turned on his heel and returned to Atkins' dressing room. He shook his head, muttering, "Me thinks she protesteth too much. Oh, I love sub-plots."

Atkins was still in Maddie's office when she returned. He studied her for a moment. The scrutiny made her uneasy, uncomfortable. Finally, he stood and said, "Didn't want to just disappear on you. It seemed impolite to do that to the Boss Lady. Hope you have no car troubles tonight. You probably can't get away fast enough today, with all the stuff that came up. Well, maybe I'll see you at rehearsal tomorrow. Bye."

Maddie stared at the now empty doorway. Was he angry? She didn't think so; he didn't sound it. Was he ignoring it? She didn't know, but who cared anyway! She put the almost finished cost sheets on Ben's desk with a note about completing them early the next morning and headed for her car.

Each day following, when rehearsals ended, Bret either dragged himself to bed or hung around the theater, actually Maddie's office. She gradually ceased being surprised when she looked up and found him leaning against the door jamb, Diet Coke for her in one hand, and his coffee, with cream and sugar, in the other. She convinced herself that her comments to Tony had gone unnoticed.

During those next three weeks their conversations touched on show business, mid-life crisis, and daughters. His time with her increased steadily, their camaraderie dissolving her inner defensiveness a little more with each passing day. Because he respected her views, she gradually felt no need to choose her words. It was the first time in long years her intelligence was validated by a male acquaintance - other than Ben and Tony, of course - rather than degraded. If there were disagreements, they questioned and discussed the points, interested in each other's opinions. He showed no need to prove himself an expert on any subject, even his forte, acting and the movies.

A surprising discovery for her was his skill in the kitchen. One day after rehearsal, when the rest of the cast had escaped to the nearest town for the evening, he prepared for the two of them the most succulent roast duck she'd ever tasted. He followed it up a few days later with a shore dinner for the whole cast.

It amazed her that on screen he made her heart beat faster with just a glance, but in person, she felt more relaxed with him than anyone else she could remember. In those weeks she grew to genuinely like the man.

———◆◆———

"What do you think, Maddie? You've been at all the rehearsals. What's your gut feeling about the action on that stage?" Ben asked as he inspected the scenery delivered that morning, scenery designed, constructed, and painted in the Genny's own set shop, located in a barn at the west end of the property.

Maddie mentally cataloged the run-throughs to that night's dress rehearsal. Bret's transition to the mind and soul of the Moor had become more apparent with each passing day. His deepening insights into the tragic figure engendered a searing emotional intensity in his Desdemona—at least that's what Maddie assumed it was - and the actor playing Iago reveled in the opportunity to add deeper shadows to a character he'd played "straight" many times.

Atkins' acting skills, obvious on screen just in the diversity of characters he'd portrayed, flowered on stage through his ability to live and breathe a character into reality. The dress rehearsal thrilled Maddie, and she'd escaped to her office to savor in silence what she'd just witnessed.

Ben had opened her office door without a knock, entered, and sat in front of her waiting for an answer. She was loathe to break the spell. He persisted, "Well? What'd you think? So good it's bad?"

She stared silently at him.

"Holy God," Ben sputtered, "it's different, intense but not bad...is it?" He felt sure in his heart that it was better than good.

Maddie continued looking out the window. "I think the world here as we know it is about to end. The performance? It's better than good, Ben; it's incredible! When the critics review this, we will be besieged for tickets, and you know very well we sold-out on Wednesday. God, Ben, Sunday we ran our first ad, the tickets went on sale Monday, and this afternoon, only 36 hours later, we're sold out! Maybe we should call in the National Guard for opening night."

"*Merde!*" Maddie greeted the cast members on opening night with the time honored backstage salutation as she dropped a rose on each of their dressing tables.

She had nothing extra for Bret. When she laid the rose in front of the fully costumed and made-up Othello, he stood, turned to her, and acknowledged softly, "*Merci, beaucoup*," tracing his finger along her chin and around her mouth.

Flustered, she hastily reentered the hallway leading to the stage and created a blockade for half the cast responding to the five-minute call. They looked at her and broke into laughter.

Confused, she walked further on towards the wings' mirror. In it she beheld Bret's "artwork". His hands and arms, covered with newly applied and not totally set brown pancake make-up, were the perfect medium for drawing a mustache and goatee on her.

Maddie raced to a dressing table, smeared cold cream over her mouth and chin and vowed for all to hear that she would get even.

By the time Bret emerged from his dressing room, everyone, including Maddie, had left the area. He headed for the wings, each footstep progressively transforming him to the Moor, altering the set of his shoulders and his gait. By the time he stepped onto the stage he was altogether Othello.

During Act One, Maddie stationed herself near a one-way window at the front of the house, concentrating on the audience, not the stage, checking reactions positive or negative. The web Atkins was weaving held the audience in rapt attention. *They know they're witnessing pure magic,* Maddie thought, and a knot of something vaguely familiar but long lost in time twisted under her heart.

At intermission she found Ben backstage. He took her aside and confided, "You were so right. We'll need all the extra security we've brought in. I feel like a prisoner! There are more guards at our property perimeters than at Sing Sing. Still, I'm nervous knowing how crazy those fans can get sometimes. How much room is left in the living quarters?"

Maddie guessed about three rooms, maybe six beds. "Call the security company and have them get four more men over here tomorrow. I want coverage inside the dorm watching him from a discreet distance, just in case. We'll say they're my guests...from New York. You and I are the only ones who'll know they're not."

Maddie made the call and then ran across the manicured lawn to check on the empty living spaces. The opportunity to get back at Bret was at hand. She let herself into his room. Wishing she could stay to hear the cursing when he tried to stretch out in his short-sheeted bed, she re-closed the door and headed back to the theater before the Act Two curtain.

Whitney drove her own car, following her mother home. *What a mob scene backstage after the show. I never saw so many women vying for one man's attention. Each one seemed to have or had a personal relationship with Atkins. He must have dated every woman in Hollywood.*

She saw Maddie's car far ahead at the turn-off but didn't speed up to close the gap. *Mom and he act like old friends. When they're together there's a quiet about them that's...I don't know...it's like two people who have known each other forever. Mom keeps insisting they're just good friends, but I can't believe that's all there is. Maybe I just don't want to believe that's all there is. Oh, I don't know.*

Maddie's brake lights flashed at a distant intersection and Whitney thought, *What's wrong with this picture? They're obviously good together. He likes her, she likes him, amen. Where are their pheromones? I know she's not dead inside, just sleeping. Is it possible he is too? Ships that pass in the night, both captains dozing at the wheel?* Her silent soliloquy took her to the end of their driveway, and she pulled in next to her mother's car.

Both women's keys were aimed for the door lock. "I'll get it," Maddie said and let Whitney walk in ahead of her. The phone began to ring, and Maddie ran for it. Whitney pulled a Diet Sprite from the refrigerator and sat at the kitchen table, trying not to listen.

"Oh, hi," Maddie said, turning to Whitney and mouthing "Bret." "Something wrong?"

He said he was checking whether she had notes on his performance that she couldn't give to him because of the after-show chaos. Whitney thought it sounded like a lame excuse for a call at midnight.

"I know you hate praise but, since I can't see your scowl, I'll say this. Your performance tonight wasn't good. It was phenomenal!"

"Maddie, that's not..."

"Don't stop me now, I'm on a roll. The part can't help but season with each performance, and I tremble to think what your final audience is going to experience in three weeks time. We'll have to take them out on stretchers."

"I guess I can take that as positive commentary from my boss. Thank you."

Maddie winked at Whitney as she asked, "Bret, where are you? I don't hear any noise in the background."

"I'm still in the dressing room. Some people stayed on after. You know, the studio executive type, and I had to play my hardest role of the night, the one where I pretended I was interested in what they had to say."

Maddie urged him to rest until his 6:00 call the next night, said good-bye and burst out laughing as she took a Diet Coke from the refrigerator. "I confidently predict that phone will ring again very soon."

"What in God's name did you do, Mom?"

She described his facial graffiti and confessed her revenge. Her gaze went to the phone a couple of times as she spoke. It didn't ring.

Whitney grabbed her mother's hands and announced the news she'd held inside all evening, though bursting to shout it from the rooftop. She'd gotten a call to screen-test for *American Dream*, a presidential race thriller. "Someone Ben introduced me to that night at Megastudios called around until he found my agent, and here I am."

"This could be your big break!" Maddie exclaimed with an enthusiastic smile. "Have you talked to Ben? Maybe he knows something about the script. This could be the right one! I'm thrilled for you." She squeezed Whitney's hand and unconsciously looked in the direction of the phone as she said, "Who's playing the would-be President?"

"Big hush-hush stuff for now," Whitney answered and sipped her drink. She thought Maddie looked different. Prettier? Younger? Could it be just more relaxed? Her thoughts were interrupted by the phone for which Maddie reached far too fast to be a casual move.

"Why am I not surprised it's you, Mr. Atkins?" she asked, winking at Whitney. "Something wrong?"

Maddie got an answer she didn't expect as Bret confided, "Something is supposed to happen that I don't feel comfortable with. I don't know what to do. Can I impose on you for help?"

"Of course, what are friends for? What's up?" she asked, shrugging her shoulders to Whitney.

Maddie listened and then replied, "Stop worrying. Have her call me, and we'll work it out together."

Whitney guessed he'd apologized for bothering her when she heard Maddie answer, "As I said, what are friends for? You can't do anything from where you are, so you need someone to do it for you. If you'd turned to anyone else, I'd be upset."

Maddie brought the phone close to Whitney's ear and shared his response. "Oh, believe me, if my legs have been radically shortened for merely doing some innocent art work, my mind boggles at your degree of punishment for upsetting you."

She laughed, and Bret added, "I'll tell her to call you tomorrow and, once again, thank you."

Whitney leaned back, remembering the way Bret's eye's followed Maddie in the crowd backstage. "Mom, it's just possible he thinks of you as more than a friend. If you keep up that 'what are friends for' stuff you just might lose a great opportunity."

Maddie looked seriously at her daughter, "Little Miss Yenta! Bret and I are friends and nothing more. He's been in and out of my life every day for three weeks, and we've discovered we like many of the same things. He's very intelligent, well-read and not just scripts - so he's very interesting. He loves classical music, and I've been filling him in on the New York music scene. You know, concerts are a pleasure he's had to forego. He feels his presence causes too much distraction, so he doesn't attend anymore for the sake of the artists' concentration. He's become a prisoner to his fame."

Whitney rested her chin on her hand, covering the beginnings of a smile behind her fingers as Maddie continued, "We share a liking for the same foods. Not good for either of our waist-lines, but I've enjoyed some great meals with him, all the better because he's been the chef. He loves to cook, but his housekeeper won't let him near 'her' kitchen. He says he gets some practice by treating his location casts and crews to at least one meal he has prepared."

"He falls short in the cleanup department, though. I've been the not-so-silent assistant who scurries in with the clean utensils and carts away the used ones. It's been really fun. I can't imagine anyone else who gets paid to have as good a time as I've had lately."

Whitney's fingers pressed tighter over her mouth, attempting to obliterate a full smile.

"He told me he has a beautiful home on a cliff above the Pacific, near Santa Barbara. Remember, Whit, when we drove up Big Sur and saw those oceanside dream houses?"

"I do, Mom," Whitney said through her fingers. "Didn't you say you'd give the world to spend the rest of your life on one of those balconies gazing at that view?"

Maddie laughed and said, "I still would but that will happen only if I win the lottery."

Whitney clenched her teeth, trying to silence what appeared so obvious to her.

Maddie went on, oblivious to her daughter's reaction.

"He's really very sweet, careful to treat a woman like a lady. You know, holding the door, pulling out a chair, helping with a coat. All those wonderful customs no one seems to observe any more. By the way did you know he has a daughter?"

Whitney had finally mastered her reactions and sat back, to all appearances casually thumbing through *Variety*. Actually, she was studying another change in her mother. Maddie was shedding her protective layer of nervous energy. The process had begun with Atkins' first phone call.

If Whitney wanted to respond she couldn't because Maddie hurried on. "His daughter! Oh, I didn't tell you! That's what he called about. His daughter is coming to see him perform next Saturday and - Oops! I wasn't supposed to tell anyone!"

"Really Mom! Like I'm going to run out and shout it from the roof tops? Please!"

"Oh, I'm sorry. I know I can trust you. He asked me for complete secrecy, and I want to do everything right."

Whitney's hand returned to once more hide her impending smile.

Maddie went on, "It seems the housekeeper is planning to pick the child up at the private school she attends and bring her to the theater. He's all hot and bothered over that, convinced the woman will get lost trying to find the Genny. He wants me to convince her there are alternatives."

Whitney couldn't resist saying, "Sure there are! How about you jump in the car and drive all over California to ease his mind?"

Maddie exclaimed, "Well, I would do it if Ben could get along for the day without me."

Whitney sat up, about to protest.

"Don't worry, I won't. We have four security guards living incognito in the actors' residence. I'll send one or two of them on a little errand."

"No, it's no trouble at all," Maddie reassured Marina.

"We have people here ready and willing to help us solve any problems that come up."

Marina wondered if this was the woman her boss had met at the party. "Fine then. I will be picked up first. I don't think Monika should be riding alone with a stranger. If I'm picked up at two, we will make it to you in good time."

Maddie agreed, "You're absolutely right about you being picked up first. I would want it that way myself."

"You have a daughter?" Marina asked, trying to build an image of this woman from her voice.

"Yes, the joy of my life," Maddie proclaimed. "She's twenty-five, but I still worry about who she's with and where she's at."

"Da. Monika has either been here with me or locked away at school so those worries haven't started yet," Marina revealed. "Mr. Atkins has been very careful about her security."

"Would she have met anybody who might be here and know who she is?" Maddie inquired while pulling out the seating plan for Saturday night's performance.

Marina hesitated for a moment. "I don't think Monika has been allowed to meet many people connected with the studios, only Mr. Cameron. And none of the neighbors are around, all vacationing, so they won't be at the theater."

"All right then," Maddie said, circling two seats in the center section and pulling a card from the box office file. "I will meet you when you arrive." As she spoke she crossed out the location numbers on the card and made a note that two seats needed to be added to the first row, figuring that putting these displaced people closer to the stage would ease her conscience about taking the best seats in the house away from them.

She replaced the chart and the card, notified two of the "New York guests" of their chauffeuring job, and was about to call Whitney when she noticed Bret in her doorway.

"Come in. Sit down." She looked for the accustomed Diet Coke and saw his hands were empty. Realizing he'd forgotten he said, "Just a supplicant today. Sorry."

Maddie thought he looked tired. "What's bothering you? No sleep last night? You're not that worried about your daughter, are you?"

"Of course I am," he stated emphatically, leaning forward in the chair. "I won't have her flitting around, not knowing who she's with, going wherever she wants!"

Maddie, thinking he was kidding said, "Right you are. Imagine, mingling with the riffraff, possibly talking to, please forgive the term, boys. Quick, lock that cell; keep her in!"

He stared at her and nearly shouted, "I'm serious! How dare you make jokes! We're talking about my daughter! I won't let just anyone near her!"

"What is your problem?" Maddie countered. "You're making no sense. She's coming here, to the theater, in the company of not just anyone. She'll be with your housekeeper. Where did all this 'flitting wherever she wants to' come from?"

"It hasn't happened yet," he admitted, "but she's leading up to it. I think she thought up this thing about promises I've made to her, to maneuver me into giving her more freedom. I don't remember if I did or didn't. Oh, don't get me wrong, she doesn't lie, but ever since she turned ten I've felt as though she's testing ways of getting around me. I'm not centered enough when I'm with her to file each sentence in my memory bank. She knows this, and I think she's starting to use it against me."

Maddie had noticed how, when he was centered on the subject, he spoke almost obliquely of his daughter. It was in his relaxed moments that her name slipped out and his love for her showed. She remembered the day Bret sat in her office and asked at what age her daughter first wore lipstick. It was as if he needed guidelines with the "girl" things but couldn't force himself to come forward and ask directly.

"Okay, we'll make this Steps to Surviving a Preteen Daughter as Experienced by Whitney's Mother. When she was eleven I'd let her wear a little bit if we were going somewhere special. I swore then that if I heard 'But everyone except me is wearing it all the time!' once more I'd scream bloody murder! I imagine it's worse now. After all, that was fourteen years ago. Boy, have times changed!"

"You said it," Bret sighed. "I can even remember when a girl wouldn't dare telephone a boy. Now I hear a girl calling for a date is okay. I give up! There's no way to keep them safe, let alone even know what they're up to."

Maddie realized his genuine concern and confusion. "Bret, I doubt she's sitting around plotting how to get the better of you. If I remember correctly, you told me she's twelve."

Bret looked up at her in surprise, not remembering having told her. *Am I talking about Monika and not even realizing it? I don't talk about her to anyone, let alone a stranger! Maddie? A stranger? Look again, Paul. She's the closest thing to a confidante you've had since...since Nancy.* His eyes widened at the thought.

Maddie noted the look, interpreted it as confirmation of her statement, and went on. "I'll bet she's a pretty mature twelve too, considering the life-styles of the children she lives with at school."

He looked at her questioningly.

"Those kids are from rich families, most of whom have a set of values which honors those who have the most and are the first to do anything. How's this for a scenario: fourteen year old sneaks out of dorm for a forbidden date. She reigns as Number One in the adoration sweepstakes until some thirteen-year old schoolmate does something more outrageous and usurps her title. It's the battle for adolescent superiority. Similar competitions exist in every school. They just get more complicated and sophisticated in a private school with all that extra supervision."

"Are you insinuating my daughter would vie for such an honor?" he asked sternly, watching her push away from her desk, rise and walk to the window.

"How could I possibly do that? I know so little about her. I had to figure out who Monika was. You never mention "my daughter" and Monika in the same sentence," Maddie answered, frustration causing an edge to come into her voice. "I have a daughter, remember? Whitney, the one whose name and relationship to me I wouldn't dream of separating. Her existence is the most important thing in my life!"

Bret heard in anger what he'd been afraid to ask about for weeks.

Maddie continued in a controlled voice, "A daughter who, through the love and support she received from the day she was born, rejected the foolishness of such competition. I like to think that was what helped her negate a need for that kind of affirmation from relative strangers."

Her anger waned as she turned and looked at him. "You obviously love your child very much, and I'm sure she knows it. That will influence all of her decisions."

Bret rose and walked toward her, saying, "Maddie, I didn't mean to speak to you that way, but I feel so inadequate at times it drives me crazy. She has a housekeeper for a mother, never knew a minute of her real one, and now I feel I'm failing her as a father. I'm there for her as much as possible, but I don't think it's enough. I'm holding on, trying to guide her, but I'm groping to find the right path. Now I feel that, when I wasn't looking, she took the lead away from me and is picking up the pace. She'll be dragging me along pretty soon."

Maddie's impulse to reach out and comfort him was almost overwhelming. She folded her arms, hugging herself instead, and offered, "I don't claim to be any kind of expert, only a survivor parent, and I don't know your daughter at all, but I have gotten to know you a little. She knows in her heart who you really are, but she is also faced with your many screen images. In fact, she probably sees them more often than she sees you in person."

Bret nodded and folded his arms too.

"Don't you think she could be a little confused?" Maddie asked.

He continued to stare out the window.

"I think she'll try many different approaches on you, all based on things she's seen on the screen. Remember too, she probably feels like she's competing with half the planet for your attention. It's never her with you in those pictures in the magazines, only some of the most beautiful women in the world hanging on your arm. Her desire to make a big impression on you must be pretty strong. After all, she is going on thirteen. How do you think females perfect those feminine wiles? They practice on Dad, so don't get uptight when she pulls a fast one or tries to con you. Better on you than on the dorm mother!"

He stared at her.

"From what you've said," Maddie ventured, staring into his eyes, "I think you're tying her too tightly. Let her spread her wings a little. It's a pity, but thirteen is considered almost adult in today's world."

Bret exclaimed, "Adult? She's only a baby!"

Maddie shook her head and gave in to the urge to touch him, laying her hand on his forearm. "In your mind and heart, but not in reality, Bret. She's growing up, and it's only natural for her to want to feel some measure of control over her own life. She's so restricted now that, if something doesn't give, she could stop dragging you along and leave you behind. Loosen up and you'll more than likely find she chooses to hold tighter to you - but on her new terms."

He sighed and looked outside once again. "I'm really no good at this at all, being a parent. What you say makes perfect sense. Yet I don't want to accept it. I'm afraid I'll lose her if I don't hold tight."

Maddie felt a wave of compassion as she looked at his profile and then glanced down at her hand on his arm, hoping it didn't look as if she were coming on, and at such a weak moment for him.

She took her hand away very slowly and returned to stand by her desk, putting distance between them. "Bret, you're good at parenting. Otherwise she'd be totally out-of-hand by now. You're experiencing your first encounter with the emerging woman in your baby. You think it's a trial for a father. Being the mother, dealing with a miniature of herself, is a truly unique torture, seeing the child running head-long at the same mistakes she's already made. Try to offer advice, and Mom's interfering; don't warn her, and Mom's accused of not caring. Different rack, same agony."

Her phone interrupted, and she was relieved for the break, the chance to back off. He wandered toward the door and waved good-bye.

Ben entered a few seconds later and waited for her to finish. "What's wrong with Bret?"

Maddie sat, saying, "Oh, he's worried about his daughter. I hope I said something to him that will help."

Ben looked confused. "Not that kind of wrong...I mean is he injured?"

"Injured?" Maddie stared at him. "No. I didn't notice anything. He wasn't limping; didn't say he'd hurt himself."

Ben headed back toward the door. "All I know is what I saw. He passed me on the staircase and was kneading his arm, like something happened to it. Like this." He laid his hand on his forearm and imitated Bret. "No idea, huh?"

VI

"*U*ncle Ben?" Whitney called out, straining to hear over the mid-day traffic lumbering by the phone booth in downtown Los Angeles.

"Oh no, I'm in for it," Ben quipped. "She calls me 'Uncle' and I know I'm about to be twisted around her little finger."

"I need to ask a favor."

Ben sat back, putting his feet up on the corner of his desk. "As long as it's not illegal, immoral, or fattening."

"None of those, but it is time consuming." Whitney switched the receiver to her other ear. "I picked up a script this morning and just finished reading it. I need to talk to you about it."

Ben winced at the sound of a siren penetrating the phone line. "Where did you read it, in the middle of the free-way?"

"Isn't this noise awful? I read it in the downtown library, and I'm in a phone booth right outside. I couldn't wait to call you. I know it's your opening night and you're probably up to your ears in last minute business. When I come to the theater tonight, can I bring it to you?"

Ben sat up, immediately interested. "Think you found something?"

"That's the funny thing! It found me! I'm supposed to screen-test next week. *American Dream*. Ever hear of it?"

He reached for a package on his bookcase. "It might be in a delivery that came a couple of weeks ago. I've been so busy with this show, I never opened it. You bring yours tonight. I'll check a few things out this afternoon."

"I think its good, Ben, but you're the expert. Maybe I want so badly for it to be the one I'm waiting for that I'm just wishing it good," Whitney offered, with a sigh lost in a horn blast.

Ben pulled at the tape sealing the package as he said, "Get out of all that pollution. Opening night or not, this is important. Go home, take three deep breaths and come out here as soon as you like. I've got your mom to pile any last minute problems onto!"

<hr />

"Lisa, I can't find a thing to wear tonight. I don't like any of these," Monika complained to her roommate, following an hour's dissection of her wardrobe, trying on and rejecting everything.

"Monika, it's your father, not a boyfriend," Lisa pointed out, scrutinizing Monika's open closet. "Everything in here is so...so..."

"Childish?" Monika finished.

"Good word. Let's see what Lisa's closet can do for you." She opened her door and selected a white mini-skirt for Monika's approval. "How's that?"

Monika's eyes lit up. "Great, but my Dad would flip if I showed up in this." She touched the cashmere gently and shrugged her shoulders.

Lisa frowned. "I'd never believe your father was such a prude unless I knew you. Doesn't he know you're growing up?" Lisa replaced the skirt in her closet and removed a rose-colored flip skirt. "This might work. It looks longer than it really is."

Monika smiled and reached for it, held it up to her and said, "I see what you mean. It is short, but...I can borrow it?"

Lisa stepped back to study her friend. "What goes with it is a matching top." She pulled out a v-necked white tunic, piped with the same rose color.

"Oh, Lisa, it's beautiful!" Monika held it up to herself. She noticed a price tag hanging from the label. "I can't wear this! It's new. You haven't worn it yet."

Lisa sat on the end of her bed and joked, "If I can't go to the theater with you, at least my clothes can. Wear it, please."

Monika gave her a hug and ran into the bathroom to change. While she was gone, Lisa took out a pair of pearl earrings and placed them on Monika's dresser.

"How do I look?" Monika asked, walking towards the mirror.

Lisa folded her arms and studied Monika carefully. "It's nothing short of perfect, but I do think pantyhose and heels would make it look fabulous."

"Oh sure! I own a pair of heels! Come on!" Monika looked down at the socks and sneakers she wore.

"All right then, your black velvet flats. They're not bad. And now, the pantyhose. Bombs away!" she exclaimed, flipping an unopened pair from her top drawer over her shoulder, hitting Monika's bed dead-center.

Monika looked uneasy. "Lisa, how can I pay you back for all this? I can't just take and use this stuff and not do something for you."

"Oh, Monikie-Moo, there is a way but...the price is high!"

"What? If I can afford it, you can have it. What?"

"It'll cost you more than money. Convince your father you want me to visit your house for a weekend."

"That's too easy! I want you to come," Monika replied, "Anytime you want!"

Lisa was surprised at the fast answer. She cuddled Snookums, Monika's white teddy bear, and ventured, "Anytime? You think he wouldn't mind? Even if it was a weekend he'd be at home? I'd love to make my mother so jealous and curious she wouldn't be able to stay away from me until she thought she'd drained every last fact about him from my memory."

Lisa Brandon's wealthy parents, with homes in four countries, spent most of their time visiting them and making side trips to unheard of places. Lisa had spent every summer she could remember in a different part of the world, mostly in the company of a nanny, even though her parents were there.

"Oh, I just had a great idea! I'll ask Dad about either Thanksgiving or Christmas. That would be more fun than a weekend," Monika exclaimed, opening the pantyhose package. She dropped her sneakers and socks on the floor as she removed them and pulled on the sheer, flesh-colored nylons.

Lisa brought the velvet shoes to her from the closet and sat on the floor at Monika's feet. "Are you sure you'd want me around at a time like Christmas or Thanksgiving? I mean it's a real family time, and I'd be in the..."

"You say it and I'll have to beat you," Monika threatened with a smile. "You could never be in anyone's way, and it would be such fun. We could go riding and..."

"Horses?"

"No, dinosaurs, you goof! Of course, horses! We have a stable and there's a beach to walk on; it'll be too cold to swim. Dad has a pool table in the beach house and..oh, I know! This would be the best part! We could sneak into the exercise barn and watch him work out. It's really funny, all that grunting and groaning."

Lisa stared at Monika, lost in her dream of such a wonderful holiday.

"Hello, Lisa! How do I look?" Monika asked, turning around in front of the full length mirror.

"Oh, yeah. You look fabulous. Monika, do you really

think he'd let me come for a holiday?" Lisa suddenly had second thoughts. "You know I was only kidding about paying me back. You don't have to ask me to visit...really."

Monika reassured her with a hug. "I'm so glad you want to come! I didn't ask you because I didn't know if you'd want to be with me, away from here I mean. You have no choices here. You're stuck with me. If I want you there, he won't say no. I think I could ask for the moon, and he'd try to get it. It must be awful not going home for the holidays."

She walked closer to the mirror, checking out the length of the skirt. "Short...but fabulous! I'm so happy you transferred here this year and you're my roommate. I love having such a good friend!"

Lisa jumped up from the floor and retrieved the earrings from Monika's dresser. "I didn't think I'd like it here but you've changed that for me." She held out the earrings.

Monika looked at her extended hand and said, "The skirt, the neckline, the pantyhose and earrings too? Dad will go into cardiac arrest!" She eyed them longingly and finally gave in to temptation.

Marina's husband, Boris, sat at the kitchen table waiting patiently for his lunch.

He was head landscaper of the Atkins ten acre estate and had finished his morning project, planting fresh greenery and flowers in the large, fluted white cement urns and wrought-iron railing boxes of a guest bedroom balcony.

"Oh, Marina, you look wonderful," he whispered admiringly as she entered the kitchen through the back door, her accustomed pale blue uniform replaced with a fitted light gray silk suit.

Remembering this was Monika's big day, the first time seeing her father on stage, he raided the refrigerator, made his own lunch and left Marina to finish getting ready.

"Where in heaven's name did I leave it?" she fretted,

reentering the kitchen, opening and closing cabinets and drawers as she passed them. "What did I do with it?"

"Can I help? What are you looking for?" he inquired, watching the woman he'd met, fallen in love with and married seven years before.

Despite residing less than two miles apart in Moscow for forty years, they did not meet until he emigrated to California and was hired by the landscaping firm that serviced the Atkins' home.

He remembered his surprise at finding a Russian-speaking person there. At last, he thought, I can talk comfortably to someone. Not long after the first hello, she informed him that they would speak only English during work hours.

At the end of the work-day, after being returned to the company headquarters, Boris would walk the three miles back to the Atkins' house, hoping she'd join him for a stroll around the grounds. Saying yes more often than no, she would speak with him for hours in their native language.

Atkins was home on a month's hiatus at the time. One evening, a week into Boris' nightly pilgrimages, Atkins called him into the dining room, offered him the use of a car and promised Marina the night off whenever she asked.

Six months later Atkins served as Boris's best man. Marina's matron of honor was her sponsor, and five-year-old Monika served as flower girl in a wedding ceremony held in the living room of the estate.

Atkins wanted to give them the unused guest cottage but they insisted they could not take such a gift, although they would be happy to rent it.

Boris admired his wife's trim figure, and she caught him looking. "Are you going to be all right until I get home?"

She walked to him, lifted his chin and kissed his cheek. His arms slipped around her waist as he said, "I was fine until now."

Marina kissed him again and said, "Well, I guess I'll have to make up for all this lost time when I get back." She looked into his dark eyes and surveyed his tanned face with its high, Slavic cheekbones and thick dark mustache.

He reveled in the scent of her perfume.

She broke the spell suddenly saying, "How can I be so blind? Look, there's the purse I've been looking for these last five minutes. I left it right here on the table."

"I guarantee I won't be so hard to find when you get home," he said softly and kissed her neck.

The front gate signal buzzed and he reached for the intercom. It was Marina's ride and he pushed the button that electronically opened the ten-foot high wrought-iron gate.

Marina kissed him again and headed for the front door, waving as she walked out of the kitchen.

Surprised at first, seeing two "civilians" instead of a liveried chauffeur and a sedan instead of a limo, she soon understood how much better this was for not attracting attention.

As the miles sped by the two men talked softly in the front seat while she relaxed and day-dreamed in the back. After heading east for two hours, they entered the heavily shrubbed driveway of the Emma Gregory Academy.

Monika, remembering a pearl on a chain her grandmother Davidoff had given her, fished it out of her jewelry box. Lisa fastened its clasp for her. Ensemble complete, she looked at the clock. "Oh, good grief! Marina will be here in five minutes!"

Lisa gave an approving nod and dropped into Monika's hand what she considered the last essential for her new image, a lipstick.

"Lisa, are you crazy?"

"I figure the neckline and skirt are strike one, the pantyhose and earrings are two. You need one more to pitch a strike-out. Let me know what happens." Lisa hugged her as Monika's name was called over the speaker.

She blew a kiss back to Lisa and ran down the hall,

depositing the lipstick in a pocket. Rounding the corner, she put on the brakes and continued serenely to the head of the long, curving mahogany staircase which descended to the first floor of the dorm building.

Marina had not seen the school before and was both impressed by the Tudor beauty of its buildings and, at the same time, disconcerted by a fortress-like atmosphere.

Entering through a massive oak door she found herself standing in an oriental-carpeted entry hall, complete with crystal chandelier and velvet settees.

Monika appeared at the top of the staircase and proceeded to descend slowly. After four lady-like steps she gave into her excitement and ran the rest of the way, helter-skelter, into Marina's arms.

Marina hugged her before stepping back and looking at her young charge. "You left the house a child and in five short weeks...Well, look at you!"

Monika felt a little uneasy. "Don't you like it? It's Lisa's, my roommate's. She's wonderful! I love her and want her to visit us and—"

Marina hugged her again, cutting off the torrent of words. "Come along or we'll be late." They walked out to the car in silence and remained quiet until they'd cleared the property.

"Do you think Daddy will get mad when he sees me? I mean, dressed like this."

"Shocked would be more like it. I think you look wonderful. There's just one thing..."

Monika looked down at herself and back to Marina questioningly.

She took hold of Monika's long, dark hair. "This needs to be updated too," and she turned Monika away from her, starting to section and braid her hair. In a minute, Marina looped the long, thick braid under itself and fastened it with two pins from her own French-twist.

She turned Monika to face her and gasped in surprise.

Monika tried to see what caused the reaction, peering into the distant rearview mirror. She looked back to Marina. "What's wrong?"

Marina tried not to stare. "You look so much like your mother! I always saw a resemblance but now, with your hair off your face, the earrings, it's a...a little shock."

"I look that much like her? Really? I really look like my mother?"

Marina nodded, took Monika's hand, and pursued a thought which had been haunting her. "Do you like that school? You don't complain but you don't say anything good either. Tell me."

Studying Marina's face for a clue to where this question came from, Monika didn't answer right away. Marina took her other hand also and added, "I need to know, Monika."

Feeling a special closeness for the woman who cared so much for her, she rested her head on Marina's shoulder and said, "I'd rather be home, I won't lie. The only thing that makes it good this year is Lisa. She's new and an outcast. They put her with me, but not because I'm Miss Popular. It's because I've been alone, the only one there who won't get involved with the stupid cliques. I was alone a lot before, but now Lisa and I are together all the time. We told each other today that we wish we were sisters."

Marina squeezed Monika's hands, explaining, "Seeing you today like this, I realize how short a time there is before you're really gone from us. In five years you'll be off to college and have your own life. And your father will feel a new kind of loneliness. I think you and I would feel a lot better if he was happy with someone in his life when that day comes. Now...did you notice how he was acting before you left, after that studio party?"

Monika nodded.

"Well, I spoke with a woman named Maddie Chase at the theater. She was very, very helpful. In fact, Monika, I think she was too helpful to be only doing her job. I think she's the one he met at that party."

"You're kidding? How does she sound? What did she say?"

"She's got a speaking voice like a singer. You know, rich, low. We only talked about getting you to the theater and back with the least trouble. It isn't what she said but how."

Monika sat up and turned to Marina. "How? What do you mean?"

"I mean...how. I heard something in her voice, something special, different when she spoke of your father." She studied Monika's serious expression and decided to ask, "I know you hope your father finds someone, but do you think he ever will if he keeps looking for another Nancy?"

Monika said, "No. I don't believe everybody has a twin even though one of my teachers said it's true. It's not right for Dad to be alone. All he has are you, me, and Boris around him. He needs more. I know it. You know it. Why doesn't he know it?"

Marina took Monika's hand again, saying, "That's why I asked you about school to see if you'd gotten used to living away and wouldn't like a change. If you had a mother, you wouldn't be there. She'd have you in a school where you could go home to her every night. Or maybe...he'd finally have a good reason to stop working constantly and be with the both of you. I saw, and you did too, that he can still be..."

Monika inserted, "Turned-on?"

"*Spaseebah*, turned on. I suspect it's this Maddie who touched one right chord. We need to watch two performances tonight, your father on stage and your father with her. There probably won't be that much time for them to be in the same place with us, so we've got to be watchful."

"No matter what happens, Marina, I'll always be coming home to you, too. I wouldn't just go off with someone else in place of you. We're a team, Marina, Boris and Monika, together forever!"

The driver interrupted, "Excuse me ladies, we'll be there in ten minutes."

Monika withdrew the lipstick from her pocket and

removed the cover. "Lisa said I might as well try everything at once."

Marina took the tube from Monika's hand. She protested softly and Marina said, "Let me do it for you. First time is the hardest to get it on right."

She admired Monika, lipstick and all, and they hugged as the car approached the theater entrance.

<hr />

"From what you've told me, this young lady is the sweetest, most beautiful, smartest, most polite female walking the face of the earth. I suppose, with such similar credentials, you two qualify as twins?" Maddie joked as Tony applied the matte brown make-up to the back of Bret's neck.

"How can I be humble in the face of truth! I hate to be a pest but would you check again to see if they've arrived?" Bret asked Maddie as he applied the glue to his forehead for his black wig.

Maddie smiled and announced, "Yes, sire, your wish is my command! I will check most carefully and report at once, oh great and mighty one!" She headed for the door and swung into the hallway.

Tony watched in silence, missing neither a stroke of application, a word, nor a nuance.

Bret asked, "Did you know Maddie before this show?"

Tony finished the neck and proceeded to set the wig in place. "Yes, in New York. I did a few shows for Ben there and she was working with him." Tony looked into the mirror, aligning the wig along Atkins' own hairline and was sealing the edges to his head when he was asked about Maddie's husband.

As he camouflaged the joining line with make-up, Maddie ran back into the room. "Exhale, Othello, your dau— guests are here, and Ben is giving them a tour of his domain. Thirty-five minutes to curtain. I'll come back before they call five." She walked to the door and turned, asking, "Tony, isn't there anything you can do to make him look...less good? I guess I mean bad. It's depressing! Look at me, all I have to do is put on these black jeans and shirt and I look like I died a week ago. He still looks great even under all that!"

Bret laughed, disturbing Tony's application. "Sorry, Tony, she's a real disturber back here. Don't complain, Maddie, at least you're clean. I feel like I crawled out of a mudhole. Oh, by the way, thanks. Now I can concentrate."

Maddie closed the door, and Bret pursued the answer to his earlier question.

She began her ritual pre-show hello to the crew. The actors she saved for last. As usual, jokes and one-liners criss-crossed the dressing rooms. Her entrance brought out the male chauvinist repertoire. She loved to join in their banter and was laughing every time she left them.

Bret sat quietly before the mirror, eyes closed, hands resting on the edge of the make-up table. He heard the door open and said, "If it's not Maddie, get out."

"What power I wield," she quipped as she entered and sat on the couch nearest the door. She looked over his shoulder at his mirror image. "All set for tonight? Any problems?"

He thought, *My biggest one disappeared. You're a widow.* Without opening his eyes, he said, "Only one. Is there any place around here I can take Monika and Marina after the show? They're going to be hungry."

Maddie answered with a question of her own. "Can you go to a place like a restaurant or diner without being recognized?"

"Probably not, but what else can I do?"

Maddie wondered out loud, "What if I send one of the security guards for something and we use Ben's living room? His house would be more private than any other place around here."

Bret opened his eyes and looked at her reflection in the mirror, asking, "Do you think Ben would mind? That would be fine, if he doesn't object."

Maddie assured him everything would be set and rose to leave. "By the way, you were right. Your daughter is beautiful."

He smiled, his teeth gleaming white against the dark make-up, and nodded. "Thanks, Maddie."

Finishing backstage, she looked for Ben, needing reassurance that his housekeeper had been on duty that day and she would be spared having to figure out how to see the show and clean the living room at the same time.

"Ben, you're going to say I'm nuts, but I want to watch from the rigging. The only view I haven't had of this show is from above. Everything is set, and I'll put on a headset so I'm available if something goes whacko."

Ben watched her climb the left wall ladder to the overhead lighting booth. Bret had made one hell of a change in her. She was positively bouncing around. If she hadn't nearly scalped Ben last week for questioning whether there was a little romance in the air, he'd have sworn there was a little romance in the air. In fact, her denial only supported his suspicions.

Maddie watched the performance from as far above any distraction as she could get without endangering herself or the show. She discovered from her lofty perch that Bret excelled from any angle, that Marina and Monika, thirty feet below, watched the stage completely transfixed, and that even from that altitude, the excitement emanating from the women in the audience was almost palpable. She willed away an unacceptable sinking feeling in the pit of her stomach at the thought of those women clustered around him after the show.

Like the techies, she waited until the audience was departing before descending the ladder. Her foot had barely touched the floor when Ben linked his arm through hers and almost dragged her backstage.

When Ben and Maddie cleared the closed curtain they were greeted by the sight of women endangering thousand-dollar designer dresses for the coveted prize of Bret's arm around them for a picture, an arm still covered in brown make-up.

Looking down at her rumpled black sweatshirt, fashionably torn jeans, and sneakers, she said to Ben, "Hold the fort. I'm going to run upstairs and change. Be back before you even miss me."

The words were no sooner said than Bret spotted her and motioned her to him. She hesitated, and his wave turned into a vocal summons, "Maddie, I need you. Come here...please."

She pulled her shirt down, trying to straighten out the wrinkles, and spotted streaks of black grease from the joints and wires of the rigging on both sides of her hands. She knew, without looking, her make-up had disappeared with the heat of the lights. What she didn't know about was the wide black streak of grease running the length of her left cheek.

Taking a deep breath, she strode toward the gorgeously dressed, perfectly made-up and coiffed bevy of beauties. Bret's smile widened as she approached and all eyes turned to see the object of his attention.

Bret could see that the usually conservative and correct Maddie was anything but and sensed her discomfort at having to pass what looked like the finalists in a beauty pageant.

He headed towards her, passing through the crowd of women like the Israelites walking through the parted Red Sea. "What in Heaven's name happened to you?," he asked, almost whispering, cupping his hand under her chin. He lifted her face to the light, turning so Maddie's back faced the silent and now staring audience.

"Thank you for that small mercy," she whispered. "I watched the show from the rigging. I guess it's dirtier up there than I thought."

He took the towel from around his neck, gently rubbed the grease from her cheek, and handed it to her. "Excuse me, ladies, I've got to get this wig and make-up off now and, as you can see, we use only pre-dirtied people to help with this job." As he took Maddie's arm, he saw the stage door open and Monika enter, followed by Marina.

Bret's grip on Maddie tightened as Monika walked toward them. "Good Lord," he whispered. Maddie searched his face. He froze for a second, a fleeting trace of shock and pain visible despite the make-up, and his hand clamped down more painfully on her arm.

All the sparkling jewelry, the perfect figures poured into silk and satin or the expensive perfume did not have the impact on Bret that Monika's appearance did. He noted her new clothes but lost any objections in the vision of his Nancy walking toward him.

Ben, aware of the change in his star and knowing Bret's concern about Monika's anonymity, sprang into action, rushing ahead of Marina and unceremoniously hustled the objecting ladies out the door to the lobby.

"Daddy," Monika laughed when the coast was clear and ran the rest of the distance. About to throw herself into his arms, she stopped short. "I can't hug you! You're filthy! Look what you've done to that poor woman with you. She's almost as dirty-looking as you!"

As she spoke Bret regained, by sheer effort of will, the composure he'd lost and smiled. He turned his gaze to Maddie and traced a few streaks of make-up on her forehead. "Don't we make a cute couple?"

Maddie hit him with the towel as she tried unsuccessfully to retreat from the strong hold he still maintained on her arm.

Monika laughed and backed away as he took a step towards her.

"Okay, then, we'll shout at each other from this great distance," he announced, at last releasing Maddie and folding his arms.

"Oh Daddy, you're so silly! Just take off the make-up!"

Bret smiled, turned to Maddie, and said, "See, she's brilliant like me, too. I'll be out in a minute, Puddin'. In the meantime, meet Maddie Chase, stellar producer, good friend and, most impressively, a first cousin of Pigpen."

Marina had watched all this from a distance, and as she caught up with Monika, she overheard the introduction. "Mrs. Chase? I am Marina. We spoke a few days ago."

Maddie wiped her hand vigorously on her shirt before shaking hands with Marina and then Monika. "I'm sorry I couldn't meet you when you arrived but there were a few technical problems that needed attention before the curtain could go up tonight. Please forgive that I'm such a mess. I don't usually look this bad but I decided to watch from over-head tonight and...well, I guess I'll have to do some fall cleaning up there."

Monika wanted to know just what Maddie did at the theater and, as Maddie finished her description, Bret opened his door. He stole up behind Monika and grabbed her in a bear hug. "Daddy, please, I love it but don't! You'll wrinkle me! It's not my dress."

While Monika chattered to him about Lisa, Marina re-approached Maddie, motioned her to join her near the stage door, and asked, "He was shaken when he saw Monika, wasn't he?"

Maddie nodded her head. "He seemed shocked. I don't understand."

"I'm not surprised, I had the same shock in the car after I'd fixed Monika's hair back. She is incredibly like her mother." Marina decided to gamble on her hunch about Maddie. "Monika's been his whole world for twelve years, his only connection to his wife."

Maddie stared openly at Marina, saying, "Are you telling me he's..? There's no girlfriend, no...no anything? I can't believe that! He can have any woman he wants! Any one of those...those beauts back here tonight would have fallen at his feet if he just crooked his little finger. He chooses to be alone? Oh, please...no...don't tell me! No, not him! He can't be!"

Marina looked at Maddie in confusion. "Can't be what?"

"Gay. It's held true so far. The nicer, the more polite, the more interesting the guy the better chance he's gay."

Marina's shocked expression accompanied her too loud protestation, "Gay?"

"Gay?," she repeated in a whisper. "Good Heavens, how could you even think that! Of course he's not!" Her Russian accent stressed her measured words angrily.

"Please, being gay wouldn't make him less an actor or a person. It just shatters that...that...well, you know...that... that... image of...of...," Maddie stammered for the right words in her wrong assumption. "I was just trying to make some sense out of him not...you know." Maddie's rising color was beginning to show through her dirt streaks.

"Oh, don't be silly! Of course he does. There are women," Marina stated, assessing this revealing reaction from Maddie. "When he speaks of them he simply says if they're willing, he's able, but none of them have gotten as far as a second date with him and none to his home."

Maddie pulled her sweatshirt down and ran her fingers through her disheveled hair, saying, "Maybe my presence back here every night while the 'willings' flaunt themselves before him has cramped his style. I hope I didn't ruin anything for him. We've been talking for weeks now but, after all, this is our business, our careers. I am his 'boss,' as he says. It's only natural we would talk together ...often." She looked back at Bret and Monika walking toward them hand in hand and felt her heart constrict.

She excused herself and headed for her office to change before going to Ben's, having accepted Bret's invitation before the show.

Ben had told Whitney to meet him at his house after the curtain came down. The door was always unlocked, so she waited for him in the living room.

"Hi, Ben. Wow, what a production! You've out-done yourself. I was here on opening night and thought it couldn't be better, but be damned, it was tonight."

Ben smiled and said, "Trying to butter-up the old man? You know I'd love you even if you said you hated it."

"I know that, " she said, getting up and giving him a hug. "Sit down, you must be exhausted - but not too exhausted to talk to me, I hope."

He sat on the couch next to her. "The script was in that package I mentioned. What role are they talking about for you?"

Whitney turned toward him, "My agent told me Ellen, the candidate's mistress."

"Figures! The general stupidity I ran into when I asked about this today is colossal! The Studio has put it into the hands of some young genius they just hired and this moron doesn't have a clue what he's doing. Can you believe he still hasn't dealt with a director? If I were the script writer, I would be after him with an ax!"

Whitney looked a little fearful. "You think the whole thing isn't worth it?"

"I didn't say that," Ben said, fixing her with a steady stare. "Who do you see yourself playing?"

"In my mind, the only real female role in it is Helen, the reporter," Whitney said seriously.

"That's my girl!" Ben declared, picking up Whitney's script from the coffee table. "You're as smart as I think you are! Learn Helen's lines. I guarantee that the powers that be will see the light before next week. I'll call you tomorrow night and we'll talk 'Helen'. Excuse me, I can't even get away from the phone down here!"

He answered his pocket cellular. "You mean in this whole complex we don't have one! I don't know why he wants it, but if it keeps our star happy, he'll have it. I want to find out why he went to you and not to Maddie or me...If you have to take the one off my office do it. A lock will be on that door before he gets back to his room tonight. Okay?...I know I can rely on you. Thanks."

Ben closed the phone and placed it back into his pocket, his forehead furrowed in thought.

"We can drop this if you want to, Ben," Whitney offered,

standing and straightening her skirt.

"No, no, no! It's no big deal," Ben assured her, taking her hand to indicate he wanted her to sit again. "I just cannot figure out why Bret wants a heavy lock on his room door, and, when he wanted it, why he didn't ask Maddie or me."

Whitney thought for a few seconds and said, "It sounds like he's trying to keep someone out. You don't think...Maybe Mom short-sheeted his bed once too often."

Ben laughed, remembering Bret limping exaggeratedly each time he ran into Maddie the day after the opening. "I think you're half right; it's a woman, but I don't think it's Maddie. I couldn't help notice how Beth hung around him from day one. Now that I mention it, if it was that obvious in rehearsal it was probably worse in the dorm. He didn't complain. I guessed he could handle it himself."

"Sounds like he's admitting failure," Whitney observed, wondering why Maddie never mentioned any Beth stories to her.

"Ready or not, here we are," Bret called out as the little party of revelers entered.

Bret introduced Whitney to Monika and Marina, asking in the same breath, "Miss Chase, where's Mrs. Chase? She hiding?"

Whitney and Ben looked at each other with one thought; it wasn't Maddie he was shutting out.

<hr />

Maddie you got what you wanted, a platonic relationship with a man, and an actor at that. The fact the man happens to be in the dreams of almost every female in the world makes it even more delicious. You've kept all that feminine wiles stuff out of it, and he's responded exactly as you wanted: no double entendres, no seduction. Of course he could be just playing another role...Actors!

She consulted the full-length mirror on her closet door, pulling her belt tighter and undoing three buttons at the neckline, studied the results and thought, *Nuts! Be what you are, Maddie! Don't try to gild a lily that's wilting in the garden.* She readjusted the belt and rebuttoned the neckline. *What's the line? "Be careful of what you pray for; you just may get it." Why couldn't I have met him when I was twenty?"*

As the car sped northward, Marina put her arm around Monika, nestling her head against her shoulder. Monika was always intense and serious after saying good-by to her father so Marina decided to take her home for the night, hoping to quiet her emotions there before returning her to school.

Monika broke her silence, saying, "Isn't Whitney pretty! I didn't expect to meet her tonight."

Marina nodded and Monika felt the affirmation. "You know something? I've often wondered why women say, "Men!" with that sound in their voices. Tonight I got the answer. I thought for sure Dad would talk about Maddie. He'd tell me what she was like and all that, especially after the way he paced until she joined us. They seem like such good friends. I've never seen him kid around with another adult like that before. He treats her like you or me! But, no! Do you know what he was talking about so seriously to me? Mom! It was spooky. He talked about Mom! Said he may have trouble because Mom wouldn't understand or have to get used to something. Oh, I don't know what he's thinking or talking about. Men!"

Marina patted Monika's shoulder, not knowing what to say. Monika shifted subjects, emptying her mind of all her impressions of the night.

"Marina, did you think he really became Othello on that stage, he wasn't just pretending to be?"

Marina kissed the top of Monika's head and agreed. "He did make that character come to life. He's a wonderful actor and I don't say that because I know him or I work for him."

Monika yawned. "By the way, did you see the way Dad smiled at Maddie— it was a special look! When we were at Mr. Cameron's house, Dad was talking to me but he'd look over at her every once in a while, and I caught her looking at him, too. I'd like to get to know her better. She might not want to, though. She already has a daughter. Do you think they might be falling in love?"

Marina hugged Monika tighter, saying, "I think your father and she have a good friendship. He's relaxed with her the way he used to be with your mother. She's attracted but is probably afraid. It has to be hard for her to tell whether it's a liking for the movie star or the man."

Monika sat up and looked at her. "I never thought of that! He's just Dad to me so I don't really think of him that other way very much. At least I don't think I do."

"She has to hunt for the real man, that is if she wants to bother," Marina said, resettling Monika against her shoulder. "Try to get some sleep now. You'll be very tired tomorrow if you don't." An hour later, she gently awakened Monika as they passed through the Atkins' gates.

Monika hugged Boris as he greeted them at the front door and she joined hands with him and Marina. "Please don't tell me not to do this. I have to sleep in Dad's room tonight. He says Mom comes there a lot and I want to talk to her about him and Maddie and Whitney." She kissed each of them good night and ran up the curving staircase.

Boris kissed a tear from Marina's cheek, and as Monika rounded the last turn, she buried her face against his shoulder. "Boris, anyone hearing what he says about his dead wife would think he was totally crazy. What can we do? He has to let go of Nancy."

He hugged her more tightly, wishing in his silence he knew what to say.

Marina couldn't control the shudder which passed through her body as she said, "Love, did you hear what she said? Nancy comes to his room? She comes to his room! I can't believe he told Monika that. God help him, he's still standing by her grave!"

VII

Maddie couldn't believe this was the twenty-fifth show, the company's last *Othello*. She watched the crew boss raise the curtain, wishing she had something complicated to distract her thoughts from the ending of the eight weeks she'd enjoyed so much.

Ben had told her he wanted to take a look at his show from different perspectives and intended to roam the house as the performance progressed. He noticed she'd been tight as a watch spring all day and realized that it was the closing and Bret's departure all at the same time. What she didn't know and Ben wouldn't tell her was that Bret was leaving that night from the theater. He'd made plans with his housekeeper for her husband to pick him up ten minutes after the final curtain. What was the matter with them? Ben had never seen two people who appeared more like they should be together. God, how he wished he could have done something to make them see the light! Talk about walking a tight rope. If he offended either one, his life wouldn't be worth living.

Oh, how he hated this whole night!

Watching his Desdemona die for the last time, Ben

remembered how close disaster had truly loomed. Beth had pursued Bret with an alarming singleness of purpose. On stage and in rehearsal she was perfect. It was after, in the dorm especially, that she showed a different side. Bret wouldn't approach Maddie with the problem and felt he'd look foolish if he spoke to Ben. Three rehearsal weeks of her appearing everywhere he turned finally drove Bret to desperation.

Ben remembered the night Bret lost his lines in the first act, four performances into the run. He'd covered like a trooper, but a tension underlying the rest of that show made Ben wonder what was really going on. Backstage all was deathly silent after the curtain came down and, when Ben entered, he remembered being stopped in his tracks by the tangible bad vibes which were obviously giving rise to the uneasy silence.

Bret had emerged from his dressing room and walked straight out the back door, leaving Ben and Maddie to placate the lobby crowd waiting to see him.

Two days later, a dead-fall bolt had been installed on Bret's bedroom door. Ben, bursting with curiosity the day after Monika's visit, had called Bret to his office and asked out-right what was going on.

"Look, Ben, I've been around this business a long time and thought I'd faced all the possible problems I could with females, but living here has created a new one for me. No place to hide."

Ben had thought Bret meant Maddie and was ready to leap to her defense, but Bret's next words stopped him. "Beth built a friendly 'hello' into a seduction scene. I tried to be kind, but that was misinterpreted as interest. I avoided her, but that only intensified her determination.

"Ben, I've never had anything to do with a married woman and I'm not starting now. I have no idea what kind of marriage she has, but this I guarantee, her husband won't be able to say one word against me. I'm locking myself in or her out, I don't know which. Now maybe she'll give up. I dropped those lines this week because I haven't been sleeping, hearing her in the hall, and for the first time in my life, I'm concerned a co-star will do something extra, shall we say, in a passionate scene."

When Ben made a move to page Beth, Bret had stopped him. "Don't, Ben, she might be more of a problem if there's any trouble. Let's see if she takes the hint from the lock."

Ben had not been able to resist saying, "Just be seen more with Maddie, and Beth might understand the way things really are."

Bret looked confused. "The way things really are?"

Ben, at a complete loss to know what to say next, had been saved by the telephone's ring.

The last night of *Othello* Ben successfully kept Maddie from the backstage area during intermission, asking her for information he knew she'd have to look up in her office.

She went willingly, thinking she could see Bret after the show and then again the next day. Ben assured her he would handle any behind-the-scenes problems between acts.

As Maddie predicted, Bret's last performance was sweeping his audience away. She looked forward to praising him and confirming her opening-night prediction about the final show after the curtain came down.

"Oh, come on, Ben. I want to get back there before the howling mob," Maddie pleaded when he requested still more from her office at the end of the show. "Bret was superb tonight and I want to congratulate him. I can give you that stuff later on, before I go home." She headed for the backstage door with Ben in tow.

Tony was packing up his makeup as Maddie swung into Bret's dressing room. "Bret, I can't tell you how wonder—" She stopped short in the doorway. "Tony? Where's Bret?"

Without looking up, he said, "Breezed in here, half

removed his makeup and, shazaam, he was gone out the back door."

Ben backed away into the crowd surrounding the other actors as Tony spoke and managed to lose himself from Maddie's sight.

Maddie walked to the back door and checked outside, admitting the roar of car engines and staccato of horns of departing audience members. She closed the door and looked at Tony, now standing in the dressing room doorway. "Did he go to the dorm?"

"I wouldn't think so. He brought his suitcases in with him when he came at 6:00," Tony said, walking the few steps to her, taking her hand and leading her back into the empty room.

She looked at the stripped area, all traces of Bret gone. "What's going on, Tony? Did he say anything to you? I mean about why he's doing this."

He sat her in a chair in front of the mirror and sat himself on the counter nearby. "Maddie, I think he didn't know how to say good-bye to you. I'd have to be dead and buried to not see what's going on between you two."

"What do you mean what's going on? We became friends, that's all! You know, it is possible for a man and a woman to be just friends."

Tony took her hand. "In the gay world, sweetheart, not often in yours. We're dealing here with the heterosexual poster boy! How could the sex thing not come into it somewhere, even on a subliminal level? Believe me, Maddie, I watched you for almost eight weeks and tried to keep all of that stuff out of my thoughts, but you two made it impossible. Such vibrations! I was convinced of everything the day he asked me about your husband, actually if there was one around. Other than that, when he spoke about you to me, it was with a kind of—I guess— awe. And you, my love, during that time turned from a lovely rosebud into a full-blown American Beauty."

Maddie retrieved her hand impatiently. "You're either writing a romance novel or you're as blind as a bat. We are— we were— just friends!"

"Excuse me! I know what I saw. And as for me being blind? If you two were any more blind, you'd have needed to share a seeing-eye dog!"

Maddie clenched her fists and Tony braced for an explosion. She closed her eyes, and when she reopened them, tears rimmed her lashes. "Tony, didn't he say anything before he left? I mean, we were together nearly every day, and I thought I meant at least a little something to him."

He watched a tear slowly trickle down her cheek. "I could lie and make up a dialogue to make you feel better, but I think it would hurt you more in the end. He thanked me for everything before he left, and that was all. He'd had nothing at all to say up to that point tonight, seemed to be just going through the motions back here."

Maddie stood and wiped the tear from her cheek with the back of her hand.

"Well, so much for that chapter of my life." She took a deep breath. "If your schedule allows, how about staying on for our next show? I know Ben would love it, and I'd like to redeem myself for being so negligent of you for all these weeks."

Tony was struck speechless as she reached out and hugged him. *I'll bet if you'd done this to Bret we wouldn't be having this conversation. Oh, why didn't I speak up to him! Maybe I could have helped. I sure wouldn't have hurt, that's obvious.*

◄●◆●►

Back at home Bret eased out of his public persona and relaxed into being Paul. He watched from the doorway as Boris slipped his arms around Marina's waist and kissed her neck as she finished at the sink. "Five minutes more, that's all I ask of you, Love," she said, tapping his nose with a damp sponge.

As he leaned away to avoid another wet tap, he spotted Bret. "Oh, excuse us, sir. I mean, excuse me. Marina wouldn't do..."

Paul smiled. "What are you apologizing for? I should be, for intruding. Just wanted to let Marina know I have to go to L.A. tomorrow— maybe another movie coming up for me— and won't be back for dinner. Why don't you two take the day off? Leave me something in the refrigerator."

They shook their heads in refusal of the offer.

"Don't argue. If I find either one of you on this property when I get home tomorrow night, I'll...well, I will...and you can bet on it. Please, go off someplace. Have fun..., " he stuffed some folded bills into Boris's hand. "...on me. You two more than earn your salaries." He turned to leave and over his shoulder added, "Carry on, Lovebirds. Good night."

Boris led Marina to a chair and set her on his lap.

She leaned against him. "I feel so badly for him. I know I shouldn't interfere, but if I don't hear him mention Maddie's name soon, I am going to call her."

"Maybe you should stay out of it, Marina," Boris warned gently and laid his cheek against her shoulder.

She ignored his suggestion. "I have a feeling she has a history as bad as Pavel's. If that's true, neither one will make a move toward the other. They'll think each other to death from afar."

Boris looked at her profile and hugged her tightly. "It is a crime that he does not have someone wonderful to come home to like I have. I felt, when he looked at us just now, he was...maybe a little jealous."

"Jealous, sad, whatever," Marina declared, "it's not a good life for him. He's chosen a road that is too lonely. He deserves some real happiness. I would very much like to look at him and see a contented man whose life is better than he ever dreamed it could be. This veneer of his, that he's satisfied, is the only piece of bad acting I've ever seen him do."

She stood and pulled Boris to his feet as he said, "I don't

know what you've got in mind, but if it can possibly make things better for him, I guess you should try it. I owe him for the only real happiness I've known in my life, this job, my wife, our home."

As he spoke he looked at the bills in his hand. "Lord, Marina, there's $500.00 here."

Marina wrapped her arms around him and whispered, "We both owe him everything. The least I can do is act on my instincts and my intuition."

"Dad, we just saw you on TV!" Monika exclaimed into the telephone. "They said you were going to star in that movie about a president or something."

Paul put down the book he was reading and stretched out to the full length of the chaise lounge on his balcony. "The name of it is *American Dream* and it's about a Senator running for President, not someone in office. Once again the press is wrong. Tomorrow's headline will read 'Atkins Cans the Presidency'. I just pulled away from that project."

Monika nodded her head to Lisa who had crowded in next to her in the phone booth. "So, that means you're definitely home for Thanksgiving?"

"Guess so. Looks like your poor, old Dad is temporarily unemployed. Just between you and me, I'm glad."

Monika signaled Lisa that Thanksgiving was okay. She hugged Monika and jumped up and down, taking Monika with her.

"What in heaven's name was that?" Paul demanded, sitting up, listening with concern to a thumping sound.

Monika signaled Lisa to be quiet. "It's okay, Dad. Lisa's here with me."

"Say no more." Paul breathed a sigh of relief and sat back again. "I can see I'm going to have my hands full with the two of you. Should I alert the riot squad?"

Monika laughed. "Oh, Daddy, you're such a nut!" She

hushed Lisa, winking as she asked, "By the way, have you heard from Maddie?"

Paul hesitated just a bit too long for Monika's liking before he answered.

"Maddie? Do you have ESP or a tap on my phone line?" Monika's eyes widened with surprise. "I only asked because I hoped you had."

"Well, if you must know, as soon as the picture deal bit the big one this morning, I called Ben to see if I could get in on the next production out there. Maddie happened to answer the phone. She asked for you."

"She did? Really?" Monika grabbed Lisa's hand in her excitement. "I like her a lot. Do you think there'll be time for us all to get together again?"

"More time out of school? Do I hear that request hidden in those words?" Paul scolded, trying to sound paternal.

"Daddy, I've given up hinting. I'm just coming out with everything from now on. I hope you will let Lisa and me come to this show."

Once again Paul heard the sound of jumping up and down. "God forbid I would say no. The two of you would probably thump your way through this phone line and beat me into submission. But you may not want to come when you hear what kind of a show this is. I even hesitated when I found out."

"Is it something awful?"

"The show's not awful but I probably will be. It's a musical."

Monika looked surprised. "A musical? You? Sing and dance?" She began to laugh.

Paul rubbed the back of his neck, his tell-tale gesture warning of either doubt or anger. "It's a stretch all right, I'll give you that, but I can do it. You'll see."

Monika, still laughing, gasped, "Oh yes, we'll see! We promise to bring only the softest tomatoes to throw at you. Oh, better yet, we'll bring a video camera. What's that old song, "Every little movement has a meaning all..."

"Hey, Missie, you will see poetry in motion! Now, after talking to you, I'm in dire need of oxygen and a wheelchair! I hope you're happy, wearing out your poor old father with a phone call! If I've recovered enough, Puddin', I'll pick you up in ten days. Okay?"

"Great, Daddy! I love you."

"Love you, too," he said and pushed the off button on the portable phone. Forgetting his book, his mind wandered back to the Genny and Maddie. He couldn't figure out what to do. At times she was so warm, so interested, he had wanted to say something, something meaningful, but he was afraid to. *Me, afraid? You bet because of those other times when she was definitely hands-off, business only, using that "what are friends for?" line. I'm so used to women chasing me. God, look at Beth! I didn't know what to do when nothing happened with Maddie. She's the only one who's been around me and done nothing. She's so different. Yet everything about her felt so familiar, so comfortable.*

I'll bet she hates me for leaving without saying good-bye. I felt as bad that night as when I dropped Monika off at boarding school for the first time. Like I was being ripped up inside. What didn't she like? What kept her from...? Well, something didn't click.

Oh, shit! Shut up and take a walk.

◆━◆

"I can't believe that car of mine!" Maddie exclaimed, getting into Whitney's. "Once a week, every week since the beginning of September, that stupid car has died on me and the mechanics tell me everything is just fine. I'm sorry to drag you all the way out here."

Whitney smiled and shifted into drive. "Not out of my way at all. I was coming out to see Ben anyway. We've been talking about the movie. I still can't believe I actually got that part and now Ben is going to direct! Do me a favor, will you? Ask Ben why Bret refused the lead. I hope it wasn't something

I said, or maybe I really do need a man's deodorant."

Whitney thought the unresponsive Maddie even more tense than she'd been since closing night. She decided that a diversion, a relaxing evening could help. "I'm glad this happened. It gives us a chance to talk. Hey, I know, let's stop for dinner on the way home."

Maddie said she'd enjoy that and then fell into a long silence which she finally broke herself, saying, "Latest news! I had...no, I'm wrong. Let me correct that. Ben had a phone call today. I just happened to answer it."

"My Lord," Whitney marveled, "Ben had a phone call! Now there's a piece of info for the front page!"

Maddie folded her arms. "Well, if you don't want to hear..."

"Sorry, but you paused for so long I thought that was the end of your story. I've heard the aged have to stop to compose their thoughts. I guessed that was what you were doing. Please continue."

"Cruel, I gave birth to a cruel one," Maddie said with a little smile.

Whitney snarled and growled.

"All right, I'll tell, you vicious child. It was Bret, and he's returning for another show at the Genny."

Whitney smiled broadly and took a quick look at her mother. "Well, well, well, I got my answer! He just can't seem to stay away, can he. It looks like, given his druthers, he'd pick another Genny show rather than play the hottest lead of the year. Makes perfect sense to me!"

"As I said, he talked to Ben. I'm not privy to the reasons for his decisions." Maddie felt a twinge of discomfort when she remembered how perfunctory Bret's conversation had been with her. Why hadn't he told her himself or called her back?

Whitney saw the dark cloud cross her mother's features but thought it wise not to comment on it. They rode the last ten miles in silence, the strains of the Adagio from

Katchaturian's *Spartacus* pulsing from the car radio, the music Maddie called the most erotic she'd ever experienced. Whitney noticed that Maddie's folded arms seemed to tighten with each ensuing theme.

She maneuvered the car into a parking space in front of Lucia's On the Water, Malibu's favorite seafood place.

"What show are you doing next? I don't remember you telling me." Whitney undid her seat belt and opened the door as she spoke. She walked around to her mother's door and watched as she got out of the car.

Maddie answered offhandedly, "A musical," and walked ahead of Whitney towards the restaurant door, removing any chance of seeing Whitney's reaction. She heard muttering behind her. "A musical? Did she say a musical?" but ignored all temptations to look back at Whitney, continuing her non-stop march to a window table.

"Mom, a musical? Does he have any musical talent? Can he dance? I can't remember ever seeing him in a musical," Whitney exclaimed, as quietly as one can exclaim, handing Maddie a menu.

Maddie opened it slowly and looked up. "Ben is the director, the boss. He hires all the actors himself. Once in a while I am called in to consult with him on a particular one. He signed Mr. Atkins up all on his very own, just like before. I am not consulted on Mr. Atkins' contracts. Ben was absolutely right last time; Atkins was more than eminently qualified to play Othello. If Ben thinks he can play Henry Higgins then far be it from me to voice any doubts. Can Mr. Atkins sing and dance? I haven't a clue!"

Whitney chuckled. "...and frankly, Miss Whitney, I don't give a damn."

Maddie remained focused on her menu. "Of course I give a damn. I just hope this doesn't hurt him—us—if it bombs. Ben's not directing since he's starting preliminary work on your film next week. He's bringing out Matt Crosley. You remember him—had some big splashy hits Off-Broadway around the time your show was on."

They ordered dinner and preceded it with champagne cocktails. Their conversation didn't touch the Genny again until the check arrived.

"Mom, I'll pay. I invited you, remember?"

"Please, Whitney, let me. We're together so little any more, I want to do something special for you tonight. You've got the juiciest role in Hollywood. Every actress in Tinseltown ended up drooling for it. You've got the best director since movies were invented, and you will have a fabulous leading man. I know Ben. He'll match you with someone perfect. Indulge the old lady. Let me treat you before you're too rich and famous to associate with us little people."

Whitney sat back. "Right, Mom. I'll make you use the servants' entrance when I buy the Hearst Castle for my little cottage on the coast."

Maddie didn't respond with more than a smile. Distractedly, she pulled two bills from her wallet, laying them on the check, and then did a double take. *I must be totally bombed! Look at that, a fifty and a ten instead of two fifties. What is the matter with me? I can't even read numbers anymore!*

"Bret-itis? Atkins Dementia? You had it once before. This must be the dreaded relapse," Whitney joked, folding her napkin and watching her mother blush. "I can't believe it! You still blush! And don't tell me it's a hot flash! You haven't started that yet!"

"Don't be ridiculous," Maddie failed to state emphatically. "That whole thing during *Othello* was just one of those...theater things. You know, that atmosphere. It's all as unreal as the play being presented."

Whitney laughed. "Mom, I can't believe what I'm hearing! He was all you talked about for eight weeks. Now he's coming back into your life. Don't you see some kind of sign here? Like, maybe it's supposed to happen between you two?"

"Be logical, Whitney." Maddie avoided her daughter's unrelenting stare with her own fixed study of the blue Pacific crashing on the beach below. "Those women who visited him backstage are his type, what he's used to, not me."

Whitney was incredulous. "Look at yourself! You're a beautiful, desirable woman, more so than any of them. He saw it, Mom. He was interested in you. Even someone with 20/200 vision could see that. Is your vision all that bad?"

"You wish it, and that's why you saw it, but that doesn't make it so." Maddie defended her conviction. "We had fun, like two friends at a...a theater camp, that's all."

"Look at him, Mom. Just take one long look at him. Woman to woman, not mother to daughter, tell me you never thought about sleeping with him."

Maddie whispered, "Lower your voice! Did I hear you right?"

"Darned tootin' you heard right. How could you not think of him that way. Even at twenty-five, I'm not immune. He's almost twice my age but, if I liked older men in that way, he'd definitely be high on my list. Why do you think you can negate such a basic instinct?"

"Because I will it," Maddie whispered vehemently. "Now change the subject!"

Whitney leaned closer to her mother. "Not until I've said my piece. You worked so hard at maintaining that friendship thing with him that, when you realized you wanted more than that you got scared out of your wits."

Maddie countered, "I can keep any relationship, including one with him, on an even keel. Why does the male have to posture in such a way that everyone sees something that's not there? Some stupid macho thing, I guess."

"You don't actually see yourself as some kind of blithe spirit who floats in and out of a man's life, leaving no lasting effects. That's totally full of ...of you-know-what," Whitney declared. "He hit all the right chords with you and vice versa. For the first time in my memory, including your go-around with Vic, you were really alive, attracted in some very deep, meaningful ways to that man."

Maddie stared in silence at the ocean, trying to deny Whitney's words, wishing she could deny Whitney's words. *Don't get all fuzzy inside again. Sure, going to bed with him has crossed my mind after every movie I've seen him in. Never once at the Genny though. I couldn't allow that kind of thinking to get started. Oh, what the hell am I going on about! If he'd wanted me he would have done something about it and probably not met much resistance. God knows, there was plenty of opportunity and he certainly knows how!*

Whitney studied her mother as Maddie continued staring at the ocean. *How could someone so emotionally hurt gravitate to someone who appears unable to reach out to her? I think I would run as if the devil were chasing me if there were even a possibility of dancing to the same dirge one more time. Why couldn't he be an untroubled man! I guess if he were he would have been grabbed up long before Mom met him.'*

Maybe two wrongs can make a right! They've both lived the negatives, so if they get together, only the positives should surface. Oh, she wants to see him again, more than she'll admit even to herself but...What if it comes to nothing again? She sighed, and gazed at the horizon.

◆◆◆

Boris and Marina stepped into the cool evening air. A wind from the Pacific stirred the branches as they crossed the tree-fringed courtyard which extended from the main house to the path leading to their cottage.

Marina spotted Paul on the cliff, his form silhouetted against the last light of the sunset sky. She stopped, forcing Boris to a stand-still and pointed to the spot.

Boris clasped her hand more tightly. "Look at him. He always paces that cliff but now he's not. It's got to be that Maddie. Now that he's going back to that theater and her, he's quieter inside. I do hope though it's not the same kind of quiet that comes in the middle of hurricanes."

VIII

Maddie watched Ben, absorbed in the script for *American Dream*. She'd entered his office to consult about publicity for *My Fair Lady* and was waiting for him to resurface.

"Sorry, Maddie, found a spot I want to talk to the writer about. What's up?"

She closed her folder and said, "I came in here on business, and now all I want to do is find out what you're doing on Thanksgiving. Your family coming in or are you going to them?"

Ben closed the script and placed it on the desk. "No one is traveling in any direction. As a matter of fact, I thought I'd just sleep the day away."

Maddie leaned forward. "Not if I can help it! I'm hoping you might join us. Tony's coming. Cooking a turkey for three is really dumb. Whit and I will be eating leftovers until Christmas. You really should take this chance to taste the unbelievable Maddie cuisine. I can't imagine I've never cooked a meal for you."

He extended his arm to Maddie saying, "Twist it, please."

She laughed and tapped him on the hand.

"Mercy, mercy! I'll come. What time?"

Her smile helped erase some of the tired look which Ben noticed increasing on a daily basis following Atkins' call. "Come early, stay late, Ben."

"You may regret saying that. Sounds like fun. Thanks, Maddie."

"See if you can say that while you're searching high and low for an antacid after you've eaten all the goodies I'm planning."

"Did I ever time my arrival right!" Tony declared as Ben emerged from the kitchen. "I got here just after everything was done."

"Well, I didn't get off that easy," Ben groaned, flopping down on an easy chair in Maddie's living room. "I opened the wine; been wrestling with that damn thing since you arrived."

"God, Ben, I got here fifteen minutes ago!"

"Did you ever try to get out a cork that has been inserted with the Son of Crazy Glue? That blasted wine is out there breathing and I'm in here gasping. All I can say is everyone just better love it!"

Whitney emerged from the kitchen and announced, "Dinner is served in the main dining salon. Tony, you have won the honor of carrying in the bird. Mom said she'll carve. Considering the mood she's been in lately, putting a sharp object in her hands may not be all that wise. Sort of like the Pilgrims inviting the Indians to the first Thanksgiving and giving them bows and arrows as table prizes!"

Lisa was playing Chop-Sticks on the baby grand in the Atkins' living room when Marina called everyone to dinner.

Monika, upstairs in her bedroom, was trying on, for the hundredth time in three days, her first pair of heels. Though only an inch high, they fulfilled her requirement, a shaped narrow heel.

With Maddie's words "loosen up before you lose her" ingrained in his memory, Paul had donned his darkest sunglasses as soon as they arrived home from school, gathered up Marina, and headed for a shoe store in the nearby village. Marina okayed the heel height, Monika was thrilled, Lisa whipped out her family's credit card to buy the latest rage in sneakers, and Paul escaped just before the salesgirl realized who was behind those Foster Grants.

Hearing Marina's summons, Monika ran full-tilt down the staircase, nearly bowling over Paul who was crossing the first floor hallway from his den. He'd been quiet since their shopping expedition, and she was afraid he was upset with her and Lisa because of all their noise and chaos.

He looked sternly at her and she stood stock still. A smile crept over his face. "Last one to the table's a rotten egg." He headed off at a full run towards the dining room.

Lisa joined Monika, and they raced en masse towards the feast.

Marina, coming through the kitchen door into the dining room, caught Bret as he skidded into his seat at the head of the table. Monika and Lisa, right on his heels, attacked him from behind. "If the two children in this house can't quiet down, they'll have to be separated from their ring-leader. One more sound and you go to your room, Pavel!"

The girls laughed and scrambled to their seats as Boris brought in the turkey.

Marina picked up the carving knife and fork from the buffet, wondering aloud, "Is it safe to hand you a pointed object, Pavel?"

"I guess we'll just have to chance it." He took the knife, stood over the browned bird and did his best "Psycho" imitation. The whole table erupted in laughter.

Though they were enjoying his little show, Marina and Boris knew the joking was an act for the girls' benefit.

Marina had noticed that whenever he was around Lisa, he was "on". Otherwise, he spent his time alone in his den or on the cliff.

Paul looked at his "family" and said, "I know we're not the most religious people on the planet, but I think it would be appropriate to thank God for all we have today."

Lisa added, "A family I visited with one year had everyone at the table say what they were most thankful for. Let's do it!"

Monika piped in, "Oh, yes! Me first! Thank you God for my crazy Dad, my Marina and Boris, Lissie-Poo, my bestest friend in the whole world and..."

Lisa nudged her and said, "And what?"

"And for someone special I met this year."

Paul stared at Monika and offered, "Lisa, your turn."

"Okay! Thank you God for letting me be here today. Thank you for Monikie-Moo; I never dreamt I would have such a great friend. And thank you for the weak moment when my father sent me that credit card."

Paul smiled, shook his head, and looked down the table at Marina. "And you?"

She and Boris joined hands. "We thank God for allowing us to find you, Pavel, for allowing us to share your life with Monika, for her friend Lisa, and for all the wonderful people who have entered our lives in the past year."

Paul lowered his eyes when his name was first mentioned by her. Her closing statement made him close them for a moment.

"Your turn, Dad, and please don't thank Him for letting someone invent film or something like that."

Paul had been wracking his brain for some innocuous but sufficient thing to say. Failing to think of anything, he was left to the thought of the moment. "Thank you, God, for everything you've allowed me to accomplish. Thank you for the wonderful people who surround my life here. Thank you for bringing Lisa to Monika. It means so much to have someone to talk to."

Monika, Boris and Marina held their breaths, waiting for him to mention Maddie.

"Thank you too for...for all this and...since no one else said it, thank you for this food. Now, dig in!"

The three exhaled, looked at each other questioningly and began to pass the serving dishes full of hot food.

"Lord, I have so much to be thankful for this year," Whitney exclaimed as Maddie sliced into the turkey's breast. "I still can't believe you're going to direct, Ben, but I wish I knew who you had in mind for the Senator."

Ben chewed on an olive thoughtfully. "Well, well, well, the ulterior motive for my presence finally comes out."

Maddie stopped carving. "Ben, how could you even think that!"

"Whoa!" Ben pleaded. "I was only kidding! Don't get hot under the collar with a knife in your hand!" Looking at Whitney he said, "I've contacted Redford."

Whitney stammered, "R-R-Robert Redford?"

"No, Sam Redford! Honestly, Whitney, if you can't say his name, how on earth can you act opposite him?"

"Oh, it'll be a trial but I'll survive it somehow!" Whitney quipped, almost panting at the thought. She looked at Maddie and whispered, "Robert Redford!"

Tony, sitting back enjoying the repartee, added, "They'll have to do you in white face to hide that blush!"

Her hands went to her cheeks. "I don't blush!"

Tony sat up and said, "Maddie, get a doctor, quick. It's scarlet fever!"

Maddie smiled and said, "That's a natural reaction to that news. All that stuff passes away fast once you get to be with the star longer than five minutes. He's human just like anyone else. Once you remember that, you're home free!"

"Oh, yes, I almost forgot, we have a tried and true veteran of the palpitation wars in our midst," Tony observed as

Ben and Whitney kicked him under the table.

Maddie finished carving and laid down the knife and fork. "Lessons should be learned from all wars. Only fools make the same mistakes twice."

Whitney couldn't resist. "Considering the number of wars there have been and are, it would appear there are a lot of fools on this planet."

Maddie looked down the table at her. "I intend to prove I'm not one of them!"

Tony cut the building tension he'd engendered, saying, "Girls, girls! I will now impress you with my great memory. Harking back to my long ago days in Sister school, I will now say Grace. Bless us, O Lord..."

Matt Crosley arrived at the Genny on the Monday following Thanksgiving. Ben had given him the "$100 Tour" and placed him in Maddie's hands from there on. They circled each other's methods, like two boxers looking for a weak spot, and found they were compatible on all the basics.

Matt let her know from the start she would be expected to be more hands-on than she was with Ben. "He knows everything and can do it twice as fast as anyone else. Me? I'll take all the help I can get! I'm good in the office end of the business, so I can help you when you get bogged down there. We'll make a great team, but I get all the glory. Right?"

Maddie smiled. "Or all the egg on your face! I'm perfectly happy in the background. As a matter of fact, I'll be very glad to be away from this office most of the time. It'll keep me out of trouble."

Though puzzled, he shrugged off the statement, laying out the scenery plans on her desk. He interrupted his study of them. "Atkins gets here in three days. Maddie, help me out. You've worked with him already. Do you ever get over the awe? I think I'll make a fool of myself when I meet him."

Maddie's eyes remained riveted on the sketches as she

stated, "Give it a day or two to pass, and then you and he'll be best buddies until the end of the show. This time he can hang around you, not me...Don't you think this archway should be more stage right? Eliza's supposed to make her entrance and cross the stage to the Professor. As it stands now, she comes in two steps away from him. What do you think?"

There's more than meets the eye here, Matt thought and promised himself a question or two to Tony. Hoping he didn't look like too much of an idiot, he asked her to repeat the comment about the scenery. He had lost his train of thought after the prospect of hanging around Bret Atkins had been dropped on him.

━━◆◆━━

Bret took the lobby staircase two steps at a time, a coffee cup in one hand and a Diet Coke in the other. He rounded the corner to Maddie's office and found it empty.

Retracing his steps, he took a sip of his coffee and headed for the backstage area.

He'd been there 36 hours and hadn't seen her yet. There might have been a welcome-back note in his room at least.

Hearing voices in the dressing room area, he headed towards them, passing his own quarters and walking further on to the chorus's room. "Aha, found you at..."

Matt and Tony looked up from Tony's make-up essentials list for the show.

"Didn't know you were looking for us! Come on in, Bret old boy. Matt, move your chair. Give the man some room."

Bret looked around the area quickly and sat in the offered seat. "Anyone want a Diet Coke? My usual taker seems to be missing."

Matt said, "Oh, you must mean Maddie. She's working everywhere on this show. No telling where you'll find her for the next few weeks. Thank God she's a versatile gal!"

Tony watched Bret for a reaction as Matt spoke.

"Oh, she *is* here," Bret remarked. "I was beginning to

wonder if she'd quit or something." He took the list from the counter and began to study it.

"Quit on Uncle Ben?" Tony exclaimed. "That will never happen! Since we have our Henry sitting here, let's turn to what tortures I have in store for him."

Matt sat up. "Did you say Uncle...I had no idea they were related."

"By marriage," Tony told him. "He's her husband's uncle?"

Bret listened with apparent disinterest, but corrected, without looking away from the list, "Her late husband's uncle."

Leaning back on his chair, Tony remarked, "Ah, yes. I remember telling you she's a widow. You asked me on opening night." He folded his arms and waited for a reply.

Bret looked at him out of the corner of his eye. "Yes, I remember."

Matt cleared his throat. "Okay, guys! I feel like I came in on Act Two. Let's change the subject."

"If you could make me look good as Othello, I don't think I have to worry about Henry Higgins. I'll see you at rehearsal tomorrow, Matt. See you later, Tony."

Tony and Matt watched him leave and then looked at each other.

"Okay, Tony, it looks like there's something I should know," Matt declared seriously. "Are Maddie and he going to give me any trouble?"

"Give you any...?" Tony exclaimed. "Good heavens, no! Whatever trouble there is will be just between them and won't interfere with the show. Neither one of them would let it! She's playing a cat and mouse game with him so nothing will come to a head until they confront each other."

Matt thought for a second and then observed, "He seemed anxious to see her. In fact, I'd say he was looking for her."

Tony nodded and shrugged his shoulders.

"Well, I'm not changing my plans," Matt declared. "I'm assigning her some backstage work once we get the show on its feet and, starting tomorrow, from the first rehearsal on she's my right hand. Whither I goest, she shall go, and that puts them in near proximity!"

Tony stood and extended his hand to Matt. "Great! Proximity! Maybe 'I've Grown Accustomed to Her Face' will take on a real meaning for him with her face back here. Matt, if you were a blond, I'd hug you!"

━━◆◆◆━━

"Monika, how are you? What a nice surprise!"

"I called Daddy's phone but he's got it turned off. Is he there with you, Maddie?"

"No. He's on stage. Should I have him call you or do you want to call him again tonight?"

Monika smiled to herself. "Maddie, can I ask you something?" Not waiting for an answer, she queried, "If you make a promise to your daughter, do you think you should keep it?"

Maddie didn't want to be accused of meddling by encouraging or discouraging her. "All I can tell you is what I've done with Whitney. If I've promised her something, I make good on it, but in turn, if she promises me something, I expect her to pay off too."

"It must have been fun for Whitney, growing up with you," Monika observed, leaning back against the hall phone booth wall. "I really like you. You're very nice. You make my Dad laugh, something not everyone can do, not even me sometimes."

Maddie needed to change the subject. "Christmas is coming soon, so tell me, Monika, what did you ask Santa for this year?" As she spoke, Bret opened the door and entered. "Hey, you're in luck. Here's your Dad, and now there's no time for your answer. Well, happy holidays just in case I don't speak to you again before then."

She handed him the phone, pointed to a sheet of rehearsal notes on the table, and left the office.

Bret watched Maddie leave, the phone in his hand but not to his ear. He slowly raised it. "Third call today, my little chickadee. What is it Monika wants and just can't seem to ask me?" As he spoke he pulled the curtain back from the window and watched Maddie cross the parking lot and disappear around the corner of the residence.

Ben turned his office chair to the window and thought, *It's been two weeks and Maddie and Bret are nowhere near as close as they were in October. Matt was nice to invite me into his rehearsals. My free days are much more pleasant spent in front of this group, but when Matt's not in charge, Maddie disappears. It couldn't be more obvious; she only stays in the same room with Bret if she's ordered to. I've seen her speaking with him, cordial, polite, proper and about as warm as Antarctica!*

Bret interrupted Ben's thoughts. "Guessed I'd find you here. I've got a major problem and need...well, someone to advise me, maybe even help."

Ben sat up and turned to face him. "Anything at all, my boy, if it's within my power."

"Well, it's Monika. I promised her that this Christmas vacation she could spend some time with me wherever I was working. I really don't want all these people here to know who she is. You know I'm paranoid on that subject! What can I do, Ben?"

"Let me think a minute, Bret." Ben tried to look as if he were searching for the answer, bringing his hand to his chin. *From my mind to your ear, God!* "My only suggestion is to approach the one person who solves all the impossibles for me, Maddie."

Bret moaned under his breath. "Why did I know you'd say that! Ben, I think she hates me. On closing night I left here running like a bat out of Hell, never said a word to her. When she answered the phone the day I called you about the picture, I got tongue-tied. I tried to pick up where we'd left off, when I got back here but...well, let's put it this way, I don't think she'll do anything to help me."

The image of his son crossed Ben's mind, and he defined what he was experiencing with Bret, paternal feelings. "I'll tell you what I assume, and I'm not going to ask you any questions. You are more than interested in Maddie, and want to, shall we say, pursue a serious relationship, but she's having none of it, probably based on that last night of *Othello*. Nothing is going to happen the way you're both carrying on now. So, listen to the man who knows her better than anyone except Whitney. The major inroad to solving the mystery of Maddie is her daughter. What touches Whitney, touches Maddie. If you do something, let's see, maybe something to help Whitney which doesn't involve Maddie, it will pull her into that circle. As to what you could do, I guess that's up to you."

Ben attempted mental telepathy, offering an obvious answer to Bret.

"The movie! I could offer to coach Whitney, after all I was studying that thing for a while. I know it as well as anyone!"

Ben grinned. "Good boy, Bret! You are a genius!"

"May I use your phone?" Bret asked. "I don't even know if the home number is the same, Ben. Help me out? I want to talk to Whitney now, before I have time to talk myself out of this."

IX

*T*he guards passed Whitney through the Genesius Theater gates and she proceeded slowly along the winding tree-lined road that led to the heart of the property, enjoying the cool sunlit day.

Life is getting weirder and weirder. Mom has barely mentioned Bret's name since he came back here and now he calls me to offer his help. Who am I to turn down such an offer! I'm sure it was at Uncle Ben's suggestion, but if Bret and Mom aren't getting along, why would Bret do it?

She pulled into a parking space near the dorm and checked her watch as she got out of the car. She was early. He'd still be in rehearsal, so she decided to look for Ben in his office.

"The Ascot Gavotte" pulsed through the open doors of the theater as she entered the building and climbed the staircase.

"Ladies, please! What is your problem?" Matt shouted over the music.

"It's the hats," an actress's voice answered. "They're either too heavy or too big or both! We can't walk, sing, and balance all this at the same time!"

Ben appeared at the top of the stairs, exasperation etched on his features. At the sight of Whitney, a broad smile displaced his serious expression. "Whitney, what a pleasant surprise! To what do we owe this honor?"

"As if you didn't know," she declared, meeting him on the top landing and taking his arm. They headed back towards his office. "Bret, coaching me! Am I supposed to believe my fatal charms lured him to his offer?"

Ben smiled. "Well, I can't think of any other reason for it." He stepped aside to let her enter his office first.

Whitney sat in one of the visitors' chairs and he took the one next to her. "I know what it is, Ben! He's hand-picking his partner. We'll be the next Tracy and Hepburn, Gable and Lombard."

Ben laughed, noting the serious expression in her eyes. "As long as it's not Martin and Lewis!"

"Come on, Ben, what's going on here? He can't have seen anymore of my work than the rest of the country, and that doesn't make me out to be the successor to Sarah Bernhardt. So where does this great philanthropy come from? Hmm, Uncle Ben?"

She held his eyes until he looked away.

"Come on, Ben, I know something's up. Seriously, what's going on here?"

He shifted uncomfortably in his chair. Hoping she would be too thrilled to care where Bret's offer came from, he counted on not having to explain his scheme to her. "You're going to get angry and tell me to butt out."

She sat up straight. "Go ahead, hit me with it. I can take anything!"

"Even when you're upset, you crack a joke! Definitely your mother's genes!" Ben said, relaxing a bit. "You've never said anything to me directly but I got the impression you like Bret and Monika."

Whitney nodded.

"Well…I'm interfering, something I swore I'd never do. I think Maddie and Bret are perfect for each other. When I got back here, just a week ago, I couldn't believe that they weren't tripping down the daisy path together. She's been avoiding him like the plague. If caught in the same room, she's nice, you know, she's Maddie. Otherwise, she's perfected the art of disappearing."

"I have no idea what's going on out here," Whitney confessed. "She tells me about the rehearsals and nothing more. I've hinted a few times but hit a wall of silence when I do. The vibes seem bad so I haven't pushed her."

Ben leaned forward, closer to her, speaking lower. "If she's around, I don't want her to hear. Bret's been trying to change her attitude and failing. Then Monika called and he knows he might need Maddie's help to do something for Monika. He and I both agree she'd probably turn him down right now, nicely, but her answer would be no."

"You really think so?"

"If you'd seen her like I have this past week, you wouldn't ask that. Now, Miss Whit, I'll make a confession to you. I've cast you upon the troubled waters."

Whitney's eyebrows went up.

"Yes, my love, I've made you the bait." Ben braced for an explosion. Whitney was not someone to be used and he knew it.

"Explain that," she said flatly.

"Bret helps you. He's working with Maddie's baby; she can't help but get involved, wanting to know what's going on, maybe even sit in on a few sessions with him and you."

Whitney's hand went up in a stop signal. "I'm the lure to bring them together? Did it ever occur to you that instead of being interested in what's going on she just might get jealous?"

"Oh, God, Whit, you don't really think that could happen?" Ben stammered, a look of concern shadowing his face.

Whitney reached for his hand. "I didn't mean to scare

you like that. Just thought you might have forgotten one possibility when you thought this up. If I know Mom at all, jealousy of me is not possible. What you have done, all things considered, is masterminded the plot of the century! How'd you get Bret to go along with it?"

"Desperate men employ desperate means."

Whitney hugged him, whispering, "You're the best. Only you could think up a scheme that kills an entire flock of birds with one stone. I get the most valuable help in the world, Bret gets to her so maybe they can iron out the kinks, she gets her eyes opened and—Mom! What a look! Oh, yeah! It's definitely you!"

Maddie stood outside the doorway trying to figure how to get through without removing the enormous white tulle and lace picture hat she wore.

Whitney added, "I think it's a real fashion statement, wearing that with a sweater, skirt and flats. It's so..."

Maddie pulled out a handful of bobby pins and hat pins as Whitney spoke. "I'll fashion statement you, Missy!" She lifted the hat from her head, carried it tilted on its side through the entrance and plopped it onto Ben's head. "Try attaching that to your hair, feel it pulling for at least a half an hour; then add insult to injury, move in rhythm with it. It's like balancing the Harvard Five-Foot Bookshelf on your head! This is what we get for not doing our own costumes! I can't find the name of the supplier in the mountain of stuff on my desk. I thought you might have it somewhere handy."

"Holy cow!" Ben exclaimed. "This thing has a mind of its own! It's much too heavy and off-balance." Removing the offending weight from his head, he handed it back to Maddie. "Let me look on the calendar. I usually have things jotted in there."

As Ben rose and headed for his desk, Maddie stared at Whitney. "What are you doing here? You usually tell me if you're coming out. Something go wrong?"

"No, Mom, everything's fine. I'm here to talk to Ben and maybe see... Keith...Keith Rand, you remember him from my college shows. Keith, your "On the Street Where You Live.""

Bret appeared in the doorway. "Goodness, it's a meeting of the clan. Don't let me interrupt."

Whitney jumped up from her chair. "Don't go, Bret. It's good to see you. Sorry you won't be destroyed by me, Senator, but I get Redford instead. Someone, please wipe this grin off of my face!"

Bret took a quick look at Maddie. She'd retreated to the far-side of the room when he appeared and was staring out the window. Taking Whitney's cue, he said, "Speaking of the Senator, I was wondering if you might find use for some of my insights on Elaine. It's a great role. I seem to have more free-time now than I did during Othello so I can offer."

Whitney exclaimed, "You're kidding!" as she rose from her chair. "Oh, but I wouldn't want to impose. You don't have to do this. You're tired after the long days here."

"As a matter of fact," Bret stated, looking directly at Maddie, "it would be nice to have my time taken up talking to someone, doing something, sharing thoughts and ideas."

Maddie turned, caught his look, and returned immediately to her study of the tree outside the window.

"When do we start?" Whitney asked looking from her mother to Bret and back to her mother.

"Nothing here that can't wait so let's go and talk about it now. Ben, I can see you later. Come on, Whitney."

She looked at Ben, crossed her fingers and followed Bret out of the room.

"Find that phone number, Ben?" Maddie asked, finally turning to face the room.

"Maddie, why..."

"Don't, Ben," Maddie warned. "Ask me no questions and I'll tell you no lies. All I want to hear is that phone number."

"Look, Bret, we've been at this one line for an hour," Whitney complained. "I still don't know what you're looking for here. She's got the Senator by the throat with the evidence she's dug up on his past. How else can she open her statements to him other than with authority?"

Bret sighed and was about to reiterate his theory on expressing power and yet leaving room to introduce other emotions of the moment when Maddie entered the otherwise empty theater. His back was to the house so he couldn't see who entered but knew who it was. "Look, Whitney, think beyond the surface of that moment. True, she's disappointed in him. She's worshipped the man from afar for years, all that he's stood for, his crusader image. Now, not only has she found the damning evidence that he was on the take, but here she bursts in on him "couched down" with her rival, in his Senate office yet. You're showing me only one emotion. There's much more at work here."

"Okay, how's this." Whitney recited the first two sentences of her dialogue.

"Too ballsy! You've established a strong yet feminine character up to this point. Come on, deep breath, close your eyes. Feel her!"

She started again and he interrupted even earlier in the dialogue. "Too feminine. He'd wrap her around his finger in two seconds. Remember, he's sitting there half-dressed. She can't be unaffected by that. She has to counter her own desires."

"Well, I think I gave you just what you're looking for and you're just being a complete..."

"That's my true nature. Whatever I am aside, I'm not feeling it all from any of your tries. Are you, Maddie?" He surprised both women.

Maddie walked down the aisle to the edge of the stage,

looked up at Whitney and smiled. "I'm afraid he's right, honey. After hearing what's supposed to be going on here, I can appreciate how powerful those opening lines can be. Establish them and you can go histrionic and not ruin the scene."

Bret, still turned away from Maddie, smiled and winked at Whitney as he said, "Let's make it real." He rose and walked to the wings. "This chair is the couch." He carried it to center stage and placed it. "I'm Redford, excuse me, the Senator. I could never hope in my wildest dreams to be Redford. I'm just a poor substitute for the moment." As he unbuttoned his shirt and removed it, he said, "This is what you face. Now think of a person you worship. Imagine they have just proven to be lower than the low. You're already dealing with disappointment and anger before you open the door. You see him and her together, as together as two humans can get, and you add rage, jealousy, contempt and...shock."

Maddie stared at Bret as he disheveled his hair and within seconds looked as if he'd been interrupted at just the wrong moment.

"Too bad there's no one here to play Laura," Bret remarked. "I could be really convincing if we could do the whole scene before you enter." He turned and looked at Maddie.

She tried to hold steady but retreated from the look, backing up to a seat and almost falling into it.

"Ready?" Bret asked Whitney, and she nodded after a few seconds.

The added dimension of his words and presence brought out the desired effect and the paragraph of dialogue went from being angry words to a moving canon of dashed hopes and dreams.

Bret and Maddie stared at Whitney in silence.

"What did I do wrong this time? I was too what? Not enough what?"

Their silence continued.

"What?" she wailed.

Bret put his arm in a shirt sleeve and said, "By George, I think she's got it! That was phenomenal! Will I have to hang around the set with my shirt off to make sure your scenes go well when you begin to shoot?" As he buttoned the last button, he asked, "What did you think, Maddie?"

Maddie cleared her throat. When something hit her right, when it got inside, tears would well in her eyes. "I'm speechless, Whitney. The difference, the dimension of what I just saw...words fail me."

"Really? I thought it was good...right. It felt so right," Whitney stated, sitting on the chair Bret had just vacated. "I didn't know what I'd telegraphed though because you both just stared at me." She looked up at Bret as he pulled his sweater over his head. "Thank you, Bret. You made it live for me and now I can feed off it. I never would have gotten to that spot by myself. Thank you, thank you, thank you!"

She shook her head to clear it and realized Bret needed her to get out of there fast, before Maddie could. "You wore me out! Yikes, I forgot I have a date in L.A. tonight and I'm running late so, see you all anon. I'll be sure to wake you up when I get home, Mom."

"I'm sure you will!," Maddie declared, adding, "I'll go out to your car with you."

"No you won't, not unless you can run as fast as me," She jumped down from the stage and ran past Maddie at full speed.

Maddie, left alone with him, had no way out of saying something to Bret

"Thank you for all this with Whitney. I just realized something interesting. After all these years, there's no such thing as an Atkins-type because you don't care about yourself in a role. It's to do with what the writer is trying to convey through all of his characters, not just yours. Your analysis of the whole work is what makes your performances so individual. You mold to the script and not vice-versa."

"My secret's out!" Bret jumped down from the stage. "Now I suppose I'll read it in the *National Inquirer* or something."

"Oh, of course," Maddie replied flatly. "I couldn't just offer a sincere compliment. You doubt my motives, think that I'd find a way to make money out of this."

"Hold it! Time out!" Bret cried. "Don't be so...!" He took a deep breath and started over. "This is the first time outside of rehearsal I've had a chance to talk to you. I refuse to waste it on stupidity."

Maddie tried to walk faster than he to the back door but he wouldn't let her get more than one step ahead. They arrived at the door at the same time and he held it open for her.

She headed for the stairs and he followed on her heels.

"I have something to say to you," Bret announced from behind as they crossed the walkway above the lobby. "I don't intend to lose this chance."

Maddie kept moving and entered her office, saying, "Does it matter that I don't have any interest in what you have to say?"

"Maddie, I'm going to say my piece, and you can listen or tune out. At least I will know I said it."

She sat at her desk, looking for something she could get lost in while he spoke.

Bret stood by the window, leaning on the frame, looking out. "September and October were two of the most enjoyable months of my life because of you. I haven't felt that comfortable with anyone in a very long time. I thought you were having fun too, in fact I was sure of it. There was one problem though. It had to come to an end here and I didn't know how to handle that. I put off even thinking about it until the night before the last show. It was then I realized I couldn't manage any kind of a face-to-face goodbye. So..I took the coward's way out and just ran for it. I figured you'd forget me in a few days, probably adopt another lonely star and brighten his or her life like you did mine."

Maddie sat stock still. Even her breathing wasn't perceptible.

Bret continued, "I expected you to corner me and tell me off in spades the minute I arrived. I even rehearsed my reactions and responses for the week before I returned. So, what do you do? Ignore me! I didn't expect that so I didn't know what to do. As usual, when faced with indecision I did exactly what I always do, nothing!"

She got up from her desk and headed away from him, going around her desk.

He waited for her to walk out but instead heard her coming up behind him. He closed his eyes and waited for...something. He didn't know what he wanted, for her to throw her arms around him or to belt him in the back and tell him off. He admitted to himself he was scared of both.

"Bret, listen to me because I'll say this only once. You couldn't have done anything worse to me than leave the way you did. I sat here for days hoping it was you every time the phone rang. By the time you did call, my hope had turned to anger. As you can see, my part in this production is more hands-on than with Ben, so my time and energy are limited until we open. Then I'll be backstage, production assisting and getting office work done as I can. If we're free at the same time someday..."

Bret interrupted her. "Since I presume you still eat dinner, I'll expect to see you in the dorm tomorrow night for the Atkins company feast. No excuses accepted. Dress is informal. Appetite essential." He headed for the door as he spoke and disappeared around the corner on the last word.

Running out on me again are you, Mr. Atkins?, Maddie thought as she watched him jogging across the space between the theater and the dorm from her office window. *Well, at least this time there's a tomorrow. Maybe I'll show up early and reassume my clean-up kitchen role. Then again, maybe I won't.*

X

The Pacific, so placid on the distant horizon, tossed and foamed its way to Maddie's feet where she stood on the shore. She looked to her right and faced a solid line of jutting cliffs and a limitless expanse of water. From her left the brisk breeze, scudding across the wave tops, brushed her face with mist.

She licked the salt from her lips and was reminded of childhood summers in Newport and on Cape Cod. *Is the Pacific saltier than the Atlantic?* she wondered as she wrapped her Irish knit sweater more tightly around herself.

Maddie sauntered back across the beach to the staircase. As she climbed she surveyed the vista, changing with almost each step until she reached the top. Wandering along the cliff, she headed to the spot where it jutted the furthest into the ocean.

Boris summoned Marina from the kitchen to join him in the courtyard. He pointed to the cliff and Marina studied the image in the distance. Turning to him, she said, "Monika must have been inspired when she decided to make him keep his promise. I think she knew he'd have to ask for Maddie's help to make it happen. Look at that, Boris! Of the many places out there, she chose the one where he always stands. Then again, maybe it wasn't Monika alone. It could be Nancy..."

Maddie looked at her watch and turned toward the house, Bret's house. Monika would be waiting to ride back to the Genny and L.A. with her.

She turned back to the ocean. *One more look. I want to remember all of it. It's so unbelievably beautiful here. My dream home on the cliffs. Well, at least I visited.*

As she headed for the house, she studied the rambling stucco two-story building with its terra cotta tiled roof. *Oh my, it even has balconies facing the ocean! If I lived here I doubt I'd leave it too willingly for any length of time. Bret has mentioned how peaceful it is, the air, the water and the quiet. It's God's own tranquilizer.*

As she sauntered up the flagstone path skirting the balustraded terrace, she remembered how unprovocable Bret had remained despite some catty remarks and digs she'd lobbed at him in the days following the rehearsal with Whitney. She'd had to defuse her anger and took it out on him beyond any decent level. All she got in return were jokes or silliness. The effect of this place must hold over for him. He had softened her up with calm acceptance and, in truth, she had welcomed it.

She took a deep breath and looked back towards the ocean. *Go with the flow, Maddie,* she told herself. *He's taking you somewhere.*

She recalled the day he broached his problem to her. The minute she thought of a solution she knew she should have forgotten it. Instead, she offered it to him. "Please...relax! You don't have to say no to her. I could pass her off as my niece visiting from New York. She'd stay with me, and I'd bring her to the theater every day."

Bret had approached the subject in a phone call so Maddie could beg-off helping him more easily than face to face.

"I couldn't ask that of you! It's too much. Thank you but no."

She pushed him to agree to do it. "It'll be fun having a child in the house again. We'll have a good time with her and you can enjoy her company in a comfortable atmosphere. She wants to be a part of what you do. All she gets to see are the end results, the movies. She has no idea of what you put into your work. Don't you think it's time she found out?"

"It would be fun for me," Bret had thought out loud. "The last two Christmases I've flown in during the day and left that night, shooting in some God-forsaken place each year. It really would make up for that."

Maddie remembered saying, "What a fantastic compliment. As much as my daughter loves me, there has never been a Christmas on which I was the first, most wanted gift on her list. You are one lucky parent!"

Bret's voice seemed to brighten. "You're right! That is what she said; she wanted me for Christmas! We wrap for the holidays...Oh Lord, excuse that pun...on the 23rd. If she came down on the...When do you think?"

"I'll pick her up on the 19th and the two of you can go home together on the 23rd."

He'd cleared his throat and said, "Maddie, how can I ever repay you? This is above and beyond the call of duty!"

"I thought I was your friend. Real friends don't need or want paybacks."

Maddie shook her head, trying to free it from her thoughts but more intruded. *There's danger when you float in that stream, Maddie. You can drown. Your tendency toward emotional suicide is alive and well. Stop it! Relax! Relax? Will you listen to me! I must be high on ozone!*

Monika came running through the French doors which stood open to the terrace. "Maddie, I'm ready. Have enough time out here?"

Turning from the view towards the voice, she answered, "My chariot awaits you. Say good-bye to Marina and we're off on your big adventure."

If Maddie had any worry about keeping up a conversation with Monika during the two-hour drive down the coast, it disappeared in minutes. The miles sped by and Monika chattered non-stop about Lisa and how things had changed for Lisa and her mother since Thanksgiving. After that holiday visit, the woman was so curious to find out "everything" about Bret Atkins she couldn't seem to be in touch with her daughter enough. Her daughter, the "personal friend" of the super star!

"And gee, Maddie, they've taken Lisa to Paris for Christmas and she's promised to bring me back a real Parisian dress!"

In the confusion and bustle of the night Monika came to the *Othello*, Maddie hadn't been able to really "see" her, other than her deep-brunette hair color. Bret being so fair, it had been a surprise.

As they'd walked to the car, Maddie realized how tall Monika was for her age and thought her a little too thin. But she probably packed on the pounds when she was home, eating Marina's cooking.

Monika's voice penetrated Maddie's thoughts. "I can hardly wait to see Dad! He's actually doing a musical! This is going to be so much fun!"

"Your Dad is quite good, and I'm not saying that because you're sitting next to me." Maddie told Monika about the hats in the Ascot number and they laughed when Maddie said, "Besides the girls' problems with balancing those giant-size pizzas, we had to get the smaller hats because when your father entered the scene he looked like he'd been decapitated. No matter where he moved, either his mother's or Eliza's hat completely covered him from the neck up. In one rehearsal he hung his coat on a chair on stage, sat in the first row in the house and recited his lines from there. "I think it works! No one can see me in the scene anyway!"

Monika stole glances at Maddie while they talked, discovering she had dark brown eyes. Pretty gold and opal earrings caught her attention, and she noticed Maddie had pierced ears, something else she wanted to talk to her father about. She confirmed many times during the two-hour ride that Maddie liked to laugh and make jokes. She particularly noticed that Maddie didn't ask her to be quiet, that she treated her like— well almost like— an adult.

Rehearsals were running later because of the up-coming week hiatus for the holidays, so everything was still in full swing when they arrived. They checked in with Ben, whom they found in the box office, and told him of Maddie's plan to pass Monika off as her niece.

"Oh, good!," Ben exclaimed. "She's your niece from New York. Can I be your nephew from Cambridge?"

Maddie threw a ticket envelope at him, to Monika's delight.

Stealing in a back door of the house, they took seats in the last row. Monika whispered questions to Ben or Maddie, fascinated by the world around her and wanting to know everything at once.

An hour had passed when Matt called it quits for the day. Bret hung back, waiting for the cast and crew to clear out, before he ran up the aisle to Monika. His face clouded as he drew nearer. "How'd you get here so fast! I saw Maddie leave this noontime and you walked in here an hour ago!" Bret didn't take his eyes from Monika as he stated, "I sent a reckless driver for you!"

Maddie thought he was kidding.

Monika knew by the tone of his voice he wasn't. She insisted, "She never went over the speed limit!"

"It's not possible to stay at 55 and make it here in that little time," he persisted, still looking at Monika.

"Well, well!," Maddie laughed. "Now we know who the speeder is in this group!"

He glanced quickly at Maddie. "Maybe when I'm alone but never with Monika in the car!"

Ben, sensing Maddie beginning to lose her cool, interjected, "So, you three going out to eat?"

Maddie looked at Monika who was staring seriously at her father. She said to Ben, "Thought it would be better to eat at home. Bret will be dropped back here at a decent hour and at a decent speed."

"Have fun, kids. Can I see you outside, Maddie?" He waved good-bye, and taking Maddie's elbow, escorted her to the lobby. "Cool down, my Maddie. His mood seemed to deteriorate with each step up the aisle. Know what's bothering him?"

"Not a clue, Ben. Maybe it's his unique way of showing me my place in this scenario, chauffeur, house-mother, and baby sitter. It's irrelevant I'm offering my house and my time to do this for them. I'm nobody's doormat, Ben, but I don't want to upset Monika. She's a wonderful girl and I won't do that to her. If he keeps this up though, I'll read him the riot act just before he goes home. It'll be my special Christmas present to him."

As Ben and Maddie spoke, Bret took Monika's hand and they walked through the lobby and out the door. "Aren't you glad to see me?" Monika asked as they headed towards Maddie's car.

"Of course I am! Why would you ask that?"

"You're acting kind of funny," Monika dared.

As she spoke, Maddie caught up with them and opened the passenger door.

Bret stepped forward and got in the back seat.

"I'll sit back there, Dad. You're too tall!"

Maddie walked around to the driver's door, saying, "Don't ruin his retreat. He seems to need to be alone." She started the engine and added, "Fasten your seat belt, Monika. I wouldn't want to lose you when I hit 125 on the Freeway." As they neared the gates, Maddie suggested to Bret, "If I were you, I'd get down. People know you're here. It's just the locals for now but we could be delayed if they see you."

"What a stupid way to live!" Bret said angrily. "I can't

make a dignified exit or even take my own daughter out to dinner! Why can't people leave me alone! Oh, just to be alone, all by myself!"

"Gee, thanks, Dad! I'd rather be with you, dodging crowds, than anywhere else. You can't mean you'd rather be all alone! What about me? What about Maddie?"

Maddie spoke up fast. "Don't bring me into this conversation. I'm just the chauffeur and house-mother here and I like those roles just fine. It's perfect type-casting."

"No, you're not any of those! You're my aunt, remember?" Monika corrected. "Let me see, that makes you Daddy's sister? Oh no, never! You don't look at all alike! Or... you're my mother's sister. That's right, isn't it, Dad? My aunt would be your sister or my mother's sister?"

Bret, sure they'd passed the gates, sat up again and stared at Maddie's profile from the back seat. Less angrily, he said, "You're absolutely right, Puddin', your mother's sister." He realized, as he continued to look at Maddie, that she was enough like Nancy in her thinking and her heart to be her sister.

At the next traffic light, Maddie looked into the rear-view mirror, and her eyes met his.

"Maddie, the light's green. Hello, Maddie," Monika prodded, shaking Maddie's arm. She followed Maddie's eyes and turned quickly to the back seat. Bret looked away just as she turned so he seemed to have been staring straight ahead. She smiled at him. *Grown-ups! He pretends she's nothing special. She pretends she's our employee. Play fantasy games with me, the West Coast champion? Wait until you hear this one!*

"Dad, Lisa and I were talking the other day and we decided it would be nice, since we're the ones who have to be away from home, if we could choose where we go to school."

Bret sat forward, not wanting to miss a word.

"We got a book out of the school library, one that lists all the private schools around the world. We each made a list of what we wanted our school to have and we found one in the book that has it all, Mount Piedmont Academy."

Maddie reacted immediately, "Monika, don't you think this..." She looked at Monika quickly, and said, "Sorry, none of my business."

Bret looked deep in thought. Finally, he said, "I think you have a point. After all, you should have a say in where you're going. Maybe we can contact this..."

Maddie burst in, "Don't agree to anything! You know nothing about that place." New Englanders knew all about it. At least one story a winter publicized its existence.

Bret closed his eyes, looking as if he were counting to ten. "As I was saying, Monika," he stated in a controlled voice, "we can contact this school and see what they have to say for themselves."

Maddie, pulling into her driveway, hit the brake suddenly, turned to him and stated, "Ask her the most basic question, will you please! Ask her where the school is! Don't be so willing to give in to her!"

Maddie gasped at her own temerity and turned to Monika, apologizing, "I'm not saying you shouldn't have a say as to where you go, Monika. You are right about that. It's not telling him where this school is that made me say what I did, before you had him backed into a corner."

"Enough," Bret snapped angrily. "You should have brought this up when we were alone, Monika. Since you didn't, it's getting out of hand with all these extra thoughts. Forget it for now. We'll talk later...alone."

"Monika, tell him!" Maddie persisted, despite a perceptibly angry sound from behind her. "Where is the school? Tell him!"

Monika turned to her father and smiled. "It's in northern Maine. Lots of mountains. The description says it can snow so much up there that often it's impossible to get through for days on end. The school keeps lots of extra food and fuel just in case."

Bret stared at his daughter while Maddie pulled the car

into the garage. "Forget it!"

"But Dad," Monika wheedled, "I'll bet Lisa's parents won't mind and if she goes and I can't, I'll lose my best friend!"

Maddie leaned over to Monika, saying, "Your father said you'd talk about it later. Don't push or he may refuse to talk about any change at all." Maddie expected tears or a pout, or at least an objection. Instead, Monika grinned from ear to ear. "Listen to you two! You sound just like parents! I say I want it. You disagree about it. He says we'll talk. I object. You tell me not to bother him. This is great! I hear kids' parents at school doing this all the time. I like it! This is perfect!"

Bret leaned forward and growled, "Please stop all this foolish talk and let me out of here."

Maddie got out and walked toward the house after she'd flung the back of her seat forward so hard it sprang upward gain.

"Look what you did, Dad," Monika scolded. "You made her mad. I think you should apologize. You've been mean to her ever since we got here. She hasn't done anything except be nice." She looked at his serious expression and it provoked her further. "Dad," she said, turning to face him and holding his arm so he couldn't move to get out, "I like Maddie a lot. Please, don't do anything to push her away. If you do, I think it'll be the first time ever I get mad at you and I don't think I'll get over it too fast."

She opened her door and turned back as she was getting out, "As a matter of fact, if she goes away from us, Maine won't be far enough away from you for a while."

Bret unfolded himself from the back seat and stretched beside the car, stalling until Monika entered the house. He closed the car door and leaned against it. *Monika's crazy about her, but Maddie's not crazy about me. She treats me so nonchalantly. Never once have I caught her letting her guard down. Wait...that's the first time I thought of that, letting her guard down. She's no more defensive than I am. I didn't recognize the feminine version.*

He sauntered toward the house, noting the quiet neighborhood and the view of the distant Pacific from the hilltop. He had gotten thrown off balance when he saw Maddie and Monika in the back of that theater. Monika looked more happy, relaxed, and content than he had ever seen her. Talk about clutching at straws! He'd had to find something, anything, to get angry at Maddie about to keep him from throwing himself at her feet and begging her to take him and his daughter.

As he walked up the back steps, he straightened his shoulders. *The others have been so easy, bed and bye. No feelings, no thought, no love. Not since Nancy have I wanted a woman as much as Maddie nor have I had so many opportunities to get what I want. Yet, I don't make a move. I've been totally alone with this woman innumerable times and not once have I steered toward anything meaningful. Help me out, Nancy.*

"Oh, that sounds like fun!" Monika exclaimed as she raised the last forkful of "Welcome Monika" cake to her mouth, a cake especially baked by Whitney for her.

Whitney had just reminded Maddie of the carnival at the church where they played and sang on Sundays. She wanted to get Monika out of the house, leave Bret and Maddie alone for a while. "You promised Father John you'd spend a fortune there."

"Oh, you're right. I completely forgot."

Monika ran to her father's chair at the dinner table. "Come on, Dad, let's.. yeh, you can't. Oh, well. Are you going Whitney?"

"If I don't, my name will be mud," Whitney joked. "Bret, how about trusting me with Monika for a couple of hours? It's only a few blocks from here. The neighborhood is good. She'll be fine."

"Well...," he said, looking at Monika who was failing in her attempt not to show how much she wanted to go. "Sure, why not. Here's some...I can't believe it, I forgot my wallet!" Maddie observed, "First thing to go is the memory, then the hair." Her wallet was in her bedroom and she sent Whitney for it. When she returned with it, Maddie asked Monika to hold out both hands, palms up, and emptied the change and bill sections into them.

"Maddie, what are you doing?" Monika squealed. "How much is here?"

"Have a blast on me, Monika. Father said he expected me to come prepared to stay all night and hand over my fortune. It's what I would have spent if I'd gone myself. Try all the rides. Maybe your luck will be better than mine and you'll win a stuffed animal."

Monika hugged her vigorously and then threw her arms around her father's neck. "Oh, I'm so glad you let me come! Let's go Whitney." She ran through the back door and waited outside impatiently.

"I'm young. I'm healthy. I can keep up with her! Oy, or die trying!" Whitney joked as she trotted to join Monika.

Bret and Maddie listened to the laughter as the girls got into Whitney's car and headed off for the evening. He stared at Maddie. She stared at him.

Maddie finally spoke, looking towards the sink. "Okay now, we've got the younger generation entertained for the time being. What can I possibly do to keep you amused for the next few hours? Entertaining mega-stars is a little new to me."

She stood up, straightened her skirt checking to see if there was anything Whitney had left undone after dinner. For once, she was disappointed to find everything in perfect order. She needed to do something with her hands, her mind, her everything! Why did she ever get herself into this?

"It looks nice outside. Let's sit out there, on the terrace," Bret suggested, standing behind her.

Maddie headed in the opposite direction, towards her

room, saying, "Wonderful idea. You go ahead. I'll join you in a minute." She ran to her dresser, combed her hair, applied some eye shadow and was twisting her lipstick up as she studied her face in the mirror. *Look at yourself, Maddie! Whatever you say or do cannot change the fact that you are a middle-aged woman. He's actually improving as he ages. You're just getting older. A raving beauty you're not, and face it, never were! Make him forget all those gorgeous women he knows? That's what I call the ultimate impossibility.*

She put some lipstick on, checked the results, and, as she walked toward the terrace, wondered in what deep, hidden recess of her mind and heart lurked her long-abandoned nerve to go out there and wrap him, heart and soul, around her little finger. *Get real, Maddie, you couldn't wrap him around anything, even with duct tape!*

XI

"*H*ello, Marina? Remember what we said about Maddie, about her being special?"

"Where are you calling from?" Marina asked, distracted by the noises, music and laughter in the background.

"We're at a fair, at a church. I told them I was supposed to call you. I'm in the house where the priest lives, using his phone. They're outside, talking. Oh, Marina, she's so great!"

"Who's great? Maddie? Is she with you? Don't tell me your father is?"

"No," Monika said, lowering her voice. "They're at Maddie's house, alone. I'm with Whitney. She's so nice! You'd better get the guest room ready, maybe two of them. I'm about to perform a miracle. Can people perform miracles or is that only God?"

Marina smiled. "It seems at Christmas time things happen that appear to be miracles. When will you be home?"

"Saturday night and I think we can expect guests for Christmas Eve, if all goes right. Say a prayer. I love you."

She hung up as Whitney knocked on the door. "All set, Monika?"

"Yes, and thanks, Father. I was supposed to call home this afternoon and forgot," Monika explained, studying the young man dressed in black. "I never met a priest before. Are you married?"

Whitney laughed, and Father John smiled despite his deepening confusion over this young girl's identity, his politely expressed curiosity diverted to other subjects by Whitney while they waited. He put his hand out to Monika, answering, "Funny thing you should ask that. Whitney tells me the women in this parish think it's, as she says, a waste that priests don't marry. We stay single so we can devote all our time to God and our people."

Monika took his hand and studied the handsome young man as they walked outside. "He's like my Dad, Whitney. Good looking and alone. Maybe my father should become a Father!"

Whitney smiled and suggested, "Maybe your father should become a husband."

Monika stopped in her tracks, yanking the priest's arm, and Whitney walked into her. "Do you really mean that? Do you think my Dad should get married?"

"Of course." Whitney studied Monika, weighing whether she should pursue the subject. "If he brought someone home and said he wanted to marry her, would you be happy?"

Monika didn't hesitate for a second. "Sure, but only if it was Maddie."

Father John stared at both of them. "What's going on here? Maddie's been dating someone? Your father? She never said a word to me, not even a hint."

"Don't feel left out," Whitney explained. "They're not dating...yet. They've met, there are sparks but...well, it's two immovable objects and a mutual non-recognition of the irresistible force."

Monika interrupted, "What? I didn't understand anything you said."

Father John translated, "Two people who aren't moving towards each other despite everything being there that should bring them together. I'll bet you're still confused. I know for a fact I am!"

"Everything's there except for one thing!" she said, squeezing his hand. "Thanks for making me think of it. Whitney, can I talk to you?"

They said good-bye to Father and headed for the car. "I didn't know if you thought Maddie and Dad were...were..."

"Interested in each other? Let's stop for a Coke and talk. It's hard to concentrate on driving and the fate of our parents at the same time."

Once settled in a back booth of a local sandwich shop, Monika looked steadily into Whitney's eyes with an intensity known only in a twelve-year-old girl. "We're saying they're interested in each other. Would you like it if they said they wanted to get married?"

"Hold your horses," Whitney exclaimed. "First we have to get them to admit out loud they like each other! I think they've collected too many scars over the years. If they can get beyond all that, and they're absolutely sure they want it, I'd be very happy for them."

"That's a real adult answer. It sounds smart but doesn't tell me what I want to know." Monika moved to Whitney's side of the table and slouched down in the seat, stating, "I don't understand what's so scary about love. Isn't it supposed to be beautiful, two people wanting to be together forever, having fun, doing whatever they like? What's so scary about that?"

"It's not the having," Whitney reasoned, taking Monika's hand in hers. "It's the real possibility of losing it once you have it. Each of them lost their dreams and had to keep themselves together because of a child. Maybe the people they reached out to during those years proved to be bitter disappointments in one way or another, and I would guess they're tired of getting hurt."

Monika smiled slowly. "Then what we have to do is put

them together as much as possible. Show them they can't live without each other and how wonderful, how painless being together can be."

"Your theory is right as far as it goes, Monika. To complete it, they've got to find everything so wonderful they'll be able to ignore any thought of losing it."

Monika's eyes twinkled as she exclaimed, "They've had over two hours alone in your house tonight. Do you think...?"

"With our luck they've been alone all this time and only discussed the high price of cotton in Cairo!" Whitney felt there was more truth than joke in her remark.

Monika studied Whitney for a moment and ventured, "You'll probably say I'm too young to understand all this but I think I know a way to get them really together."

Whitney's eyebrows went up and she looked at Monika with added interest.

"Put them under the same roof with Marina. She can move anything, even... immobular objects?"

"Immovable," Whitney corrected her.

"Immovable. Please, if you'll play along and act as if you're having this brain-storm with me, they'll go for it."

"I'm your slave," Whitney stated and they shook hands on their promise.

The wavering light of the large table candles afforded Maddie with enough camouflage to scrutinize Bret. She sat on the glider and he on one of two wicker rockers facing the Pacific, now defined only by the shoreline lights in the distance.

Bret stared at the horizon and sighed. In the waning light, Maddie thought he looked sad. "I miss so much with Monika," he said softly, as if to himself. "I have to arrange a simple trip like this as if it were the invasion of Normandy. By the time all is set, the whole thing has lost its charm. I would give anything to have a second face I could pull on and go out again like a normal human being. I like people. After all, if it weren't for them, I'd probably be playing dinner theaters. But I'd love for them to leave me alone once in a while."

He looked towards her. "Classic example. Last spring Monika wanted to go to a real theater with me and eat popcorn out of a tub like a normal American kid, not have to watch new releases in our screening room at home. Would you believe I had to buy out a local theater to do it without creating a crowd problem for the owner? There we sat, me, Monika, Boris, Marina and 500 empty seats. Now that's a typical day at any theater! I wonder if she feels like she's living with the family freak that has to be hidden away?"

Maddie had a new insight into the scope of his isolation. "I had no idea! I imagined people like you led these idyllic lives, going to glittering parties, jetting off on a moment's whim, doing anything and everything possible." She looked away from him as that all too familiar sympathetic warmth, the one that consistently got her into trouble in the past, enveloped her heart.

He went on, "There are only two things of any importance in my life, Monika and acting."

Here it comes, Maddie. Outside relationships are not on his important list. Well, tell me something I don't already know!

He paused, lost in thought. "I can't trust my impressions...about people, I mean. More often than not I get slapped in the face with ulterior motives just when I think I can trust." He glanced at Maddie but couldn't see her eyes in the deepening shadows.

He doesn't know yet that he can trust me. I give my time, offer my home, ask nothing in return and get mistrusted. Perfectly logical to me! She gazed fixedly at the darkening pink and blue streaked sky.

"Do you realize I could make an absolutely lousy picture and it would still gross millions! I am at a point in my career where the public will pay to see me do just about anything. I find that totally depressing."

"You wouldn't—couldn't—do a lousy job and you know

it," Maddie observed still staring ahead of her, telling herself to say what she felt, not what might please him. "You're a consummate actor. If movies are depressing you, maybe it's time to take a break and make a complete move back to the stage. Personally, I hope you continue your stage work, even take it to the East Coast. You and Ben could give Broadway a welcome transfusion of American blood!"

"You think I could do that?"

"If your bank account can survive the drop in salary, you should treat yourself to facing those New York critics and showing them how a real actor does it. Maybe movies wouldn't look so bad to you with a heavy dose of live performance buoying up your return to them."

Bret leaned towards her. "Do you really think so? For so long, I've needed to talk to someone who...who knows the business."

Great, I know the business! He can't see that I see so clearly what makes him tick, that he wants Broadway so much he can almost taste it! Maddie leaned her chin on her hand, wondering where she was hiding when fatal charms were given out. *If I had even one alluring quality, I wouldn't be sitting here now...listening to...*

Suddenly, he rose, walked to the far end of the terrace, stood for a moment and walked back towards her. Sitting beside her on the glider, she felt his warmth against her side. *Oh, please, please, say something about us. Do something...reach out to me! You have to do it first! I can't. I have to know you feel something for me before I can let go! Hug me. Do something, please!*

"I've just made a couple of big decisions," he announced, rocking the swing with his heel. "First of all, you will stop calling me Bret."

"Oh, really. What do you want me to call you now? Mr. Atkins?" she asked, her heart beating a staccato in anticipation of what might come next.

"Very funny," he quipped, nudging her with his elbow.

If he slaps me on the back, like I'm one of the guys, I'll positively kill him!

Maddie closed her eyes and held her breath. "Bret is a business name. He's work and the public image. I told the cast to call me Paul because it's my real name, Paul Davidoff. We were going to be living like family for a month and I hate family or close friends calling me Bret. So, first decision, call me Paul from now on. Second decision... I'm going to talk your ear off."

She exhaled slowly as her heart descended from her throat and he proceeded to meander through a retrospective of his films, beginning at picture number one, critiquing himself through the years. What he had to say would have been exceedingly valuable to any student of cinema.

I should have had the foresight to put on a wire instead of wasting my time with lipstick and eye shadow. She closed her eyes, trying to quell the residual excitement which persisted. His soft, low voice lulled her and she drifted away on it.

"Maddie!" Once again he changed the subject unexpectedly, jolting her from her quiet place with no idea how much time had passed. "I've talked for ages, completely lost track of time, and you've stayed here without dying of boredom or telling me to shut up. I'm amazed at how comfortable I feel with you. It's like being with Nancy again!"

Maddie, still distracted in trying to collect herself, asked, "Nancy?"

"My wife, Nancy."

She turned away from him. *Nancy! Being with me has to be like being with her to be any good? I will not have my identity planted in her memory, even just for a friendship!* Turning, she looked at him. *What an idiot you are, Maddie! You let yourself imagine he could possibly be interested in you, even though you vowed you wouldn't. Look at him! If he came from another planet, we couldn't be less suited for each other. Now, put the icing on the cake, Maddie! I had a husband I don't want to remember and he's looking for his wife's twin. Two aliens!*

She demanded her head rule her heart and asked, "You know why you feel comfortable with me? We're kindred souls. I don't think either of us has a truly close friend outside of our families, someone we can talk to. You've found I'm as careful as you about who gets close. We recognize our mutual poverty. What could be more comfortable?"

He stopped swinging the glider and Maddie knew she had to move away from his closeness if she was to remain in control of herself. She got up, walked to the edge of the terrace and turned in his direction. "I'll be very honest with you. It hasn't been easy, associating with Bret Atkins. I've been a fan of yours for ages..."

"Ages?"

"Whitney can't remember when you weren't around. That qualifies as an age."

He groaned.

"As I was saying, I've been a fan of yours for...years. Better? I knew I'd have to be an expert at controlling things like fainting and hyperventilating in order to be with you at the theater. Now, I don't think about it at all because you're a part of real-life, not a fantasy anymore. So, I didn't give off the usual breathless vibes you get and your over-all reaction to me has reflected it."

"Reflected what?"

She turned away from him to steel herself to say, "That friendship is our agenda. Actually, it's only logical. The whole world knows you, and I'm not certain my mailman will recognize me tomorrow. People who surround you, the rich, pampered, powerful, are from a completely different world than mine. I've never moved in those circles. It's the workers, the ones who make theater happen, the underlings, the ones you and your peers hire and fire; those are my people and I love them. Talk about two different worlds."

"You make it sound like *Upstairs, Downstairs*! I'm not the master, and you're not the maid!" *She can't be serious!* "I thought you saw Paul, saw inside to the real me. No, I didn't just think it, I knew you did," he stated emphatically.

She stared across the dim-lit terrace, focusing on the shadows rather than on him. "I don't know what I'm supposed to... What do you want from me?"

He approached her slowly, saying, "I don't...I guess I want...You're so special, Maddie. You remind me so much of Nancy. We loved to sit and talk. I guess I always did most of the talking and she'd just listen. Look what we've done right here tonight. You reacted the same as she used to."

Maddie looked down at her hands resting on the wrought iron railing. *His wife again! We've been out here almost two hours, alone, and all I've accomplished is to remind him of his dead wife. If I'm so like her why doesn't he...he didn't even try to hold my hand! What a stupid fool you are, Maddie, even thinking for a second he would be attracted to you. Let me out of this! I want to be anywhere else but here.*

She moved away from him but he followed her. She sat on a wicker chair and he brought another close to it, sitting directly in front of her. He placed himself so he effectively trapped her. She prayed she wouldn't scream while he extolled his wife as his closest friend and advisor, his lover, his critic, his very life and reminisced about the caring relationship he and his Nancy had shared.

Their marriage was everything mine wasn't. Nancy lived my dream with him! Maddie fought to show no emotion. *Running away will solve nothing. I can't escape from myself!*

In that moment of silence he sat back and stared at her. *It's only logical we stop at friendship? She didn't say that's what she wants though. Come at her out of the blue. See how she reacts.* He stretched his legs far enough so that his feet touched her chair and stated, "It must have surprised you that, in the many times we've been alone, I've never made a pass at you."

Maddie's already simmering low self-esteem and insecurities boiled over. She lied in a too loud, tense voice, "Good Lord, no! I never dreamt you would."

"Why not!" he demanded, sitting forward, trying to discern if she was serious or if it was another one of her jokes.

Maddie, feeling increasingly vulnerable, sighed heavily. "Men your age don't bother seducing women my age. You, more than anyone else I know, can get any sweet young thing or out-and-out sex goddess you take a fancy to. Young or sexy I'm not! To tell you the truth, if you'd tried anything, you would have choked on my dust as I headed for the hills."

"Jokes! Always jokes!" he exclaimed. "I'm sorry I raised my voice but I couldn't help it! You have a quick line put-off for serious things. Now, I want an answer, a real answer. What would you have done?"

"I, no doubt, would have fallen for it and disappointed the Hell out of you!" she said quietly though shaken by her unintentional admission of a deeply hidden secret. The only lovers she'd had, her husband and Vic, had concentrated on self-satisfaction, not mutual gratification. She feared her lack of sexual sophistication was an acute handicap.

Before Paul could go on, Monika and Whitney ran through the kitchen and burst onto the terrace.

"And what, pray tell, have you two been up to on this heavenly, starlit night?" Whitney asked, winking at a giggling Monika. "Anything we should tell the media?"

He waited for Maddie to answer but she remained silent, lost in a private nightmare of herself in bed with him, unable to respond, torrid as an iceberg.

"Here's your headline: Atkins Swings in the Hollywood Hills." He moved away from Maddie and walked to the glider, pushing it into motion as he sat.

Monika ran to him and sat on his lap. "Come on, Maddie. There's room for you!"

"Last time I swung with anyone, Kennedy was President. Just another of the many things at which I'm out of practice." She turned to Whitney and asked if she would drive Bret back to The Genny. "Monika needs sleep. I'll take care of her." She called over her shoulder as she walked across the terrace, "Meet you in the kitchen after you say good night, Monika."

Maddie continued on toward the house and Paul, wanting to stop her, stood, forgetting Monika was on his knee. He caught her before she fell and hugged her to him saying huskily, "Sorry, you know I'd never hurt you. You'll always love me, won't you, Puddin'?"

Monika returned the hug and nodded her head but her eyes sought out Whitney who looked towards her mother's departing figure and back to Monika in confused silence. She hugged her father harder and looked over his shoulder at the sky. *Star light, star bright, first star I see tonight. Wish I may, wish I might, have the wish I wish tonight. Maddie and Dad, please, oh please! Maddie and Dad.*

XII

"*O*h, Maddie, please," Monika begged, beseeching her father with her eyes to speak up.

"I think it's a great idea," Paul responded. As Monika pulled Maddie to a wicker chair, Paul added, "Join us for Christmas. We've never had company other than my folks over the holidays." Monika stood in front of her seated quarry and commenced a litany of reasons why Christmas would be so much better for them all if Maddie were at the Atkins' house. "And last, but not least, you're not going to have a big Christmas tree. We've got the biggest one ever and we all can help trim it and..."

"Hold it." Maddie smiled, taking Monika's hands in hers and bringing her around to stand next to her. "I would love to come, but—don't say a word until I finish, Monika—but I have to do a Mass with Whitney on Christmas Eve. Father is depending on us for music. And besides, I've never missed a Christmas with my daughter. As far as the tree is concerned, I'm sure the shipping company will finally locate my missing ornaments, and we'll do it right next year."

"Can I talk now?" Monika let out the breath she'd been holding. "The Mass...can't you get someone to do it for you?"

"It's too late now. Everyone who can carry a tune on a tray is already hired to work on Christmas."

"I knew you'd say you couldn't go because of the Mass," Whitney chimed in, as she reentered the room from her bedroom. "I just called Father John, and he said he'd love for me to do it alone. Now I can experiment without you turning up your nose at the newer music." She turned to Monika. "One problem down; one to go." She faced Maddie again. "You go, and I'll get up there after Mass. You'll have your baby with you on Christmas Day."

"I wouldn't hear of you driving up that coast alone at night!" Maddie protested. "It's far better if I stay here."

Monika's broad grin at Whitney's solution fell to a frown with Maddie's arguments.

Paul stepped in. "She wouldn't have to drive up alone. Ben is planning to join us on Christmas Eve. I'm sure he wouldn't mind waiting for his favorite niece to finish up at church and the two of them come up together."

Maddie looked at Whitney for support, but she simply smiled in response. "I guess you've removed all the stumbling blocks. It's such an inconvenience," she said to Paul. "I mean for Marina. It's not fair to ruin her holiday."

"She doesn't celebrate her holiday until January, the

Russian Orthodox calendar," Paul explained. "It's the only winter holiday she's ever known. She and Boris disappear after New Year's week every year. So, now that that's cleared up, why don't the three of us drive up the coast on Saturday, after rehearsal."

Maddie looked again at Whitney, and still finding no help there, said, "What can I say?"

Monika hugged her. "Yes! You can say yes! Oh, it's going to be so wonderful! Dad, come over here with me. We have to make some plans." She led him to the far side of the terrace.

Whitney approached her mother, "Do you think you could look about half as excited as Monika. It'll be fine—really it will. We'll be together on Christmas and that's all that counts. If you should need to escape for a while, and that place is as big as you say, you could wander off alone to 'sightsee' without raising any eyebrows."

"That would be fine if there wasn't a major complication. I haven't told you about last night yet. We'll talk later, after he's gone."

Paul and Monika approached them. Maddie rose quickly. "Whitney, would you please take Bret..."

He cleared his throat and stared at her.

"Oh, I forgot. Will you take...Paul back to the Genny and I'll stay with Monika." She expected Whitney to question the "Paul," not knowing Monika had already filled her in on the name-game.

"No need to drive me, Whitney," Paul said, looking at his watch. "Ben had to come to a meeting in L.A. tonight and he's picking me up any time now. You're off the hook."

Ben called "Hello" as he came around the house to the terrace and joined the foursome. What a great looking family they'd make but something wasn't quite right. He noted the subtle division, Chases to the left, Atkinses to the right. This pudding clearly needed a little stirring!

Maddie told Monika to say good-bye to her father so he wouldn't keep Ben waiting.

"I'm in no hurry. Kissing good-bye should never be rushed." Ben noted Maddie's deliberate departure from the scene camouflaged by her collecting the dessert plates and glasses from the table and heading for the kitchen. Not escaping his attention either were Paul's eyes following her every move.

Paul had noted a subtle change in Maddie, a certain reserve, which had settled on her after their talk. He dogged her steps to the house and quietly informed her, "I haven't forgotten what you said last night. I have every intention of finding out what you meant." Knowing he could say or do nothing substantive until they were alone again, at his home, he turned on his heel and was gone.

"We should have lots of fun," Ben agreed, as Monika regaled him with her plans for him over Christmas.

Maddie smiled and glanced towards Monika, asking Ben with her eyes not to instigate more talk about the visit.

Ben greeted Monika with a hug when she and Maddie arrived at the theater and asked her what she really, really wanted for Christmas. "Don't answer me right away! I'll give you all morning to think. Tell me before you leave this afternoon." The shouted question of a lighting technician interrupted them and he rushed across the stage.

That morning, like the three preceding it, Monika watched her dad rehearse. She also studied Maddie working with Matt, fascinated by all the unseen details involved in making a show run. *Everybody seems to love what they were doing. What a nice thing to get paid for doing what you love. I'll try out for the theater club next term. If I can't act, I'll be a Maddie.*

Two hours later Ben and Mark wished everyone a merry Christmas and happy Hanukkah and dismissed cast and crew until January 2. It had been a day of technical flukes and potential cast disasters, a day everyone was glad to see come to an end.

Monika and Maddie waited outside, walking the triangle formed between the dorm, the theater, and the car. As they headed from the theater towards the car for the third time, Paul emerged from the dorm.

Maddie fished her keys out of her pocket and headed for her car, trying not to stare at him. *Cream turtleneck, brown slacks...and cashmere too. If only, just once, he would look bad, I could hold on to that image and make my life easier!*

At the driver's door, Paul silently extended his hand for the keys. Maddie hadn't gotten the silent treatment in ten years. Her husband had been the world's champion at it. How dare Paul act like him! She had thought he was nothing like him! Maddie crawled into the back seat, sliding over behind Monika, muttering all the way.

Not even Monika spoke as they rode through the narrow roads of the Genesian compound. She couldn't wait until they were home. Marina was going to have a harder job than Monika had thought. She was so sure this time down here would do something good. Instead, her dad was scowling in the front seat, and Maddie was so ticked she was talking to herself in the back!

Paul slowed the car as they approached the huge iron gates at the entrance. About 100 feet back from them, he pulled over, parked and got out.

"Dad, what are you doing?"

Maddie looked at the gauges on the dashboard, painfully aware of her car's recent erratic history. "What's wrong?"

He closed the door, stared seriously at Monika for a moment, and then headed for the gates on foot. He knew Monika was smart enough to stay put and that would force Maddie to stay with her.

Maddie's heart rose to her mouth as the swarm of fans rushed forward.

Monika's eyes opened wide and she visibly tensed.

"What in God's name is he doing?" Maddie gasped under her breath.

The Security Captain deployed his force and the local police were galvanized into action. Paul continued to the gate, said something to the crowd, and the noise level, which had penetrated the cocoon of the car deadening any hope of Maddie or Monika hearing his words, died down a little. He signed autographs, posed for pictures and shook hands for the next fifteen minutes. Those iron gates standing between him and the fans couldn't prevent one of the hand shakers from breaking his wrist or, if there was a real nut out there, slashing him.

"Daddy used to do this, but there are so many people now, he hasn't done it for a long time."

Maddie rubbed her face with both hands, as if to erase the panic, and tried to think of something she could do. She jerked her hands away as the car door was pulled open. "What the hell is going on here, Maddie?" Ben shouted over the crowd noise.

"He did this on the spur of the moment. Neither of us knew what was going on when he pulled over." Maddie asked him to get in so they could talk. "Do things look under control over there or is it just my wishful thinking working overtime?"

"Looks it," Ben said, eying the area ahead. "He'll be okay, I hope. You've had quite a day, Monika."

Maddie looked towards the gate again and saw Paul heading back to the car. Ben exited the driver's seat and Paul looked surprised to see him but didn't miss a step. In fact, the two men stood talking for a few minutes while Maddie and Monika sat in silence. Paul escorted Ben to his trusty golf cart, and, before getting back into the car, watched Ben drive over the first hill.

The crowd at the gate parted as they drove through. "Wasn't that display just a little foolish, considering your daughter is in this car?" Maddie demanded, fright making her sound more angry than she intended.

Paul ignored Maddie and explained to Monika,

"Thought I'd give them a break, give them what they wanted. You know, I really feel good when people who like me show it. They're so pleasant to deal with; they like me and there's no question about it, no mysteries. I guess I never see the people who don't like me. They stay away. No, I take that back. Sometimes there will be someone who is stuck in the middle, the gray area dweller, the one who doesn't like me but is forced, for one reason or another, to be around me. Just like fog...I ask a question and get completely lost in the vague answer. It's like walking into the pea soup fog that sometimes blinds us at home."

Monika tried to lighten the mood, suspecting through her confusion that his comments were directed at Maddie. "Hey, Dad, you could get elected President tomorrow. Those people don't like you; they love you! I could be first daughter. Marina could have her own housekeeper and Maddie—"

Paul interrupted, "...can be spokesperson for our administration. She's so good at enigmatic statements."

Maddie steeled herself but said nothing, closing her eyes and mouth, staying out of everything. *I'm going for Monika,* she reminded herself. *Poor little rich girl! Has everything but what she really needs and wants. Oh, shut up, Maddie. It's just for over Christmas, three days at the most. Make her happy, break her heart in the new year when the show ends.*

It wasn't long before the distances lengthened between traffic build-ups. Maddie concentrated on the coastline as they headed north. She could study the scenery on this trip since she didn't have to watch the road, and she didn't want to look unoccupied. Despite Monika's attempts to include her in her front seat small talk, Maddie remained silent.

By three o'clock they pulled up to the gates of the Atkins' residence and Maddie realized how much she'd overlooked her first time there. The long driveway into the property was lined with flowering shrubs which formed a privacy screen for the Mediterranean-style house, situated on the higher of two cliffs. A stone fountain, surrounded by neat symmetrical gardens of red and white flowers, dominated the central courtyard.

Paul helped Maddie from the back seat but hadn't a word for her. *Merry Christmas, Mr. Scrooge. Are all men alike? I really thought you were different. More fool you, Maddie!*

Marina greeted them with a huge smile at the front door and a tray full of Christmas cookies, hot tea, coffee, and cocoa. She was delighted to see Monika. It was obvious she'd seen something in Paul's face because she refrained from speaking to him, waiting to be spoken to first. She served the drinks and snacks in the living room, listened to Monika's minute-by-minute account of her stay with Maddie and Whitney and studied the still silent Paul with short, probing glances.

"Come on, Maddie," Monika coaxed, taking her hand and pulling her from her chair, "I want you to see your room. It's just down the hall from mine so we can have those fun bedtime talks while you're here too." She turned to her father, "Dad, did I tell you about the great talks Maddie and I had before we went to sleep each night?"

"No. Glad you had fun...Marina, I'll be in my room until dinner. Absolutely no calls or visitors and that means you too, Puddin'." He got up and walked out without another word.

Monika lost her battle against a frown and shrugged to Maddie. They followed him up the staircase. He turned to the right and disappeared through the French doors at the end of the hall.

Maddie watched in silence and realized Monika was staring at her. "Come on, Maddie, your room is down here." They walked to the second door on the left and Monika swung it open with a flourish.

"Oh, my heavens," Maddie whispered as she entered a room she fell in love with instantly. It was a dream of silk curtains, pleated bed canopy and matching spread, everything coordinated to the pastels of the French Aubusson rug.

Monika ran across the room and threw open lace-curtained French doors, revealing a balcony rife with flowers, bobbing their heads in the breeze, and a view of the Pacific that seemed endless.

Maddie sat on the edge of the chaise lounge near the bed. Monika approached and looked at her worriedly.

"I'm fine, Monika, just overcome by all this! It's the most beautiful room I've ever seen! Did you choose this one for me?"

Monika nodded and suddenly sat next to Maddie, hugging her. "Please, don't get so mad at Dad that you'll leave us. Please!"

"Where did that come from?" Maddie asked, holding Monika tighter and then leaning back to see her face.

Monika turned away, fighting tears, and walked to the balcony doorway silently.

"Excuse me for a few minutes," Maddie said, deciding there and then to settle what was bothering Paul, knowing very well it all centered on her. She walked to his door and raised her hand to knock but hesitated. Hearing Monika step into the hallway, she willed her knuckles to strike the wood and waited for an answer but none came. Knocking again, she had the same results. Turning to Monika she was given a signal to try the doorknob. Maddie shook her head but Monika persisted. Finally, she turned the knob and the door swung open, far further than she'd intended.

His room was large, the mahogany furniture heavy and gleaming in the late afternoon light. An over-sized maroon leather chair was turned toward one of the two bay windows, it's back facing the door. "I said no visitors. Go away before whoever it is gets into more trouble than they want!"

Maddie closed the door but placed herself inside the room. She walked slowly towards the chair, the thick oriental carpet deadening any sound. Peering over the high padded back, she saw his hands first, closed into fists on the chair's arms. Stepping a little to the side, she could see his profile and the shine of a tear on his cheek.

She froze in a tumult of emotions. *I should never have come near this room. I shouldn't be seeing this. Can I get back to the door without him hearing me?*

"Nancy?" he said, pushing himself up suddenly from the chair. He turned and saw a confused and scared Maddie. "What the Hell! How long have you been...God, I can't even find peace in my own home!"

Maddie turned and retreated as fast as she could toward the door.

"Come back here!" he demanded but she didn't stop. As she reached the door, he swung it shut in her face with a slam. He stepped in front of her and she turned away, looking for another way out, declaring, "No one speaks to me in that tone of voice! Who do you think you are?! I come in here to—"

"To what?" Paul demanded, walking towards her.

She backed away, matching his forward motion with her retreat. "To...to try to make peace with you...for Monika's sake. This is supposed to be a happy time of the year and you're acting like...like...Scrooge!" On the final word, her back hit a wall.

"Are you all right? You heard me say I didn't want to be...."

"I told you why I came in here. You didn't think I was coming into your bedroom for...! Well, of all the conceited...Words fail me!" Maddie stated angrily, holding firmly to her spot, and, despite her declaration of speechlessness, proceeded with an angry diatribe. "I have more respect for myself than to throw myself at anyone! You didn't get the response from me you expected the other night and you've been like a caged lion since. Now you're stuck with me in your house. If you'd been honest and open enough to admit that...that you're unhappy having me anywhere around you for the holiday, I would get some good motivation for trying to pretend I'm having a good time."

Paul stared incredulously. "You even argue like Nancy. It's incredible! If you have a mole on your left hip..."

"That's it! I'm out of this house!" Maddie snapped and vowed she wouldn't let herself cry though throughout her life, when she was truly angry and upset, tears were uncontrollable.

"What's the problem? Nancy?" Paul asked, confused by her vehemence. "I couldn't pay you a higher compliment than to compare you to Nancy."

Maddie grabbed him by the shoulders and tried to shake him. "Wake up! Look at me! For God's sake, look at me! I'm not Nancy! I'm not your dream come true. I'm just plain Maddie. The truth for me is that I'm so far out of my league with you, it's pitiful! I'm not beautiful. I'm not famous. I'm not Nancy! Just me, myself, and I. Like it or not, I'm me. Me! ME! Why isn't Maddie, just Maddie, good enough?...I'll tell you the truly pitiful part for me. You've turned out to be just like every other man in my life. They've all expected me to be someone or something else. Maddie was never enough for them. I didn't realize it before, but I've been living a fantasy; this whole thing with you at the theater has been a fantasy. I thought you liked Maddie, me. I thought you were so different!"

Paul was stunned and while he was lost in a chaos of thoughts, Maddie stepped around him and ran for her room.

Monika, waiting in the hall, jumped out of Maddie's way and ran into her father's room. "What happened?"

"All I said was she's just like your mother and she went crazy."

"Oh, Daddy," Monika said, hugging him. "Why can't she just be Maddie. Why does she have to be someone else too?"

Paul held her at arms length. "That someone else happens to be your mother!"

Monika tried to get closer but he held her back. She almost whispered, "My mother is dead, she's not here. Maddie is."

He stared stonily at her for a moment, grabbed his jacket from the end of the bed and left the room.

Marina tried to enter and he brushed by her in the doorway. Monika clung to her and told her what she'd heard and said. "If you're all right, I'll look in on Mrs. Chase. See if I can't make things better. Why don't you watch television now?"

Monika kissed her cheek and headed for the den on the first floor.

"Mrs. Chase, I may talk to you?" Marina asked, tapping softly of Maddie's door.

Maddie stopped packing the clothes Marina had unpacked less than an hour before and walked to the door. "There's really nothing to talk about, except maybe a train or bus schedule back to L.A."

"Please, listen to me. You must know some things but first I ask you to excuse my English. I can get mixed up when I have much to say. Now, before you make any moves, please come with me." She led Maddie onto the balcony. In the late afternoon the trees appeared etched against the winter gray sky. Marina pointed to the other cliff.

"What's so unusual? He's standing on the cliff. So what?" Maddie tried to appear disinterested but her eyes drifted involuntarily back to the cliff.

Marina folded her arms and planted her feet firmly. "You are not stupid, Maddie. He is not stupid. Why is understanding each other so hard? He knew when he met you at the studio party you were— special."

"He talked about me after the party?" Maddie pulled her gaze away from him and to Marina.

"He didn't have to say a word to me or Monika. It was easy to see the change in him, that something had happened. We started to count the times he talked of that night. We were like—like detectives, finding clues and they all pointed to you." Marina watched Maddie wander to one of the flower urns and pretend to smell the flowers, all the while adjusting her angle to better see the cliff.

"He's all right out there, isn't he?" Maddie inquired, remembering his mood.

"My husband watches, but Pavel doesn't know it."

"Pavel, Russian for Paul, right?"

"Da! Gavareet po Ruski?" Marina inquired, amazed there might be yet another shared likeness to Nancy.

"I speak very little I'm afraid; used to work with some Russian musicians and learned a little from them. I wish I'd had time to learn more and speak it well but...you know how crowded life can get sometimes."

"I also know that planning to make something happen doesn't work. Monika felt if she got you here in Pavel's house, you and he would—you know—fall in love. She made plans to leave you two alone at the right time. And the magic of the season, the holiday. She thought it would make something good happen. Well, she was right, something happened, but it came too early and went all wrong. Please, tell me what he said that made you so mad. I am not nosing—no, no—prying. I think I already know and, if I'm right, I need to—to tell you some things so you can understand."

Maddie was loathe even to remember let alone talk about it. She thought of Monika, looked back to the cliff and reconsidered. "I'm not being disrespectful, but please tell me something. Was Nancy some kind of a saint?"

Marina sighed. She had thought right, and now she was going to try to correct a wrong. "If I didn't know Nancy for the months she was alive after I came to work, I would say she was a— sorceress who'd put a spell on this man forever. The only power she still has over him is his memory of their life, the life he'd dreamed of and shared with her, that lasted only three short years. They weren't together long enough to have the bad times every marriage goes through. It was a beautiful time, and to him she was perfect. He wants that back. Even after twelve years, he wants it back."

"Marina, I am not Nancy. I can't be someone else, especially someone I never knew. If I have that image in his mind, what will happen when I disappoint him for the first time? It'll happen, sure as there'll be daylight tomorrow, and he'll experience something worse than pain. I'll have let him down, but so will Nancy. Am I to be condemned twice for every minor flaw? I...I can't...I won't put myself up as a target for that kind of grief." Maddie glanced back at the cliff, almost silhouetted in the now deepening shadows. "Marina, may I confide in you?"

Nodding her head, Marina led Maddie back through the doorway to the bedroom, insuring that Paul wouldn't see them. She knew he would be heading back towards the house any minute. Maddie sat on the edge of the canopied bed and gripped a bed post for stability as she confessed for the first time aloud what she was really feeling. "Marina, I've never been so scared. Without the gory details, believe me, my life has been one thorny patch after another where men are concerned. I vowed off any more serious involvements a few years ago. In August I found out I was going to be working with a man I've adored from afar for twenty years. I fought every urge in my battered body, but couldn't prevent the inevitable. My dream man turned out to be more perfect than I thought. Marina, I figured he hung around me because he didn't want to talk shop with the other actors. I never once thought it was because he was truly interested in me."

Marina stood closer to the bed. "And why wouldn't he be interested?"

"Look at me! I can't compete with the kind of beauty that surrounds him, with people who have the money to look perfect, with the club crowd, the ladies who do nothing but pamper themselves, shop, do lunch, and look gorgeous. I grew up and lived most of my married life in the suburbs. I've worked every day since my husband died. I'm peanut butter and jelly; he's caviar."

"You're talking about outside things," Marina pointed out. "And the caviar— He worked his way up to it but still prefers tuna fish. Let me tell you something about the people around him. He sees gorgeous women every day, true, but he says their beauty stops at their faces. He's looking for beauty on the inside. You are an attractive woman, but it's what shines through you from your heart and soul that is your true beauty. It shows—in your eyes. That's what he saw the night of the party."

Maddie remembered the effect his eyes had had on her and shook her head to clear away the still resultant fuzziness. "It would be better for everyone concerned if I just get out of here before one of us says something we can't take back. I have to work with him for five more weeks and it would be easier if we were at least on speaking terms."

Marina looked Maddie directly in the eyes. "You haven't said what I wait to hear, that you're not in love with him."

"Ah, yes, I almost forgot. Russians tend to be brutally frank and to the point. All right. I don't think I am yet, but I could very easily fall for him if I knew he felt something for me, Maddie, not me Nancy-nearly. If I leave right now, I'd honestly miss Monika more than him. She at least accepts me for what I am and likes what she's found."

"Please, Maddie, don't leave before dinner. I've worked all day on this, and I will ruin the recipe when I put hemlock in his portion because our guest-of-honor is gone. He is a good man. Please, give all of us another chance, at least through dinner."

Maddie rose and kissed the housekeeper on the cheek. "For you, I'll stay. Should I wear formal or just everyday armor to this battle?"

"Armor? Oh, battle—armor. Da! Please, anything but blue if you want to change his thoughts. It was Nancy's favorite color."

"Thanks for the warning and thank you very much for the talk. I promise I'll come to the table an observer, not a combatant. I'd like to see something different from him, something oriented to me. Oh well, if I don't, I won't be disappointed because I really don't expect it."

Marina closed the bedroom door as she left Maddie. She had watched Paul on the cliff far more closely than Maddie knew. *He wasn't pacing. That was all Maddie in his head out there. I won't talk to him. He needs to figure out what's going wrong himself, with no help from anyone except his own heart. Oh, da, he's hooked!*

She descended the staircase humming "Jingle Bells." Monika and Boris came from two different directions at the unaccustomed sound of her voice.

"Come on you two," Marina ordered, clasping hands with each of them. "Help me finish getting the food ready and to the table. Monika, keep your fingers crossed and your mouth closed if anything starts up between them at the table. This is going to be a tough test for him and her."

Monika, groaned, "Wonderful. If he flunks, so do I!"

XIII

*T*ony and Ben ran into each other in the lobby short-ly after the last cast member left. "Have a nice holiday, Ben."

"Thought you'd already left, Tony. Heading back to the Big Apple?" Ben inquired as he checked the last areas of his domain before leaving it closed and alone for the holidays.

"No. Everyone of any importance to me is working,

believe it or not! Only problem is they're all on the road. It's some kind of show biz miracle when everyone you know can pay the rent. Thought I'd go into L.A. Any restaurant recommendations?"

Ben checked the circuit breaker box hidden behind a framed artist's rendering of the Genesius Theater as he said, "Hey, no one should be alone on Christmas. Get your bag packed and we'll leave here tomorrow at five. I'm sure Santa can find you up at the Atkins spread."

Tony hesitated just long enough for Ben to add, "Don't worry about being one too many. His place is almost as big as the dorm. You've mentioned New York so many times in the past week. We all thought that's where you were headed. If he'd suspected you were going to be alone, I know he would have asked you."

Tony couldn't stop the smile which lit up his face. "I'd love to, if you think it's all right."

"I'll give him a call, and we can drive up tomorrow. First we'll go to dinner and then to church."

Tony stared at him.

Ben smiled and said, "You old reprobate! It's time you got a little religion back in your life. Whitney's singing at St. Francis, and after that the three of us will head north. Maddie's already there."

"She's gone to..." Tony exclaimed, "what's going on that I don't know anything about?"

Ben locked the house doors and, putting his hand on Tony's shoulder, walked with him to the main entrance. "According to Whitney, not as much as she and Monika expected. I guess getting her up there, into his house, is their last ditch effort. I drove him home from Maddie's two nights ago and expected to hear something from him. Not a blinkin' word!"

"And Maddie?"

Ben turned serious and paused on the top step, "Whitney says Maddie's told her anything serious between he and Bret is impossible. Something about her identity or some such thing. I don't understand any of it anymore."

Tony linked his arm through Ben's and they headed for the dorm. "You know, Ben, I would bet my membership in the Gay Men's Chorus that those two haven't even kissed yet. I think if that situation's remedied, things will move towards some kind of conclusion. It shouldn't be hard at this time of the year."

Ben looked sideways at him.

"Don't glare at a genius at work, Ben. We have a purchase to make before we pick up Whitney. Mistletoe! It may sound like a stupid idea, but look at how stupid this whole situation is. The plan's so dumb it will probably work!"

Maddie descended the staircase dressed in her power color pant suit, cardinal red softened only by the fact it was a shimmering velvet.

Monika ran down behind her. "Wow, you look like a beautiful Christmas gift! Dad will..." She wished she hadn't started the sentence.

Ignoring Monika's last works, Maddie took her hand as they continued descending the long, curving stairs, and said, "Thank you so much; glad you like it. By the way, I'm putting a present under the tree for you, but it's just a little something for the day. Your real present is that you and I are going shopping before I go home. Maybe we can find something as pretty as that outfit you wore to the *Othello,* or you can pick out whatever you would like."

"Then that means you're not going home after dinner?"

Maddie smiled at her and said, "Not on your life, pussycat. I came up here to be with you, and that's exactly what I intend to do."

Monika smiled happily, and in her excitement, she almost dragged Maddie across the hallway.

Maddie had been trying to identify the aromas coming

from the kitchen since she left her bedroom. By the time she reached the dining room doorway she was ravenous for whatever the unidentifiable delicacy was that smelled so good.

Paul was already seated at the head of the table. His back to the entrance.

Maddie hesitated, suddenly afraid she would lose her temper again if he so much as looked at her, only then realizing how hurt she really was. Trying to put as much distance as possible between herself and him, she walked to the far end of the long table and sat to the right of the empty chair at the opposite end.

"If you read the place cards, you'll find you're in the wrong spot," Paul instructed Maddie as Boris led two people, an older couple, into the room.

Maddie took advantage of the upset of Paul and Monika greeting the newly arrived guests to look for her name. As she hoped, it was opposite Monika, and as she feared, it was to Paul's left.

"...and Mom and Dad, I'd like to introduce Maddie Chase," Paul said as Maddie arrived at her assigned chair.

All she heard was her name, missing whom she was being introduced to. She extended her hand to the gentleman. "So nice to meet you..."

Monika suspected Maddie hadn't a clue who she was meeting. "Poppa, this is the lady I told you about. You know, at the Genny."

Maddie smiled. *Oh, good grief! It's Paul's parents!* "Merry Christmas, Mr. and Mrs. Davidoff. What a pleasant surprise. Nobody mentioned you would be here tonight."

"Please, no formality here," Paul's father said, sliding Maddie's chair out for her. "Call me Pete and this is Anna." Sitting next to Maddie, he looked at Paul, winking, "This is what I call a beautiful surprise. What a nice addition to our holidays!"

Anna and Monika talked about school. Pete talked to Maddie about the Genny. Boris and Marina were busy with the food in the kitchen. Paul's silence appeared to be discounted by everyone else but Maddie.

Uncomfortably aware he was actually watching and listening, she wondered whether he was waiting for his father to marvel at how much she reminded him of Nancy!

Marina entered, placed a covered silver platter before Paul and Maddie and stood back from the table. Paul turned to Maddie and said, "Why don't you do the honors?"

Without looking in his direction, she lifted the handled cover and finally recognized the aroma, Peking duck.

Monika laughed at the look of pleasure which crept over Maddie's features. "Dad remembered how much you said you liked this and so rarely have it because you keep forgetting to order ahead. Look at all the different parts to it! How do you put all this together?" She walked behind Paul's chair to Maddie and watched her fold the meat, sauce and scallion inside the thin Chinese crepe.

"Okay, Nana and Poppa, I'll make yours. Maddie's so great! She makes almost everything fun, even eating!"

Maddie, for a moment, forgot the tension of the afternoon. Monika's happiness became infectious as she began filling crepes for everyone at the table, forgetting only one person, herself.

Maddie reached across to her with the one she'd made before Monika took over. Monika leaned forward and took a bite. Laughing at her "Mmm, good!" Maddie took the next bite.

Looking down the table to Marina, Maddie asked, "Did you make this yourself? Marina, this is the best I've ever tasted. You are truly a genius!"

As she spoke, Paul cupped her hand holding the food in his. She turned to him as he moved it towards his mouth. While his eyes held hers, he bit the last piece from her fingers.

Maddie was sure her face matched the color of her suit as his incredibly sexy move and look engulfed her. *Thank God I'm sitting down. I'm melting like ice cream in 100 degree heat! I can't ever remember feeling such...feeling so...Oh, what are you going on about! He's probably pretending I'm Nancy!*

Marina saw everything coming to a sudden halt at the table and she nudged Boris. "You'd think all we were having is the duck. Come on, love, help me bring in the rest of the meal." As they made their way to the kitchen, Marina stopped and, as if in after-thought, said, "Oh, by the way, Maddie, would you mind coming to the kitchen and testing a side dish for me. I want to check something out with you before I serve it."

Maddie left the room in their wake. Marina led her straight to the patio door and opened it. "Get a breath of fresh air. I thought you needed to get out of there for a minute."

Maddie nodded a thank you, unbuttoned her jacket and welcomed the cool air as it crept through her silk blouse. After taking a few deep breaths, she ran her fingers through the damp hair on her forehead.

Marina walked up behind her and observed, "Paul sparked enough heat to rise from you to thaw Siberia. Come-on now, button up, and take this into the table. Boris, the wine, please. I'll take these serving dishes."

Maddie, carrying a serving platter laden with a Marina lobster specialty, walked through the door first. Marina winked at Boris as they brought up the rear.

Paul studied the shelves laden with videos of the latest Hollywood hits as his parents settled themselves onto a large, soft couch. The screening room was lit by a recessed light over the wall shelves and a lively fire in the fireplace.

"Monika certainly is into the spirit this year," his mother observed, watching her son avoid facing them. "She had that tree half trimmed before we arrived. Every other year its been totally bare. I'm glad, really. It took half as long to finish it. Whew, it feels good to sit down."

Paul's silence continued.

"You didn't tell us you'd have company when we

arrived," she continued, determined to make him talk. She looked at Pete and nudged him to speak up.

Pete leaned toward the coffee table, picked up his after-dinner Drambuie and sat back before speaking. "You've said enough tonight to fill a one-page, stamp-sized book, Paul. It seems obvious there's something you have to tell us."

Anna kicked his foot at his bluntness.

"Well, there has to be something! After all, someone new has entered the scene."

"What would you like... adventure, romance, comedy? Got 'em all here," Paul observed, ignoring both his father's comment and innuendo.

Placing his glass back on the table with an audible bang, Pete declared, "We ate dinner with a mute, and now you want to stay that way and shut us up too with a movie. Forget it. We can see you at almost any hour of the day or night on the cable. After driving for a couple of hours to get here, we do not intend to look at you on a screen while you're sitting in the same room with us!"

"Now, now Pete," Anna soothed. She refocused on her son and commented, "Your father's right, you know. If we weren't at that table talking and laughing, I haven't any idea what your guest would have done. It would have been very uncomfortable for her."

"She's not my guest, Mom. Monika asked her here."

"Don't you dare try to stop me, Anna," Pete demanded, sitting forward as Anna pinched his arm. "I'm going to have my say. There is enough heat between you two to...to start a fire, and that's not some kind of hero worship I saw in Monika's eyes whenever she looked at Maddie. Your daughter is clearly in love with this woman. She's chosen her mother. As for you..."

Anna stopped him with a wave of her hand. "Since you opened this to discussion, I want my say too. You were watching Monika, Pete, but I was facing Maddie...and you, my dear son. I could see you judging and weighing every word she said. What became obvious early on was that she was purposely ignoring you. Just when I was convinced she had absolutely no interest in you, you pull that Tom Jones food stunt and the poor woman nearly fell apart! What I particularly loved though was the way you were completely out of reach to everyone, especially her, after that. I felt like I was witnessing some sort of torture and my own son was the anguish-master."

Pete stared at her. "Subtle, Anna, very subtle."

"Now look, Pete, I don't have to or even want to know what's going on in Paul's life that he doesn't choose to tell me of his own free will. But when it touches me directly and, when I see how inextricably Monika is wound into this, I have a perfect right, and, I think, a duty to speak up."

Paul paced while his parents spoke, his arms folded. "I was afraid this would happen. I have never had so much trouble over one woman!"

Anna glanced quickly at Pete and their eyes met for a second in mutual understanding. "Paul, come here, sit beside your mother."

He walked toward the couch but stopped a few feet short of it.

Anna patted the cushion next to her. "I think it's obvious you need to talk. Our son's happiness is the most important thing in our lives. When you've turned to us before you seemed comforted by our insights and actually on some occasions have taken our advice. How about a good, old-fashioned talk?"

Paul turned and walked towards the door. "Would everyone please leave me alone! I can handle this myself. You seem to forget I'm an adult capable of handling...Oh, Hell! Who am I kidding! I can't handle this at all. I don't understand what's going on!" He returned to the couch and sat next to Anna.

Pete retrieved his glass, saying, "Other than finding out ourselves that she's charming and obviously likes Monika, she's an unknown entity. You've never mentioned her to us."

"I know I haven't. Since the night I met her, nothing has been the same for me." He told them of his time at the Genny and the friendship which grew between them.

"Monika appears on the scene, meets Maddie and after that, whenever I talk to my daughter on the phone, the first question out of her mouth is, 'How's Maddie?'"

His mother put her hand on Paul's forearm, saying, "It's very important how Monika feels, but it's far more important, in this case, what's happening for you. You haven't said a word about what you and Maddie feel for each other."

"Mom, I decided to find out what Maddie feels while Monika was visiting with her, just this week. Granted, I didn't come right out, point blank, and tell her how I feel but she has to know by now how interested I am. She's so different. I wouldn't pull any of that Hollywood star stuff on her. You know what's amazing? How much she reminds me of Nancy."

Anna stared at him in concern and asked, "Paul, you didn't mention that to her, did you?"

"Well, of course," Paul answered defensively. "I couldn't give any woman a higher compliment."

"Please, take this as my candid observation, not disrespect," Anna said seriously. "You may think it's a wonderful thing but all it does is create huge problems for her. I'm more than twenty years her senior, but if I were in her shoes with someone like you, I'd resent not being appreciated for just myself. She's a professional in a business that requires a strong individual identity. She's probably had to fight to establish hers. There's obviously a deep sensitivity in her and that is what makes her special, unique to herself. You're telling her she's not unique and that her main worth to you is that she's a carbon copy of someone she never knew. What kind of a life has she had, Paul? Where's she from? Was she married?"

Paul's troubled look increased. "She doesn't offer much about her past. I guess I never really asked. I do know she was married. She has a daughter, an actress. I think I'm afraid I'd fail to measure up to Maddie's husband. Maybe he was some kind of god to her."

"Paul, listen to yourself!" Pete declared. He put his arm around Anna's shoulders. "You've been doing to her what you're so afraid will happen to you. Has she reacted any differently than you would have?"

"Oh, what an absolute idiot I am," Paul moaned, slouching back against the couch. "Not four hours ago I compared her to Nancy and she got so angry I thought she'd be gone before you arrived."

"First time you mentioned her?" Anna asked, stroking Paul's arm where she had been holding it.

"First time she reacted. At least the third time I mentioned her. Okay, Mom and Dad, how do I erase what I've said to her and straighten this out?"

"Daddy! Come here! Quick! Help!"

Paul bolted from the couch with Pete and Anna following close behind, running towards Monika's voice. They found her in the living room, at the Christmas tree. Maddie was perched precariously on top of a step stool, her right arm extended into the upper branches and a look of panic on her face.

"I wanted that ornament you brought back to me from Spain way up high so the long crystals could hang down. Maddie tried to put it near the top for me and her sleeve caught on a branch." She ran to her grandmother as she pleaded, "Don't let her fall!" Paul grabbed the desk chair and placed it next to the step stool. "Dad, if you go upstairs and walk along the balcony, you can free her from above. I'll make sure she doesn't lose her balance." He stepped onto the chair and put his arm around her waist, saying, "Lean on me. I've got you." Though she didn't look it, he was surprised to feel how rigidly she was holding her balance.

Pete appeared above, knelt and reached through the banister railing. His fingers found the offending twigs caught around the sleeve button on Maddie's jacket. Paul reached up and supported Maddie's arm while his father worked from above, tracing the twigs to the main branch and snapping them off at the joining point. Once she was released, Paul tightened his grip on her waist and arm, lifted her to his chair, stepped down first, and helped her down to floor level.

Maddie was embarrassed, and the release of tension made her hands shake. "Monika, that was a show and tell lesson on how to get everyone's attention on a moment's notice. Please do not imitate!"

Pete came huffing and puffing back into the room. "You all right, Maddie? That tree's a vipers' nest up there. Lethal to all comers. Who got this woman-eating tree?"

"Guilty, right out of our own woods," Paul admitted, moving to renew his closeness to Maddie. He approached her and gently rubbed her arm. Relieved that she didn't pull away or hit him, Paul gently, subtly moved her toward the couch. He asked Monika to get her some cold water.

Anna commiserated, "Oh, you poor dear. Come, sit down."

Maddie looked into Anna's eyes and realized how much Paul's eyes resembled hers. "Please, don't worry about me," she said, recovering her composure. "I'm fine. Really! I don't usually have trouble with heights, but you'd never guess it by that performance!"

Paul sat beside her and rubbed her back very lightly. "She's a wizard at the theater. I've seen her up on the top light rigging."

"That's got to be forty feet off the floor!" Pete exclaimed.

Paul stared at him. "That's right! How would you know that?"

Monika returned with the water, handed it to Maddie and sat on the floor, leaning against Maddie's legs as Anna revealed, "We were at your closing night performance."

"Why didn't you come backstage?" Paul exclaimed. "I had no idea you were there."

Maddie couldn't resist. "Who were they going to see

back there that night? You left faster than if a fire was chasing you. Remember?"

His hand stopped in the middle of her back and she turned to him. "My parents know how stupid I am. Do we have to broadcast it to my daughter too?"

Discomforted more by the fact she liked his touch than by the fact he had the nerve to do it after that afternoon's scene, she replied, "Some things are so obvious they don't need words. Now, before I get myself into anymore trouble, I think I'll say good night." She stood, smiled at Pete, Anna and Monika, and started to leave the room.

"Can I still come to your room before I go to bed if I stay up later?" Monika asked, following Maddie to the door.

Maddie hugged her and kissed her forehead. "Of course, you silly goose. The fact I'm in bed doesn't mean I'm asleep. Actually, I think I can guarantee you I'll be awake." She turned back to the living room and wished them all a good night.

Monika returned to where they were seated and wedged herself between her grandparents. She looked intently at her father. "Maddie told me she's staying here only because of me. Dad, do you think you could apologize for yelling at her this afternoon?"

Pete and Anna tried to hide their impending smiles as Paul slouched back against the couch, mumbling, "It takes two to make an argument."

His father cleared his throat.

Paul looked at him sheepishly and continued, "But...I was in the wrong and I promise I'll talk to her in the morning."

"No, Daddy, do it now."

Paul reached across the coffee table and took Monika's hand in his. "I promise you I'll do it, but let me pick the time and place. Right now and in her bedroom? No. She'll be better able to tell me where to go in the morning, after a night of murdering me in her mind."

Monika sighed and leaned her head against Anna's arm.

"Have faith," Anna soothed. "If your father can successfully talk his way out of doing Hollywood's nearly mandatory nude scenes all these years, I'm sure he can find the right words for Maddie."

Paul, as Anna spoke, stood and walked to the tree. He plugged in the light cord and shut the room lights off from a master switch. "Boris does the best job getting those lights so evenly spread out."

He returned to the couch and Monika switched over to sit next to him. "I promise you, Puddin', this is going to be the best holiday ever. Everyone in this house will be smiling on Christmas morning...or else!" He stressed the "or else" with a throat-cutting motion.

Pete smiled at Anna. "That's what I like to hear, the true Christmas spirit." He imitated Paul's gesture, singing, "Peace on earth and mercy mild..."

XIV

A stack of brightly wrapped gifts decorated the corner of Ben's desk. He picked up the top one and tilted his chair back as he read the label, "To Marina and Boris, From Ben." Shaking it gently, he thought, *I wish I had a clue what I'm giving everybody.* A knock on the door interrupted him.

Matt stuck in his head. "Just leaving for the airport. Wanted to say Merry Christmas before I left." Seeing Ben was alone, he walked towards the desk, eyeing the beribboned presents. "You got or you bought?"

Placing the gift in his hand back on the stack, Ben quipped, "Me get? That naughty and nice stuff knocks me right off Santa's list every year!" He glanced at the gifts. "I didn't even buy these. Remember when Maddie disappeared for a few hours yesterday? This is some of why. She ran to the nearest mall and shopped for me and herself, unexpected extras on the gift list, the host, hostess and entourage."

Matt checked his watch, sat down and lit a cigarette. "Car doesn't get here for another fifteen minutes. So...I heard you're all heading back to the Atkins' place. I'm all confused! What is going on between him and Maddie?"

"You're confused!" Ben stated, tilting his chair back to upright. "I swear if by 11:59 on Christmas night those two haven't come to a meeting of the minds...or whatever...I'm going to shoot them both and put us out of their misery."

Matt took a long drag on his cigarette. "She avoided him for weeks and then, all of a sudden, he's at her house night after night. Now she's with him for Christmas and, from what you told me about the incident at the gate, she's probably not talking to him. You're going to walk in on that? Maybe I should wish you a safe Christmas; you may need a flak jacket!"

Ben laughed at his image of Maddie and Bret lobbing bombs at each other from opposite ends of Bret's property. "Tony's bringing a pacifier. Mistletoe! Maybe to ensure success he should bring enough to blanket the ceiling of every room."

Shaking his head, Matt ground out his cigarette as he stood. "Oh, I'm so stupid! The first thing I wanted to say was thank you for the case of Scotch. I never got out of this place to do any shopping, but I intend to bring you back something from Hawaii. How's about...a coconut?"

"Giving me a choice? How's about a hula girl!"

Matt laughed as he headed for the door. "You old dog! On your behalf I'll conduct intensive interviews, comb the islands for just the right one. If my search fails, I'll have had one hell of a good time looking."

Ben laughed. "Go my son! Have a blast! Enjoy, enjoy." He stood and stretched, feeling stiff after spending three solid hours working on the *American Dream* script.

Below, on the circular drive in front of the theater doors, a limo waited, engine running. Matt trotted down the steps to the open car door. He looked up to see if Ben might be at his office window and waved when he spotted him.

Ben returned the good-bye, checked his watch and discovered it was later than he thought. Time to collect his suitcase from his golf cart, pick up Tony and head towards LA.

◆◆◆

Waking at dawn from a dreamless sleep, Maddie focused on the first gray light of morning highlighting the intricately pleated canopy suspended above her. The rays of silk fabric emanating from a central knot reminded her of the sun. She heard the siren call of the Pacific and surrendered to it. The balcony she'd dreamed of awaited her just beyond the French doors.

Finding a blanket in the antique carved trunk near those doors, she headed outside and settled onto a chair near the balcony's far edge. She cocooned herself within the blanket's warmth and filled her lungs with the crisp, cool air. The waves breaking on the nearby shore created the perfect background music for her idyll.

Her eyes grew accustomed to the slowly graying darkness and she oriented herself. The terrace lay below her to the right, delineated by its white stone balustrade, opalescent against the deeply shadowed lawn.

She scanned the edge of the cliff on which the house stood, from beyond the terrace to the area around the beach directly in front of her. A rock promontory, jutting straight into the Pacific, formed the lower elevation. Thick woods, to her left, arising unexpectedly from the seemingly infertile landscape, created a wall of deeper darkness.

Silhouettes formed in the strengthening light and the form of a man standing near the edge of the rocky cliff became apparent. *It's got to be Paul. He must have been there when I came out.*

Maddie let her thoughts run rampant as she stared at the unmoving figure. *Plotting my tortures for the day? I'll be one step ahead of you! First, no more finger food. If it can't go on a fork, I'll go hungry! Second, both feet will remain rooted to the floor. Third, my back will be firmly pressed against something every time you're within ten feet of me.*

She sighed as reality intruded upon her resolutions. *The way you looked at me when you took that food....no man ever seared into my soul the way you did last night...only in my wildest dreams... and then what happened? You shut off like a burnt-out light bulb!*

It suddenly felt too warm and Maddie loosened the blanket. *Look at me! I can't even think about it without getting all hot and bothered! Combine that with holding me so close at the tree...and that back rub! I can fake what's on the outside but my reality is the mess inside. If I didn't leave that room when I did, there was definite danger I'd throw my arms around him...look into those eyes and kiss him until we...until he...until he called me Nancy.*

Stop it, Maddie! She closed her eyes, blocking him from her view. *Get a grip! Admit it, you've met the man of your dreams...yes, my dreams and everyone of them illustrated for me in that chronicle of his life with Nancy...Nancy. You're a tough act to follow, Mrs. Davidoff. No, I'm wrong. You're an impossible act to follow! I should hate you...but I don't. If anything, I guess I'm jealous. Yes...jealous...but not because you stand in my way. No, that's far too normal for me! It's that even in death he can't let go. You two were so joined, so tied up in each other. All ties attached to me have been of the strangling type. Right now, I wish I'd choked on them years ago!*

Paul turned to face the impending sunrise over his house. Streaks of pink and vermilion brightened the sky above him. He knew that in a matter of moments the off-white stucco house would be bathed in the colors above, a sight he anticipated whenever he was home and the weather cooperated.

He studied the sky above the house but was distracted by a white almost spectral object on the balcony nearest him. Too far away to determine whether it was animal, vegetable or mineral, he walked towards it.

As he drew nearer to the house, the form took definition and he realized it had to be Maddie. He waved to her but received no response. *You're looking in this direction. Are you so angry you won't even wave to me?*

He walked through the gardens extending out from the balcony and waved again. *Still won't wave, huh?...and I'm supposed to apologize to you? Well, my dear lady, we'll see about that! We're having that talk here and now.*

Entering the house soundlessly, he climbed the staircase two steps at a time and stood outside her door, listening. *What are you waiting for? You already know she's up!* He knocked gently. Silence. He knocked again, more forcefully.

Maddie heard the first knock but as if in a dream. Lost in thoughts of Paul and Nancy, everything else receded to nothingness. The second, more strident knocks, got her attention, and, thinking it was Marina, she called out, "Come in. It's opened."

She closed her eyes and breathed the clean air again.

"May I join you?"

The unexpected sound of Paul's voice jolted her. "What are you doing here?"

"Last time I checked, I live here," Paul answered softly.

"You're out on the cliff! How'd you get here without me seeing you coming?" She pulled the blanket around her more tightly. *I wonder how odd it would look if I pulled this over my head. Only the Wicked Witch of the West looks worse than I do in the morning! No make-up! My hair isn't combed! I wanted to make an unforgettable exit, leaving him with a memory of me that would make him wish he'd won instead of lost. Now all he'll do is laugh...hysterically.*

"I waved at you as I walked up but you ignored me."

She buried herself deeper inside her coverings. Only her eyes and forehead showed and she gazed intently at the nearest planter.

Receiving no response, he noted, "If you were that lost in thought, I suspect I was a big part of it."

Her eyes darted from the flowers to his face. "And why should you think that? After yesterday's..."

"That's exactly what I want to talk about," Paul interrupted. "I'm sorry I acted that way with you. I shouldn't have raised my voice—"

"Try yelled!" Maddie interjected indignantly.

He took a deep breath. "...yelled at you. I realized this week, with Monika, how little control I really have over my own life. I mean, I don't really live. I'm a prisoner for all intents and purposes. You, not me, pulled all the strings to make her visit happen. That incident at the gates was my pathetic attempt to show you and my daughter I can initiate some kind of action, that I can control what's happening to me. I was wrong to do it with Monika there."

Maddie's head rose little by little out of her cocoon as he spoke. "It would have been less scary had we known what you were up to. Oh, I'm sure I would have had some choice words for you but you would have done it anyway, and I would have been left sitting there with my heart in my mouth."

He stared silently at the ocean.

Maddie went on seriously. "I shouldn't have entered your room. Monika seemed upset...I mean she was in my room and asked if I...well, I thought if I talked to you we might be able to reassure her we weren't going to kill each other. Instead, I caused..."

"You caused me to face a few things I've been avoiding," Paul interrupted.

Maddie's eyes followed him as he walked to the railing. He stood half-turned from her, looking down at the terrace.

There's so much more to him than just the actor and father. His fame and money have purchased him loneliness in one of the world's most luxurious isolation booths. He sees Monika growing up and away from him. More loneliness. What's he got then? His career, this place and Nancy, none of them able to soothe a fevered brow or keep him warm if the world turns cold.

She stood and held the blanket around her. "I'm starved! How's about letting me get dressed and I'll meet you downstairs. We can figure out how, when, and where I can take Monika shopping before I go back."

Paul walked slowly toward the balcony doors. "You're not angry with me?" He turned back to see her face when she answered. She shuffled along, hobbled by the blanket, and stopped beside him. "No, I'm not angry, but I do have one request. Can we take a few steps back in time, like to *Othello*, and get back to having some fun? I think it's safer ground, don't you?"

Accepting the olive branch, he smiled, nodded his head and left the room. *Perfect! Thank you, Maddie, for taking it back to before the time I made the first mistake, comparing you to Nancy.*

He walked downstairs and met Marina in the kitchen. She reached for one of the frying pans suspended from a rack above the work island, noting, "My goodness, you are up early this morning."

"So's Maddie," he reported as he removed two glasses from a cabinet.

Marina stopped breaking the eggs she was going to prepare for scrambling. "How would you know? How would you know she was up unless..." The words escaped before she could stop them.

"Because I'm psychic!"

"I think you said it wrong. Don't you mean psycho?" she quipped, relieved to find his mood improved and herself not corrected for her impertinence.

"Ho, ho, ho! Very funny!" He lost the race to the refrigerator for the orange juice pitcher and retreated from her threatened slap, stepping back with his hands up. "We mended our fences this morning. I assure you, everything will be peaceful. I'll behave myself."

"If that's true, it will be an early Christmas present for us all," she commented as she poured the juice and handed him a glass. "I don't usually criticize you..."

"Did I hear you right?" Paul laughed. "I guess you call it the freedom to express your opinion! You've done everything short of crucifying me!"

Marina put down the juice pitcher and looked at him seriously. "You wouldn't think it criticism if your conscience wasn't guilty. Now, as I was trying to say, if you got up this morning still in yesterday's mood, I was going to remind you of your guests, your family, your daughter, the season. I'm glad I didn't have to."

"So am I, believe me!" Paul answered, smiling at her. "Now, there are things that need to be done today. Don't look stricken. I'll do them. I just need some information. Monika and Maddie told me they want to go shopping. Is there a shop in the village or do we have to go further away?"

"There are a couple of nice stores in the village. I'll run and get Boris up so he can take them this morning," she said, wiping her hands and taking a step towards the back door.

"No, no. Don't bother him," Paul said, "I'm taking them myself."

Marina stared, stunned.

"I'm giving myself a gift, a day with my daughter and Maddie. We'll wear track shoes just in case we have to beat a hasty retreat."

Marina, at first glad he was attempting to normalize his life, was suddenly engulfed with worry.

"Now, don't fret," Paul comforted her, putting his arm around her shoulder. "If we don't come running back in an hour, you'll know everything is fine and you won't see us for lunch."

"Are you sure..."

Paul squeezed her shoulder and stepped back towards the dining room door, hearing Maddie coming across the hall. "Marina, I finally accept that I can't go on trying to find the past so, to quote a wise someone, "Today is the first day of the rest of my life."

XV

Monika squinted as she gazed into the center of the Christmas tree making fuzzy halos form around the colorful lights. She sat in front of it, cross-legged on the floor, listening absently to the hum of voices around her.

Her father, Ben, and Tony were getting sillier with each sentence as they tried to out-do each other's old jokes. Maddie and Nana talked softly, comparing notes on grown children. Poppa had cornered Whitney near the fireplace, but they were too far away for Monika to hear more than a few words here and there. She could tell by Poppa's smile though, he was having a wonderful time. *This is the best Christmas ever... ever!*

It's just like a big family get-together. So what we're not all related!

Tony broke into her happy haze, whispering in her ear, "Out in the front hall is a box full of mistletoe. Don't you think it's time we find some good use for it?"

"Oh, great!," Monika cried out, bringing the room to an abrupt silence. She scrambled to her feet and dragged Tony toward the doorway.

"What was that all about?" Paul asked, missing the opportunity to deliver his punch line as half his audience left the room.

Ben stretched his legs and leaned his head against the sofa back. "It's Christmas Eve and no one is accountable for his actions—too much excitement in the air, especially for twelve-year-olds and those who think they still are!"

Tony and Monika reentered, hands behind their backs. Tony resumed his position next to Paul, and Monika squeezed herself between Maddie and Anna. Both Tony and Monika draped an arm along the back of their couch.

"What are you two up to?," Anna asked quietly, noting the impish smiles on their faces.

"Nothing!," Monika insisted, leaning against Anna's arm and looking up at her innocently.

Anna glanced over at her son just as Tony's hand came up behind Paul's head, mistletoe hanging. She chuckled and tried to cover it with a cough.

Maddie had been sitting opposite Paul, inundated by mixed memories, the warmth of her childhood Christmases contrasted with the discomfort of cold, silent holidays spent with David. Changing her focus to Anna, she'd been able to break away from that and distract herself.

It was another element, she found more disturbing because of its resistance to distraction and dissipation. It had begun during the day while the three of them strolled the village streets, Paul and she licking ice cream cones with as much abandon as Monika. Paul had been completely relaxed, completely himself, and she liked what she saw, liked the warmth he engendered around her heart.

Under the strengthening spell of the tree's soft lights and the relaxing comfort of Marina's delicious meal, Maddie finally surrendered herself to memory of the warmth of him next to her all afternoon, the inner peace his voice created as he talked softly to her, the exultation of feeling...actually feeling.

Despite her haze she began to realize that Monika and Anna were staring at Paul and she turned towards him. He was unaware of the leaves and berries just above his head that made him resemble an over-sized Christmas elf. Maddie burst out laughing just as Ben leaned back and blew him a kiss.

Paul turned to his left in time to catch Ben and his eyes widened in surprise. Tony, seated on his other side, yawned and stretched his free arm as Paul looked towards him. The twinkle in Tony's eye told Paul something was going on and he raised his hands in surrender, hitting the mistletoe above him.

"God, no one let my agent know about this!" Paul exclaimed, regarding the distaff couch in dismay. "I can't get a woman to kiss me even with the sure-fire stuff nearly growing out of my head!" As he spoke, Monika mirrored Tony, raising a cluster behind Maddie's head.

Anna glanced quickly at Paul.

Standing slowly, he announced, "I refuse to participate in the flagrant neglect of tradition exhibited by the females in this room," approached Maddie, leaned over and, while cradling the back of her head with one hand, kissed her tenderly on the mouth, prolonging it just enough to show her it wasn't a casual kiss.

In her excitement, Monika dropped the berries onto Maddie's head while Whitney stood watchfully silent, ready to rescue her mom if she detected any bad reactions.

The earth didn't move for Maddie, it stood stock still. He'd taken her by surprise and she'd been too stunned to react. Fearing he'd gotten nothing out of it, she wanted to bring his mouth back onto hers, showing him how much she'd longed for this but all too aware of her audience, she didn't.

He straightened up and with a theatrical flourish, delivered the memorable line, "Merry Christmas to all and to all a good night" and left the room, heading for the staircase.

Every eye turned to Maddie. Whitney, walking toward the couch where Maddie sat, remarked, "I think it's bedtime for every one, especially my little mother. She's had a busy, busy day and we wouldn't want her to look tired on Christmas, now would we?"

Maddie, relieved at the opportunity to escape their scrutiny, playfully slapped Whitney's proffered hand and stood up on her own.

Monika unplugged the tree, kissed everyone good night and took Maddie's hand, asking Whitney, "You don't mind if I talk to Maddie for a while...oh, I'm sorry... she's your mother and I..."

"Be my guest, sweets. We've had a lifetime of talks already. The change in subject matter must be refreshing for her."

Boris had locked the house earlier, before he and Marina had said good night and left for their own place. Everyone headed for the staircase without any detours. A round of "good nights" filled the landing and then scattered down the hallway as the group dispersed to their various bedrooms.

Maddie suggested Monika put on her pajamas and come back to her room, and she watched as Monika raced down the hall, unbuttoning her sweater as she ran. Looking down the hall to Paul's room, she thought, *He'd never come to my room with this many people in the house. Would I dare go to...* She hastily let herself into her room and headed straight for the French doors to the balcony.

Hand on the doorknob, she prayed, *God, keep me away from his room! I feel like I can't breath!* A blast of damp, cool air swirled around her as she pulled the door open. It was much colder than she thought! All the better to dampen that fire inside. *Come on, Monika, get back here. Keep me occupied.*

As if she'd heard her summons, Monika knocked. Maddie closed the balcony door. "Come on in." She wondered whether Paul would be out on the cliff in the early morning.

Monika ran in and leaped onto Maddie's bed, landing with a resounding thunk. "Guess I'm getting too heavy to do that anymore," she observed, laughing at the thought of crashing through the bed, onto the floor. "Look at you, slowpoke, you haven't changed yet. It's freezing in here!" She jumped off the bed and gathered up an afghan from the chaise lounge. "Were you out on the balcony?"

Maddie headed to the dresser for her nightgown. "Just wanted a breath of fresh air. Tell me, where did you get that mistletoe?"

"Tony," Monika replied, and then, turning the conversation toward her own hidden agenda, she asked, "Was Whitney always pretty? I mean, even at my age, was she pretty?"

Maddie stepped into her bathroom, answering from there as she changed. "She went through a stage where she was all arms and legs, from about 11 to 13, but then everything seemed to catch-up. She was tall for her age, like you, and didn't quite know what to do with those extra inches for a while. You seem to have skipped that awkward stage. You're quite graceful. That mistletoe...who had the idea of holding it over our heads like that?"

"Tony. Was Whitney a good student in school? Did she get into all the school shows and stuff?"

Maddie walked out of the bathroom, a wide, full length nightie swirling about like a white cloud. "Everything from the littlest angel in the first grade Christmas show to Annie Oakley in eighth grade to Juliet senior year in high school. I felt like I spent half my time in auditoriums or theaters when she was in school. I'm not complaining, I really loved every minute of it...and yes, she always got good grades.I expected you to run over and give your dad a kiss when Tony put the mistletoe over his head."

"Why? I can kiss him any old time. I think I'll try out for my school's theater group. I really like what I saw at the Genny this week, both on and off stage. I don't know if I can act but, if not, there's plenty of other things to do and still be in the theater, right? Why didn't you get up and kiss Dad?"

Maddie sat on the edge of the bed and Monika, huddled under the cream-color crocheted afghan, sidled over so Maddie could get under the covers. "Tell me, how did you like your day?," Maddie asked.

Monika's question hung in the air, blatantly ignored. She looked at Maddie, yearning to ask what she felt after his kiss but answered the question instead. "It was great! Dad and I haven't been in the village together since I was ten. Oh, and going to church made it more special. It was so pretty in there with all those little lit trees along the walls and the manger under the altar. And did you notice that all the figures were dressed in real clothes? And the halos had little diamonds in them to make them shine?"

Maddie's mind returned to their conversation in the church parking lot. "They leave your father pretty much alone up here. We had very little bother shopping or at Mass. The people were surprised though to see him in that church." Maddie visualized the Spanish-style, stucco church nestled into a hillside on the outskirts of the village. She had stood admiring it as Paul wished Merry Christmas to a few people who couldn't resist saying hello.

"He made a deal with the town when we moved in," Monika had explained. "He'd make sure they could keep their quiet life here by not being seen too often in the village. You know, the tourists, they'd figure out real fast he lived nearby. In return, the people who live here would have to be quiet about where our house is and keep all their own "fan stuff" down. He thanks them for cooperating by helping out with their charities and school funds, things like that."

"You mean contributes?"

"Not only that. If they need to raise a lot of money, he'll go to whatever they've planned. They can use his name to attract money but they have to have their dance or whatever at least 25 miles from here. If the press finds out what's going on, it'll be because somebody talked and that will be the end of everything, for good. They don't want to have to give back or lose the money so they keep quiet. We moved here when I was six, and he's done at least one of those affairs every year since then."

Paul interrupted Monika's explanation. "Home we go?" After finishing with the group he'd opened Maddie's door and then jogged to the other side with Monika.

"Yes, yes, yes!," she'd piped up as she clambered through his door into the back seat. "I have gifts to do up and put under the tree before Whitney gets here!"

He'd started the engine and backed out of the parking space, saying, "That was a nice service. I've never been to a Mass before. I'd forgotten how wonderful Christmas carols sound in a church. So much more meaningful, so beautiful."

"The choir was excellent. It was a lovely service," Maddie agreed, looking back at Monika. "Thank you for inviting me up here. What a relief not to have to play! That in itself was a perfect Christmas present, a terrific gift, Monika, and you didn't even have to wrap it!"

She'd leaned forward, against the back of Maddie's seat, as Maddie went on. "Remember the church where you went to the fair? The children there act out the Christmas story each year. It's very cute. Something funny always happens."

"Like what?" Monika asked.

"Last year the tallest and oldest shepherd wasn't happy with his minor role, being equal to the other kids, so the director told him he could be the head shepherd. Taking his title to heart, he quietly but deliberately moved the other kids' stuffed animals over to himself as the narrator told of the shepherds coming down the hills to Bethlehem. None of them dared object but, when he tried to kidnap the last lamb, so over-stuffed it barely fit under the arm of the boy holding it, that kid turned and hit the bigger kid–*whack*–over the head with it. Even Father cracked up. I was laughing so hard I couldn't see the notes. No doubt, Whitney will have a tale to tell about what went nuts tonight too."

Paul and Monika laughed.

"How come you're Catholic?" Monika had asked suddenly.

Maddie turned to her in surprise, saying, "Well, I've always been. My parents were Catholic and had me baptized when I was a week old."

"Why wasn't I baptized, Dad?"

Paul rubbed the back of his neck debating with the truth and finally admitted, "To be honest with you, I wasn't feeling too religious after you were born."

"Oh...yeah. Well, do Catholics have to marry Catholics?" Monika asked, moving between her father and Maddie so she could see both faces.

Paul stared at the road.

Maddie responded quietly, "No."

"Your husband was a Catholic?"

"No."

"But you still got married in a church?"

"Yes."

"Why? He didn't have to, did he?"

"It didn't matter to him but it did to me."

"What did he do for a living?" Paul had ventured into the interrogation he'd wanted to initiate himself for weeks. He sensed Maddie was not talking about a subject she liked. Her answers had become unnaturally terse; she was not a mono-syllabic person.

"He was a lawyer."

At least she answered, so Paul persisted. "You mentioned once you grew up in Boston. Like I would think you were from Nashville with that accent of yours? Did you stay in Boston after you married?"

"Yes..." Maddie was helpless to control the change in herself whenever her husband's memory came up.

Paul checked Maddie's expression quickly. She'd become tense and he speculated at a possible reason with, "The holidays can be rough sometimes. After so many Christmases with...I don't even know his name!"

"David," Maddie said flatly.

"...with...David...it must still be a difficult time for you, even after ten years. I know its tough for me though we only had three Christmases together. My memories become more intense in December. Do yours?"

Maddie had ignored Paul's question and looked over her shoulder at Monika, knowing the sight of her happy face would brighten her own unwelcome discomfort. "I hope all the chaos the Chases, Ben, and Tony bring to your holiday will be a welcome distraction for you." She needed to stop the questions. "Oh, by the way, Monika, have you heard from Lisa?" Maddie knew Lisa had called the night before and that Monika would talk on and on about her if asked.

"Maddie. Maddie! Are you still awake?" Monika nudged the unmoving figure next to her.

"Huh?" Oh, sorry, honey. I was lost somewhere in the middle of... a wave of longing suddenly engulfed her and she sat up. "You know what I think? You should stay here with me all night. Let's have a slumber party. Want to?"

Monika sat up and hugged Maddie as hard as she could. "Oh, Maddie, I'd love to!" She abandoned the afghan and got under the covers. After Maddie shut off the light and settled in the bed, Monika slipped her hand into hers.

Maddie stared into the darkness above her head. *I'm using you, Monika. As long as you're here I can't go to him there. Hold on tight to me!*

Pete paced the width of the bedroom.

Anna gave up any hope of falling asleep. "Do you get paid by the mile? Please Pete, come to bed. I'm exhausted and you must be too."

"What's your take on Maddie?" He maintained his walking tempo as he spoke.

Anna sighed, accepting defeat, and sat up, rearranging the pillows behind her back. "She's a lovely woman, pretty, intelligent, professional..."

"I don't mean that! What do you think of her with Paul?"

"Well, she's not your typical show biz type. She seems solid and obviously thinks Monika is wonderful."

Pete stopped walking and turned to face her. "I said with Paul, not Monika."

Anna stiffened at the exasperation in his voice. "What the heaven is bothering you? Change that tone or you're going to have the Christmas from hell tomorrow!"

"I'm sorry," Pete apologized, walking to the bed and sitting next to her. "I didn't mean to say it that way but I hate being confused. What the hell is going on here. The woman is attracted to him. He's obviously very interested in her. Monika's crazy about both her and Whitney, but..."

"They obviously haven't done anything about it," Anna said, finishing his thought. "Monika told me she and Whitney plotted this whole thing to get them under the same roof, hoping. Monika wants them together so badly it's almost frightening."

"That truly scares me! The child's already planning her future with a new mother and the two adults are acting like dense heads," Pete declared, standing once again. "I cornered Whitney tonight..."

"Hmmm, yes! I noticed."

"What's this? Oh, I love it! She still gets jealous!" He returned to the bed and kissed her cheek. "Nearly one third my age is just a little too young for me! Now, as I was saying, what's so obvious to everyone else is positively a blind spot with them. She told me those two have been playing a cat and mouse game for months. Isn't he aware of how Monika feels, how deeply she's into this? That child could really get hurt if they don't do something one way or the other."

Pete looked at Anna and her attentive look in return signaled him to continue. "It seems Maddie didn't have a happy marriage and was badly hurt since then by someone. Whitney said the Great Wall of China pales to insignificance compared to what her mother has developed as her defense system."

"Bunk! Right now that wall is about as substantial as a house of cards! All Paul needs to do is take a firm lead and she'll fall apart!"

"Oh, aren't you just so sure! Did you know that kiss tonight was the first time they've done it? Whitney told me as we were coming upstairs. Our son, Mr. Macho, voted the Sexiest Man in the World, has been alone with her, hours on end, and this is the first time they've kissed! What's wrong with this picture?"

"Shh, you'll wake everyone up!" Anna whispered fiercely. "What's wrong is Nancy. She's his Great Wall. You heard him just last night. He's known deep inside he's met the woman he wants but has run face first into his own wall and to make matters worse, he told her. Imagine comparing her to Nancy! Now that you tell me about Maddie's past, I understand why she's reacted the way she has! She needs affirmation, to be made to feel needed and wanted for herself, not because she reminds him of someone else."

Pete looked at her questioningly.

Anna took his hand in hers. "He made a mistake, bringing Nancy too much into the picture, and now he'll have to undo it. First, he's had to place Nancy in her proper niche. Considering how long he's clung to her, it's got to be difficult for him to take the step out from her shadow. Next, he has to find a way to bring Maddie into the light too. She couldn't and wouldn't come if called, and dragging her would have scared her off. He's now doing exactly what he should, making her want to take the chance. You saw her at the table last night. She was teetering on the edge. His rescue at the tree couldn't have been better timed, and while he was rubbing her back, she got so turned-on it was palpable!"

Pete stared at her in awed silence.

"That kiss tonight," Anna went on, "finished her off. I'll bet you that right now he's out like a light, having his first good sleep in weeks, feeling that all he'll have to do tomorrow is crook his little finger and she'll be at his side. As for Maddie, she's probably spending the worst night of her life, longing for more and knowing he can't come to her with a house full of guests and family. I wouldn't be surprised if she's biting the bedpost even as we speak."

She patted his hand and wriggled her way back down to a lying position. "Now, please turn the light off and come to bed. Honestly, you men make so much work out of such simple things!"

Pete walked around the bed, sat down and turned off the table lamp, muttering, "Females! Think they've got us all figured out! What's so disturbing is they usually do. Come here, woman! How can you be so sexy and so smart too?" He took her into his arms and their bodies pressed together.

Anna sighed in contentment as his hands slowly caressed her body. "The smartest thing I ever did was marry you...Aaahhh, yes...yes, Pete...mmm. Paul would lose his Sexiest Man title in a second if his fans found out about you."

◆◆◆

Whitney closed her door after seeing Maddie close hers. She walked to the gilded mirror over the dresser and brushed her hair, each stroke bringing a broader grin to her face. "Oh, those walls came a tumblin' down!"

Sitting on the edge of the bed, she remembered how quiet Maddie was when they arrived from L.A. and how her immediate concern was relieved on seeing the sparkle in her mother's eyes.

Paul seemed changed too, more intense, but it differed from his work attitude at the theater. It was from a deeper source. Whitney knew without asking that something was and had been happening.

She was too keyed-up to go to bed. Walking to her door, she opened it slowly and checked the hallway leading to the staircase. All was quiet. Slipping off her shoes, she dropped them behind the door and headed on tiptoe towards the stairs.

About halfway down the flight she heard a sound above her, turned to check, and discovered Ben and Tony on the top step. They caught up with her, the pale light of a crystal bright moon shining through the tall, triple windows above the hallway guiding their way.

Whitney whispered, "What are we turning into, the three stooges or the three musketeers?"

Tony came up behind her and whispered, "Darling, we're the three graces. We cause, we effect, and we're totally delightful."

They reached the bottom step and headed towards the living room and the tree. Whitney warned, "Both of you, hands off the presents. I'll bet that's why you came down here!"

"Us?" Ben asked in mock horror. "The real question is what are you doing here? A little bit of the same?"

She closed the living room doors, Tony plugged-in the tree and they settled onto the couches. Whitney said, "I'm so wide awake I don't think the strongest sleeping pill could make me blink."

"Well, it worked," Tony exclaimed softly. "Mistletoe be blest!"

"I think something was already cooking when we

arrived," Whitney observed, tucking her legs under her. "I never saw Mom look so alive! Her eyes were positively dancing when we walked in. There was so much confusion with going to our rooms and meeting everyone, Mom and I never had a chance to talk."

Tony sat back. "Oh, nuts! The mistletoe was wasted."

"No way!" Whitney corrected. "Believe me, that was their first kiss. If it wasn't, she would have looked a little guiltily at me and blushed. She was totally surprised but managed to hold onto that control of hers. The important part is that automatic closed-off look she hides behind, the one I've seen so often in the past, was erased. Whatever happened since yesterday seriously weakened what was left of her defenses. You provided the knock-out punch. You done good, Tony."

The three of them lapsed into silence and Whitney recalled their trip up the coast that evening. After 8:00 p.m. Mass was over she'd found herself in the back seat of Ben's Mercedes, cramped into a corner by myriad packages. Moving one from under her elbow, she'd commented, "I would say you over-bought a little. Who are all these for, the Seventh Army?"

"Who do you think? Maddie bought them. I haven't a clue what's in any except the ones in my pocket, for you and your mother." Ben said, signaling to make a turn onto the shore highway.

Tony nudged Ben. "You got something for Whitney? Don't I remember naughty and nice having a lot to do with whether you get a gift?"

Ben met Whitney's gaze in the rear-view mirror. She ogled him menacingly and he retaliated, "Oh, she's right on the borderline now! It's a real problem but...I guess I'll weaken."

"She did do good work tonight," Tony remarked. "She can't be all that bad, I guess. Boy, have times changed! Those kids in that Christmas program were a howl! My Christmas pageants, when I was growing up, were solemn. No picture taking allowed. God forbid it would ever be done during the Mass, and especially no Mary picking up the Baby Jesus by the foot. How did you keep a straight face up there, let alone sing, Whitney!"

Ben added, "That littlest angel with the big tinsel halo, the one that held the stick with the Star of Bethlehem hanging from a string, she was adorable, especially when she dropped it onto Joseph's head!"

They laughed and Ben continued, "She's a natural. Made a crucial show biz decision; which is more important, playing the role by keeping that star in place or dropping everything to fix her drooping halo and looking good for the cameras!"

"Maddie would have loved it!" Tony quipped. He lit a cigarette and said through the smoke, "Laughing and applauding in church! Unbelievable!" He recalled his parochial school days for them, when that kind of behavior was grounds for a poke in the back and detention for a week from Sister.

Whitney leaned her elbows against the back of the front seat and said, "I saw you two trying not to sing. Ha! You lost the battle on 'Silent Night.'"

Ben told them about his only other foray into a Catholic church, Maddie and David's wedding. "Such a formal event, even the kiss after the vows was eliminated."

Ben's voice cut through Whitney's thoughts and brought her back to the living room. "I've been trying to find the right time or place to tell you something, Whitney, and there just isn't one."

"Oh, God! You sound like a death knell, Ben. What's going on?"

"*American Dream* is turning into a nightmare," he reported disgustedly. "You've heard me say over and over what an idiot this new guy in the studio production office is. Well, he finally screwed-up royally and guess who got the brunt of it?"

Whitney nearly choked trying to say, "Not Robert Redford!"

"No, no, you're safe there... for now. It's worse! He's put off the major money people! You and I both know a studio alone can't invest millions nowadays, so they're blessed when they can woo a willing and able investor. Well, the upshot of all this is...we're on hold. Thank God for the holidays. Something may crack before New Year's. At least we might be able to set a date by then."

"How long do you think it might be before we start?" Whitney asked, looking at the tree, not Ben.

"Could be a week, could be a month, could be scuttled for now if nothing happens for too long. Redford could take another project. Who knows!"

Tony nudged Ben, pointing out how intently Whitney was staring ahead of her.

Switching couches, Ben took one of her hands in his, assuring her, "Don't worry, love. We're going to do this film, one way or the other. You'll have your chance or my name isn't..."

"Ben, I just turned down a good paying role in an independent. It was no great shake of a part, but it would have paid my bills."

Tony leaned forward. "Need a job, little girl? Perfect! The wardrobe man could sure use some help with that cast at the Genny. What do you say, Ben. Something's better than nothing."

Ben looked at Whitney and smiled. "What do you say? Fair warning though, you know you'll end up being a go-fer for Tony too. Knowing him, he'll take full advantage of you back stage."

"Go-fer, chipmunk, squirrel! Who cares! Can you afford to put me on the payroll?" Whitney asked, smiling faintly back at Ben.

He relaxed, relieved she trusted his commitment to the film and that her chief concern was only temporary unemployment. "Oh, I think we could find a dollar or two to throw your way every once in a while."

She reached out and hugged him, saying, "Thanks, Uncle Ben. You always go out of your way to help me. I wish my Dad had been more like you. He loved me, but I never felt he approved of my theater work. He never got involved. He didn't come right out and say anything to me for or against it, but I'm sure he let Mom know how he felt. She supported and encouraged me enough for any two people though. Then, I was lucky enough to feel your good influence buoying me up from the first day I met you in New York. Now I have Bret Atkins as a personal coach. I've got to be the luckiest actress on the planet!"

Tony sat on the other side of Whitney, took her free hand and said, "Don't tell old man Cameron but we're going to have us one great time working together. This actually makes me look forward to getting back to work. Oh, incidentally, don't tell him what I said about having a great time. I figure if I gripe and moan enough about how over-burdened I am, he'll pop out some guilt money for me. Shh, not a word to him!"

"You know what?" Whitney stated. "Suddenly I feel like I could sleep for a week."

"So do I," Ben agreed and Tony nodded.

They shut off the tree and strolled out of the room together.

Tony placed himself between Ben and Whitney as they started up the staircase and quipped, "And so to bed. Time to let those visions of sugar plums dance in our heads."

"Just what kind of a nut are you?" Ben asked, chuckling.

"Oh, Ben! You cut me to the quick! A nut? Let's get this straight...*Mon Dieu!* Did I actually hear myself say the word straight? You've got me so upset I don't know what I'm saying! Listen and learn, Ben! We're the granola company; Whitney's the flake, you're the nut, and I am the fruit!

XVI

It's an earthquake. No, never on Christmas!, Maddie reasoned after feeling the bed shake under her. Suffering through a mostly sleepless night spent listening to house noises and the pounding surf, she'd finally managed to doze off as the sky began to brighten.

"Maddie, come on. Get up," Monika pleaded, pushing against the side of the bed with her knees.

More aware of the movement than the voice, Maddie mumbled, "It *is* an earthquake! Oh, who cares! If it's my last moment on earth, I choose to spend it in bed." She turned over, pulling the covers almost over her head.

Monika renewed her efforts and called out, "Maddie, let's go!"

Suddenly wide awake, Maddie jumped from the bed, grabbed Monika's hand and headed for the door.

"What are you—," Monika gasped.

"You're supposed to get out of the house in an earthquake. Come on!"

Monika pulled on Maddie's arm, laughing. "I thought you were kidding me! You really thought it was an earthquake?"

Maddie stood where she was, poised for the next earthly convulsion. After a few quiet seconds she stared at Monika, finally realizing there was no danger. "Okay, I'm up. What time is it?"

"Six."

"That late? Last time I looked at the clock was long ago at 5:30." Maddie headed, yawning and stretching, for the bathroom, and Monika sat on the bed, waiting impatiently.

"You're going to take forever!" Monika complained when she no longer heard the shower.

Maddie padded into the room, wrapped in a huge white towel, and gathered her clothes from the dresser and closet. As she headed back to the bathroom, Monika persisted, "I'll be too old and weak to open my gifts waiting for you to get all beautiful."

"At my age, Monika, getting beautiful is an all day, major project. I'm aiming for presentable. Well, at least clean. I can do that in fifteen minutes. Time me! Hey, do me a favor? I couldn't find my opal earrings in the drawer. Would you look in my suitcase? See if they got caught on the lining or something."

Monika got the bag from the closet, carried it to the bed and unzipped it. Empty, but two long, closed pockets on either side needed investigation by hand, not eye. Reaching into the left one, she found a small picture folio. Forgetting the earrings, she sat on the edge of the bed and studied the photos, mostly of Whitney as she was growing up and a few of mother and daughter together. Remembering the earrings, she plunged her free hand into the other pocket and found them hiding in a corner. "Got 'em, Maddie. Want them now?"

"No, honey. Thanks. I'll get them when I come out. I'd hate to lose something I love that much. Ben gave me those when we worked together in New York."

As Maddie spoke, Monika restudied each picture in the folio.

Maddie emerged from the bathroom dressed in deep

green velvet tights and a cream silk tunic on which she'd left the top three buttons opened. She saw the folio in Monika's hand but didn't remark about it. Taking the earrings from her, she walked to the dresser mirror to put them on.

"How come there aren't any pictures of your husband in here?"

"Mustn't have been any good ones around when I put that together," Maddie answered as casually as possible.

Monika got up and stood behind Maddie, meeting her eyes in the mirror. "Maddie, you've hardly talked about him. Do you really feel that bad that he's...are you divorced?"

"No, honey, he died. That part of my life is over and reminders of it are of no help to me now. I'd rather not dwell on that subject. I entered a whole new life ten years ago, my dear young lady, and that's all I concentrate on now." She took the book from Monika's hand and lobbed it into the suitcase.

"Good shot!"

Maddie picked up her perfume atomizer and directed a spray towards her open neckline.

"Fifteen minutes on the nose and you look great! I'll go get Dad!" Monika headed for the door on the run.

Maddie studied herself in the mirror, pushed an errant strand of hair back from her forehead, and softly promised herself, "I don't care if I make a spectacle of myself today, Paul is going to hear about and feel what's going on inside me." Her eyes narrowed with her next idea. *If he acts as if the last two days never happened or...he just turns off...* She swallowed hard and stated, "I can always put one of those cliffs out there to good use."

"And push me off?" Paul inquired from the doorway where he stood with Monika. She hadn't given him a chance to do more than put on a robe.

No one was safe from her now, and she took off down the hall to wake up her grandparents, Ben, Tony, and Whitney.

Maddie looked at the totally unglamorous Paul

Davidoff, unshaven, uncombed, little more than half-awake, leaning on the door jamb. *He looks good enough to eat! Only a total idiot would allow herself to starve at this banquet!*

She walked to him, a herculean victory over her desire to run, and smiled. "Merry Christmas, Paul." Putting her arms around his neck, she kissed one cheek, then the other, his forehead, and from there traced a line of kisses to his mouth.

When they finally parted, he was breathless, speechless. She whispered, "That makes up for last night."

Finding his voice, he wondered, "What was wrong last night?"

"I was so shocked when you kissed me, I couldn't get my act together. You must have gotten nothing at all out of it!"

Paul laughed, hugging her to him. "I was in such a panic, afraid you'd belt me, right there in front of my parents, I didn't even notice. All I knew was I was finally doing what I wanted to for a long time and getting away with it."

Ben, plodding down the hall in robe and slippers, caught a glimpse of what was going on as he headed toward the staircase. He stopped just beyond the open door to Maddie's room, grumbling, "I want to see this Atkins character! What a way to run a hotel! You get a wake-up call when you don't ask for one, in person yet, and are expected to be bright-eyed and bushy-tailed before any vampire worth his salt needs to return to his crypt! Where are you, Atkins? Get out here and explain yourself!"

Paul stepped into the hall and stood behind Ben. "Hey there, is that the Grinch I see before me?"

Maddie sat on the chaise lounge near the door, her heart racing. *I have never felt anything like this! After David's degradations' and Vic's egotism, I thought my desire had died of starvation. What a Christmas present! To find out it's not dead, it's just been sleeping! Ha! It's running rampant! I had to fight off an almost uncontrollable desire to rip off both our clothes and make love right in that doorway!*

"Well, hello Mom! Merry, Merry Christmas! You look

like you could fly," Whitney exclaimed softly as the last of the little troop made their way to the staircase.

Maddie hugged her tightly, whispering, "You've just interrupted one of the most erotic dreams I've ever conjured up. Oh, Whitney, it's happening...what I've dreamed of is happening! I need you to tell me it's okay with you."

Whitney laughed, holding her mother tighter. "Okay with me? It's been okay with me since the party at Megastudios! And that Monika! She's a regular match-maker!"

Maddie sat back, eyebrows raised, looking at Whitney.

"Monika and I talked about you two getting together back in October. She's the one who had the idea that if you both were under this roof and Marina tied a few loose threads together, the two of you would finally see the light. Paul didn't object to your coming up and I made sure you couldn't say no. It worked and I couldn't be happier for you...or for me."

Maddie's expression hadn't changed as Whitney spoke. "I got lost somewhere! You two maneuvered me here?"

"Not just you, him too. A few of Santa's helpers stepped in along the way, Tony and his mistletoe, Ben and his ride up here. Marina had the hard job, though, finding a way to talk to you so you'd understand more about Paul. She must have done it because look at you now!"

"We made that easy for her," Maddie stated, filling Whitney in on events since she'd left the house two days earlier.

"You're not upset that we all did what we did? I wouldn't want you to think we were inter—"

Maddie hugged her again. "Thinking got me into the mess I've been in for years. Paul saw what was hiding inside me, tried to bring it out, and I fought him every inch of the way. Now, following my instincts...Well, look at me!—a walking advertisement for casting caution to the winds. I gave up my battle yesterday and feel reborn."

Whitney stood and pulled Maddie up. "If a kiss can do

all that, I'm almost afraid of what making love—"

"Stop!" Maddie ordered. "Finish that sentence, and you are going to have to pull me off of him when we get downstairs!"

As they walked down the hall, Whitney observed, "Paul is one incredibly sexy man! I wouldn't have been surprised if you two had started an affair in the fall. Your generation, though, was brought up to wait to have sex. Now you're sure how you feel about him, and I can't even imagine how wonderful your love-making will be. Nothing could ruin it for you."

"Mom, I've dated more guys than I care to remember. I know you're not naive and think I'm any different than the rest of my generation; I've slept with some of them. There's something you told me years ago that I dismissed then as hokey, that a relationship between a man and a woman should be first based on solid friendship and you compared that strong relationship to a well-baked cake. You said sex is the sweet frosting to decorate it. Put frosting on a half-baked cake and you get a disaster waiting to happen; the outside looks good but the structure is weak."

"I hope I remember all of this part. The cake can be eaten by itself and taste good. It won't be as sweet without the frosting but nevertheless satisfying in its own way. And...oh, yes, frosting with no cake under it is a formless lump. You can eat just the frosting too but, after a while, it gets sickening. Know what? You were right, I can see now you were absolutely right!"

Maddie took Whitney's hand and said, "Life taught me some hard lessons after I made some basic mistakes. It turned me into a regular philosopher, I guess! When Monika asks for good advice on the subject of sex, you can repeat that for her."

"The first thing I'll tell her is to look at her Dad and you, perfect examples of doing it the right way," Whitney declared as they entered the living room.

Anna was losing her battle to corral the scattered shreds of discarded wrapping paper and place them in a rubbish bag.

Paul sat on the floor by the tree. Monika had draped discarded ribbons over his head and shoulders.

"Somebody get the camera," she called.

"If anyone moves I'll severely maim them," Paul threatened good-naturedly. "Honestly, a picture like that, even under lock and key, is bound to leak out eventually. Thanks but no thanks!"

Spotting Maddie and Whitney as they strolled in, he shook the bows from his head, seemingly embarrassed.

Maddie took a seat on the end of the couch closest to him and gathered the fallen ribbons on her lap. "Monika, can you find a paper plate? And some scissors? I'll show you something pretty you can do with these."

Faster than it seemed possible, Monika got up, raced to the kitchen and returned, plate and scissors in hand. She sat next to Maddie, watched her slit a hole in the plate's center and draw through the long streamers attached to the bows. In no time she had created a large, colorful "bouquet". Tying off the ribbons under the plate, she handed it to Monika. "Voila! I think they look far prettier like this than on your father's head!"

"How do you know all this stuff?" Monika exclaimed, taking the bouquet to show it to everyone in the room.

Paul started to get up but Maddie stopped him. "You can't go anywhere until you open my gift," and she pointed to the large gold and white box under the tree.

He pulled the package toward him as she continued, "What do you get the man who has everything?"

"Only almost everything," he corrected, winking at her. "I hope to change that situation very soon."

"Be good! Open your gift."

"Oh, I'll be good," he whispered provocatively.

"Oh, Lord, Paul! Please stop it. There are all kinds of people here," she whispered pleadingly. "Come on, let's see if you like it."

He ripped the paper from the box while staring at her.

"Like it? I'll love it!"

His double meaning provoked Maddie to poke him with her foot, a movement Monika caught as she came towards them and she smiled triumphantly at Whitney who was standing behind the couch.

Interest centered on Paul as he lifted the box cover. His smile turned to a grin as he lifted out an Irish-knit pullover sweater. "Did Monika tell you I wanted one?"

Maddie shook her head. "I thought it might be good for those walks along the cliffs. When I visited here to pick up Monika I walked there and, when I thought about a Christmas gift for you, I remembered the ocean breeze. I hope you like it."

"You bet I do," he declared studying the various patterns combined in the garment.

Marina and Boris appeared in the doorway and announced breakfast was on the table. Whitney and Monika headed straight for Marina while the rest walked towards the dining room. "Merry Christmas" they said in unison and their smiles were so wide Marina didn't need to ask if everything was going well. She looked at Paul and Maddie and lost any remaining doubts. Running to Boris, who was standing by the dining room door, Marina gave him a very American thumbs-up sign. He responded with an enthusiastic "Right on!"

"You must be starved, Paul," Maddie said, ruffling his already ruffled hair. "Come to breakfast."

"Not so fast, my pretty! I haven't given you your gift." He pulled a silver and red package from his robe pocket and handed it to her.

The box was the size of her hand and she kidded, "Well, at least it's not another coffee pot!" She unwrapped it, revealing a black velvet box. Slowly, she lifted the hinged lid and peered at the widening gap as if the contents might escape if she moved too fast or took her eyes from it. "Oh, Paul," she sighed as the opal pendant necklace resting on its black velvet bed came into view.

"I noticed how often you wear those earrings and figured I couldn't be wrong. You obviously like opals." He took the pendant and chain from the box and, facing her, placed it around her neck, fastening it blindly behind her.

She touched the pendant with its fiery center stone set into an oval of diamonds. "Oh, Paul, it's exquisite, but...it's too much. It must have cost a fortune!"

"Not for you to worry about." He stood, taking her hands to pull her up to him and kissed her on the forehead. "Is the smell of that coffee and bacon making you hungry?"

She nodded.

"Come on, let's attack the dining room." He put his arm around her waist as they walked toward the assemblage of happy eaters.

"Maddie, look at what Paul gave us!" Anna exclaimed excitedly as Maddie sat down. She pulled an envelope from Pete's robe pocket, handing it across the table, and hugging herself in happiness.

"The South Pacific. Oh, how wonderful!" Maddie studied the itinerary which outlined week-long visits, beginning the end of January, to Tahiti and Bora-Bora. She looked at Pete and teased, "Should I send warnings to the males down there that you're coming? You're going to drive those native girls crazy, Pete!"

"Fat chance I'll let him out of my sight!" Anna declared, hugging his arm.

"Fat chance I want to get out of your sight," Pete answered, kissing her on the tip of the nose.

Maddie smiled, reminded of her own Mom and Dad, so like them, happy together and full of life. *I thought life just went that way. You met, married and lived happily ever after. Some are lucky enough to do that. Maybe my day is coming!*

"Thinking about me?" Paul asked softly, his voice dispersing her thoughts.

"Indirectly. Your folks are terrific. They remind me of mine. Incidentally, that's how I got you the authentic, hot-off-the-needles sweater in such a short time. Mom and Dad retired to Ireland a few years ago so they air expressed it."

"There's so much I don't know abut you," Paul said, laying his hand on her forearm.

Maddie looked into his eyes. "It'll all come out eventually...if you stick around long enough to hear it." She looked away from him, fearing he wouldn't and found Monika and Whitney to her left, poring over a newspaper.

"Okay, we've got it!," Whitney announced. "Listen up, folks! The movie caravan will leave from the front door at 1:00. Outstanding film featuring a *REAL* actor..."

Paul straightened up and put on his Atkins smile.

"...Sean Connery. Oh, honestly, Paul, who here wants to see you? And...you two are not invited! Mom, you look like you could sleep for a week, so take a nap while all is quiet. Paul, our special Christmas gift to you, an afternoon of peace and solitude. Enjoy!"

While Paul and Maddie talked quietly in the dining room the rest of the group went to the living room and gathered up their gifts before heading upstairs to dress.

Shafts of sunlight filled the breaks in the cloud cover and scattered across the land and water. Maddie wrapped her Irish sweater more tightly around herself as strengthening winds buffeted the cliff she was descending.

The lower cliff had two pathways and a series of staircases leading to it. One set rose to the higher cliff on which the house sat and the other wound its way down to the beach.

Maddie had reached the lower cliff when she heard Paul calling to her from above. Waiting at the staircase she was about to descend, she watched him run to catch up. He was wearing the sweater she'd given him, and he linked arms with her as they started downward to the beach.

Once at the bottom, he gathered her into his arms, kissed and then held her and she rested her head on his shoulder. They separated slowly. He took her hand and they walked toward the tide's edge and sauntered toward the end of the property.

"Maddie, you've seen me on the screen as this hot-shot lover, women falling at my feet. Some of those scenes make me look like the greatest thing since...well..."

Maddie nodded, plunging her hands deep into her pockets.

"I've got some bad news for you. That stuff is all choreographed. I couldn't bring myself to do most of that in reality. The thought of us together is obsessing me but I'm afraid you'll say forget the whole thing afterwards."

Maddie stopped, forcing him to, and stared in wonder at him. "Remember when you asked what I'd have done if you tried to seduce me?" He nodded. "What do you think I was talking about that night when I said I'd bore you to death! I've had only two lovers in my life, one worse than the other. I'm afraid I don't know enough about how to please you or even what pleases me! Oh God! I can't believe I told you that!" She turned away to face the water, wishing she was disappearing in quicksand.

He turned her to face him and hugged her tightly. "You're absolutely wonderful! You don't know enough about...It's so perfect! We're both worried about the same thing!"

Maddie would not be assuaged. "What will you do if I freeze up on you. What if I can't..." Maddie couldn't look him in the eye as she confessed, "My husband said I was frigid."

"Sounds like he was blaming you for his own inadequacies."

Maddie searched his eyes. "What if he was right?"

He held her by the shoulders and looked deeply into her eyes. "I can't imagine how the woman I'm holding, the one who responds like a ten alarm fire when I kiss her, could possibly be frigid. Self-conscious? Scared? Yes. Frigid? No!" He framed her face with his hands and kissed her gently.

Maddie'd heard the reassurances she so desperately needed. She held him as close as she could and responded with an intensity that shook them both.

"Make that a fifteen alarmer! Let's go to the house...everybody's out, even Marina and Boris are at their own house. Maddie, I'm not pressuring you to...you tell me when you're..."

Maddie took his hand an led him toward the stairs. "You are the most wonderful thing that's ever happened to me." They climbed to the top and walked slowly toward the house in silence. Maddie was far from quiet inside though. The closer they came to the house the more agitation she felt and as they reached the terrace, she fretted aloud, "I don't know what to say or do! When it comes to this sort of thing, I'm a much better follower than leader. It's what I've been used to, I guess. What would you like me to do?"

"Oh, I'm sure I'll think of something," Paul said softly, close to her ear. He took her hand and led her into the house and up the staircase.

She looked at the door to his room and then at him, hesitating. He raised her hand to his lips and held it there, assessing her state of mind.

Paul pressed her hand to his heart. "I can say all the right things when someone writes the words for me. Now that it counts, I love you is all I can think to say...I love you."

His words caressed Maddie's heart. She looked at her hand and his on his chest and whispered, "I love you too, more than I can ever find the words to describe."

Their arms wound around each other and she melted against him. "Maddie, if you have any doubts about making love, tell me." He'd had no idea her emotions had taken such a beating until she inadvertently confessed it on the beach and feared he might be taking things too fast.

Positive she was the one and trusting that his love would heal her, he added, "I wouldn't get angry if you said you want to wait. This is something for us to share, not do selfishly. I want you to want it as much as I do. Tell me what would be right for you, go to my room or back outside to finish that walk?"

Maddie felt light as air and held onto him to keep from floating away. She'd heard the words she'd only dreamed and they'd cut through the last threads of her fear. "I feel like a virgin. I don't know how I'll react. I've never truly enjoyed...And then there's those firm, perfect bodies I've seen on the screen with you. They're probably no different than the ones you've been with. Well, I can't compare. Ha, I can't even come near them."

He slid his hand down her back and around to her breast. "Thank God! You feel like a woman, not some kind of silicone Barbie doll!"

A fire she thought had long ago been squelched flared through her when his hand covered her breast.

Words were no longer necessary. She was radiating her desire for him. They walked together through his bedroom's double doors and she waited silently while he closed and locked them.

He led her to the bed and, after sliding her cardigan off, started to unbutton her blouse. "No one ever did this to me before," she said softly.

He stopped, his hand frozen in mid-motion. "If you'd rather..."

She closed her eyes and threw her head back, sighing, "This is a dream coming true! God, how long I've waited for this moment!" She looked at him again and fingered the bottom edge of his sweater. "You'll never know how much I want you!"

He quickly pulled the sweater over his head. She began unbuttoning his shirt and whispered, "Help me make this good for you. I want you to want more, not feel 'Well, maybe next time.' Tell me what to do."

"Just let go, get lost in us, forget everything else. That's what I'm doing right now, and it's working wonders for me."

Maddie focused on his whispered words of love, his touch, his gentleness. She wouldn't believe until then that any man could be so caring or cater so much to her needs and pleasure. His hands didn't just touch her. They were breaking off the hard edges of hurt and defensiveness that had formed over the years, molding a new Maddie.

His tender, compelling urgency brought her to an awareness of what she was capable of giving and newly tapped well-springs of passion arose and overflowed within her. Her most intense feelings and reactions came from the incredible pleasure he took in her. He responded to her with an intensity of desire and passion she never dared even dream of experiencing. It was the first time she felt fulfilled as a partner and reveled in the new found knowledge of her own sexuality.

Lost in the wonders of what she was feeling, she lay next to him, barely breathing. His hand cradled her head as he said, "Are you all right, love?"

"No, I'm not. I'm dead," she answered opening one eye. "I just died and went to heaven."

He laughed and held her close again, luxuriating in the way she pressed herself against him from her head right down to her toes.

She kissed his neck and ear, whispering, "Is it true that men over forty have trouble with a second time?"

"I can't tell you from personal experience, but I've read the same thing."

Maddie pressed her leg against his and suggested, "Let's find out."

"What if I can't?" Paul wasn't sure of anything happening.

"I bet you can. Besides, trying for a couple of hours will be fun anyway. As she slowly drew her fingers up his thigh, he knew she was going to win her bet. She knew it too and whispered, "You really are the sexiest man alive."

Marina and Boris, walking up the path from their house, had seen Paul and Maddie crossing the lawn to the terrace. An hour later Marina, beyond keeping her curiosity in check, made a reconnaissance mission to the second floor.

She ran downstairs, nearly knocking Boris over as she raced towards the kitchen. He had come into the dining room, worried when she hadn't returned sooner.

"She's not in her room and his door is locked! They're in there and not discussing great books, I'm sure."

Boris hugged her, saying, "I'm inspired to discuss a few novels of my own." He swept her off her feet and carried her toward the back door.

Marina laughed softly. "Only ones with happy endings."

XVII

"I found out only last night, and with so much going on, I didn't know when to tell you" Whitney explained as she and Maddie walked along the beach.

"*American Dream* isn't going to happen?" Maddie questioned, looking seriously at Whitney.

"Come on, Mom, keep walking. I didn't say it was canceled, just postponed." She recapped Ben's explanation, adding, "And so it comes to pass that you are now my boss."

"How did I come to that?" Maddie asked, this time stopping altogether.

"Oh, I forgot to tell you the rest! I'm going to be working with wardrobe and Tony for the *My Fair Lady* run. He said he needed an assistant and, viola, here I am! At least when and if word comes that they're ready to start shooting, Ben and I will be ready to take off—together."

Maddie smiled, glad to see this set-back hadn't disappointed Whitney too much. "This will be wonderful! I get company back and forth each day, maybe even a chauffeur. Oh, life is getting good-er and good-er."

"It sure is," Whitney teased. "You look like you just won the lottery. Everything you dreamed of and more?"

"What do you mean?," Maddie asked, skipping a stone over the wave tops.

"What do I mean? Obviously something happened since we took off for the movies. If you tell me you two compared notes on the disadvantages of home ownership, I'll skip you across a few waves. Don't deny it. You went to bed with him."

Maddie faced her and suddenly reached out to hug her. "Oh, Whitney! I had no idea I could respond like...He was so gentle, so caring...He made it so easy, so...comfortable. I found out it didn't have to hurt. It was so wonderful...so... Whitney, for the first time in my life, I feel really wanted, needed...to quote a song, 'He makes me feel like a natural woman.' Like a woman, Whitney, not a thing."

"Mom, I couldn't be happier for you. When's the wedding?"

"The wedding!," Maddie exclaimed, stepping back and staring at her daughter.

"Of course, that logically comes next, unless you're planning to just live together. I don't think that would work with Monika, do you?"

Maddie heard little of the last statement by Whitney. She was stuck on the word wedding. "I'll cross the wedding bridge when I'm asked. If I'm asked. You know, it may have been wonderful for me but it took two to dance that tango and maybe he didn't like my choreography."

Whitney took Maddie's arm and pulled her to start walking again. "If that was the face of a disappointed man, I'll eat my sweater. Both of you were grinning like Cheshire cats when we walked in. You obviously pleased the lord and master very much."

"Oh, I do hope so." Maddie looked up at the graying sky. "It's almost dark. We'd better go back," she said, trudging towards the staircase.

"Mom, I'm thrilled for you. I hope someday I'll meet that someone who will make me feel the way you do. The sooner the better."

Marina folded the spread from Anna's bed and placed it carefully on the upholstered bench at its foot. "I think it's a good idea Maddie and Paul have time to themselves. I'm sure Monika would love to spend a few days with you."

Anna indicated she wanted Marina to sit and talk to her. "You live here with Paul and know more than I do. Do you think Maddie can be happy with him? I mean, do you think Nancy will come between them? He was going on to Maddie about her even as lately as a couple of days ago."

Marina looked calmly at Paul's mother. "Maddie's been hurt enough to know what she won't put up with. If anything, I think he may have more trouble with her independence than she will with his dependence."

Anna's interest was piqued. "What do you mean?"

"Maddie put in long years getting where she is today. Add to that, the man she works with is a relative. She will not abandon him just because Paul wants her to stay at home for

Monika. Oh, believe me, she loves Monika like a mother but, she loves Ben too. It takes the two of them to manage that theater, and I don't think she's going to abandon her end."

Anna's maternal instinct pushed to the surface. "Well, Paul is right. He needs a mother for Monika, not a career woman."

Marina smiled and pointed out, "And Maddie needs a full-time husband, not a gypsy movie star. Please, don't think I am insulting you or your son, but Monika needs a full-time father too. There's much to be sorted out and settled and maybe even more between just the two of them we know nothing about."

Anna helped Marina close the drapes. "They looked so happy when we came in. I really don't want to see either one of them get hurt."

Monika carefully carried a tray full of home-baked cookies and followed Marina and Boris into the living room where the Christmas guests had gathered by the tree.

Paul removed the accumulation of newspapers from the coffee table so Marina could place a coffee carafe, cups and saucers on it. Boris followed her with a carafe of hot cocoa and a dish of marshmallows.

Monika knelt by the table, placed a marshmallow in a cup, poured cocoa on top and crowned her concoction with two more marshmallows.

"Why don't you have a little cocoa with your marshmallows," Paul teased.

"Oh, Monika that looks good," Maddie exclaimed, peeling off her sweater and walking towards the table. She and Whitney had come in from their walk just in time for the special snack. "How about making me one."

"Daddy, you want one too?"

"You think I need a second career as Fatty Arbuckle?"

"Oh, Daddy! Marina, give him black coffee."

Maddie protested, "Too much caffeine. Make his a glass of water. No, make that half a glass. We can't have him bloating."

Anna settled back with a steaming cup of coffee. She said under her breath to Pete, "Talk to him now. He can't say no with all these people around."

Pete sat forward and said, "Paul, I'd like to ask something..."

Monika interrupted, "Dad, Nana and Poppa want to take me to Disneyland. We can leave tomorrow and spend a few days, and we'll be back for New Year's Eve. I've never been there, and I'd love to go. I know I came home to see you, but...it is Disneyland and I've always wanted to go. And, besides, you've got Maddie."

Maddie turned to Monika immediately. "Because I'm here doesn't mean you should feel..."

Monika leaned over and hugged her, exclaiming, "Oh, Maddie, I don't feel I have to go, I want to! Do you think I'm jealous?"

"I hope not."

Paul cut in. "So, you want to go off and leave us alone and unloved, do you? Well, we'll survive somehow, I guess. Who am I to stand in your way! Mom and Dad, good luck. She'll run you ragged. When are you leaving?"

Pete stared at Paul, surprised at such a quick affirmative answer. "We thought we'd take the train from the village tomorrow morning. Driving to L.A. would make it like any other trip; the train lends an air of adventure. We'll come back on Saturday. Are these plans okay with you?"

"Fine with me," Paul said, looking quickly at Maddie. She was fighting the melted marshmallow blob in her cup as she tried to get a sip of cocoa. "I'll drop you off at the train station."

"Oh, by the way," Ben interjected, "We'll be leaving too. Have to get back to the Genny tomorrow."

Maddie looked up in surprise.

"Whitney's got a few lessons to learn," Ben continued, "if she's going to work with Tony and she needs to study the inventory and change schedules for our cast before they return."

Maddie looked from Ben to Whitney to Tony. "I really should go with you."

"To do what?," Tony inquired. "If we need anything from you, there's always the telephone. One of us can figure out how to use it."

Paul thought Maddie looked a little lost in this talked-about exodus. "Well, my sweet, I guess we said something wrong. Everyone is abandoning the ship. Want to keep me company here?"

Maddie smiled, relaxing a bit. "Well, I guess so. It's a dirty job but someone has to do it." She looked at Whitney and said, "I hope you're not leaving at the crack of dawn."

"It's up to Ben," she answered, looking over at her dozing uncle. "I would guess we won't get away from here much before mid-afternoon. Ben needs his beauty sleep."

"Are you sleeping here tonight," Whitney asked, as they walked upstairs and entered Maddie's bedroom.

"Well, of course! Where else would I be?"

"Mom, please don't be coy. It's definitely not you."

Maddie looked at Whitney for a second before walking toward her dresser. "I guess it wouldn't be right. Well, you know, his parents, my daughter, his daughter—it wouldn't look right. It's those old ethics at work. Besides, I wasn't invited."

Whitney had seen the look in Paul's eyes every time he glanced at Maddie and had no doubts he was in love with her mother. *This night is not going to pass without them getting together in some room. He'll show you how to stop doubting yourself and him. I haven't a clue how but he will. Anyone who can make such a change in you can accomplish anything he wants. Walk on water, leap tall buildings in a single bound.*

The morning of the Davidoffs' departure Maddie sat in the kitchen in Boris's accustomed seat. Marina, clearing up the last traces of their breakfast, made her final cleansing wipes on the table. "You look like you are a million miles from here," she commented, unsure Maddie even heard her.

Staring fixedly at the condiment-laden lazy Susan in the center of the table, Maddie was lost in thought. She heard Marina's voice but not her words. "Marina, I'm so confused. I need to talk to someone. Whitney can't help; she's never been married. I need someone who's..."

"Someone who's been married and then found another." Marina finished Maddie's sentence as she rinsed the sponge.

"You are a very wise woman, Marina. Know anyone who fills that description?"

Marina turned and looked seriously at Maddie. Despite a dozen years in the United States, her life in Russia had schooled her well in survival through secrecy and silence. It still took strong determination of will for her to open up to anyone but Boris. She approached the chair next to Maddie, saying, "Me, but it was a very long time ago and very far away, another life."

Maddie found herself staring at the housekeeper. "So Boris and you met here?"

"At this house. We were married in the living room." Marina sat down, knowing what Maddie's next questions would be.

There seems to be no end to the surprises . "Marina, please don't think I'm prying but will you tell me about your first marriage? Was it happy?"

"Happy at the beginning. He was in the Army, away more than home. They changed him, trained him to kill, made him hard and cold. Everything just fell apart. We were divorced before our daughter was born. In fact, he never saw her; wasn't interested, I guess."

Maddie was surprised. "You have a daughter? What's her name? Where is she?"

"Natalia. She died of pneumonia when she was two."

"Oh, I am so sorry!" Maddie reached for Marina's hand. "Now I understand why Monika is so dear to you." Maddie paused, checking Marina's reaction to such a devastating memory.

"Boris changed me, took away so much of that hurt that now I can think of it without pain."

Maddie tightened her grip on Marina's hand. "I feel selfish going on with this."

"Please, don't. I will try to help, if I can," Marina reassured, confirming her sincerity with a reciprocal tightening of her hand.

"Well, if you're sure. Maybe, you can help me. Your first marriage must have left its scars on you. I'm still a mess after mine and it's been ten years, ten years of feeling nothing inside. Marina, I'm so confused."

"About the...shaking in your head and heart this morning?"

"Yes! Marina, you do understand."

Marina patted Maddie's hand. "Maddie, I questioned hard my feelings for Boris too. I know what you're thinking. You wonder if what you feel is real or just...pleasure, no, joy, at the idea you're still alive...inside."

"Oh, Marina, yes, that's exactly it! Obviously you figured it out. You and Boris married, and you seem to be as happy as can be. Not that that's even been mentioned—marriage, I mean."

"Everything's too perfect, Marina. Life has taught me I can't be this happy and stay that way. Maybe what will come up and ruin it for me is the realization that I'm just enjoying the physical stuff, the sex, and ignoring a lot of other important issues."

Marina moved closer and said, almost whispering,

"When you were dating your first husband, were you filled with a passion that wouldn't let go, night or day. Every time you saw him, you went crazy?"

"Yes, but I'm almost ashamed to admit it because I was so wrong."

"That part doesn't matter, right or wrong. You felt that before; now look for something the same but also very different. I'm not going to tell you how it's different because then it won't be your feeling alone. Just watch what is going on inside you while you're together for these days."

As if on cue, Paul came barging through the back door, flushed from running up the hill from the garage. "Good morning, girls. Got the travelers off on their adventure to Disneyland. Plotting and planning something?"

Marina stood immediately, smoothed her apron and said, "I'll have your breakfast on the table in a few minutes."

Paul looked at Marina and then Maddie, asking, "Why do I engender fear in her heart every time I find her sitting?"

"Because I'm not paid to sit," Marina answered firmly.

"How many times have I told you to relax, take it easy. I won't die if I have to wait for a meal or find dust on a table. Sometimes you make me feel like a task-master."

Marina turned to Paul. "Pavel, I am not a member of your family. I am paid to do certain work here, and—"

"Stop right there before I get angry!" Paul retorted, walking towards her, softening his serious face with each step. "What do I have to do to make you realize you are one of the family, stop paying you or maybe adopt you?" He put his arm around her shoulder and hugged her.

"Oh, Pavel, stop it! What if Boris walks in!"

"Okay, okay!" Paul backed away from her saying, "If this makes you feel better; get that food on the table in ten minutes...or else! Come on Maddie, you have to figure out for me what I can possibly do for an 'or else.'" He took Maddie's hands as she stood and led her towards the dining room, saying in a low voice, "I go through this with her at least once a year. Watch, by this afternoon she'll be ordering me around again as usual."

Maddie looked away from his stare and concentrated on the glass of orange juice Marina placed in front of her.

"Those thoughts look like they're worth a lot more than a penny," Paul commented. *Later today I get her all to myself and the day starts off with something obviously wrong. Only one way to find out.* He felt a knot beginning to tighten in his stomach. "What would you like to do today?"

"Nothing until Whitney, Ben and Tony leave. Then..." She looked at him. *I've got to say what's on my mind. No more hiding everything behind yet another wall, silence.* "...then I'd like to talk with you."

"Not here and now?" Paul asked, feeling the knot tighten even more.

"This isn't the time or place. Well, good morning, Tony."

Maddie slumped against the doorjamb as Ben drove away from the house.

Whitney was once again crowded in the back seat, this time beside the "Santa loot" she, Tony, and Ben were taking home with them. Maddie returned a wave when Whitney blew a kiss through the back window.

Paul put his arm around Maddie's shoulders. "Are you all right?" he asked, concerned at the seriousness that had deepened in her during the day.

She nodded. "You should have seen me when she moved out here and left me in New York. She lived on the East Side and I was on the West but we saw each other almost every day, even if only for a few minutes. How I hated to see her go! It was six months of lonely hell for me. That's really sick, isn't it?"

Paul hugged her tighter. "Not for someone who's had only Whitney for so long. Maybe it will lessen now with someone else in your life." He looked at her until her eyes finally met his. He put his mouth near hers.

"Can we have that talk now?" she asked, moving away from him.

He hesitated, thrown off by her reaction. "Sure. Let's go to the terrace. It's not too cool for me. How about you?"

"I'll be fine," Maddie said. *I'm stewing so much inside I wouldn't be cold at the South Pole!*

He settled himself on the wrought iron settee, patting the cushion next to him for her to sit with him. Instead of accepting his invitation she walked to the railing and turned to face him, arms crossed.

"We've got to talk about Nancy," she announced, using every bit of her strength to make herself do it.

Paul reacted immediately. "I haven't mentioned her! It's been you and only you for days now."

"Mention her or not, she's very present. I can't ignore her. Am I like her or not."

Paul left his seat immediately and walked purposefully to her. "You are Maddie, only Maddie. I finally woke up to the fact that no one can be someone else. It was the stupidest idea I've ever had and I regret ever mentioning her to you."

"Look, Paul. I realize now that we're approaching this relationship from two completely opposite directions and I'm afraid we're going to crash head-on. You told me about her because she was so special to you, so incredibly a part of you. I've never mentioned David because..."

"You don't have to say anything."

"Paul, I do have to; I need to. David nearly destroyed me emotionally. I hadn't a clue what he was really like until after I married him. He was determined to own me, keep me as nothing more than a slave to his ego and whims. Eventually, I gave up arguing, crying, begging. Silence became my armor in that losing battle, and it somehow fooled him into believing he'd won. In reality I had retreated inside myself in a desperate attempt to survive and became a spectator at my own torture. You had three years of bliss. For all intents and purposes, I was in solitary for fifteen years. Then, he died in a car accident ten years ago. By that time I was incapable of almost any feeling but fear. I really thought I had died inside."

Paul listened in dismay, fighting the urge to stop her confession but at the same time wanting her to delve even more deeply into it.

"Then came Vic. You must know him, Vic Steele. He's been in a couple of your films."

Paul nodded, remembering a tall, model-handsome man whom he had thought could be a better actor if he would allow himself to be less aware of his looks and take more risks with his characters. The women on the set adored him, and Paul was pretty sure Vic knew each one of them in the biblical sense by the time shooting ended.

"Well, he looked sideways at me, and I fell like a boulder off one of your cliffs. I was liberated by David's death and wanted to make up for every minute of lost time. I couldn't go to bed fast enough with Vic. He was charming, witty, handsome, all the requisites but, in his own way, he was worse than David. As long as this little bed buddy gave in to him on everything, he was wonderful. If I tried to make things better for myself, do a few things my way, he was like a roaring lion. Once again, I was silenced, getting nothing but pain and frustration out of the relationship."

"I'd had a double dose and found it two too many so I swore off any serious relationships from that point on, drowning myself in study and work. It's really amazing how you can sublimate your most basic drives and convince yourself you're happy with cerebral substitutes."

Paul didn't have a clue what to say, whether to soothe her or sympathize or what.

Maddie was not about to stop until she reached the end. "Then I met you. God help me, I met you, my big-screen dream man for so many years, the only one who made me wonder if everything was really turned off inside me. How could my heart skip a beat during your love scenes if every inner feeling was dead? You made confusion for me. One magic night a few months ago my hand was resting in yours and I was so shaken I couldn't utter a sound. All those screen memories came flooding back. If I was going to spend weeks successfully working with the real you, I had to put all that stuff behind me and concentrate on the reality; that you were just another actor at the Genny. When you began showing up in my office, I wished you away, afraid you'd ruin my idyllic image of what you were like off-screen. Instead, what happens? You turn out to be even better than I thought, just short of perfect. Looking back, I realize I was already in love with you by opening night, not with that Bret Atkins persona, with you. My proof was when I short-sheeted your bed. I could never do that to Atkins. I felt I had to be the most wonderful, intelligent, witty, sophisticated woman on the planet for Bret Atkins, like the women on the screen. I'd never try to get him mad, never play a joke on him."

Paul smiled. "I beat you. I fell in love with you at the Megastudios party."

Maddie turned toward the ocean and said, "I don't think it was me you fell for. I was just an image of Nancy. If there wasn't something about me that made you think of her, I doubt you would have paid an ounce of attention that night or throughout the whole run of *Othello*."

Paul left his seat, turned her, forcing her to face him. "She has been my criterion for a woman for twelve years now. Naturally I look for similarities. She's all that ever made me happy. Why wouldn't I want it to continue with someone like her?"

"I can't be her!" Maddie insisted. "It actually scares me that you've talked about her so much but I had to ask Monika to show me her picture. I expected to find her shrine in your bedroom and there's not even a snapshot there. That's what's forced me to talk to you. She didn't die, Paul. To you she's very much alive. She lives on in you...and...I can't compete with her."

Paul leaned against the railing, shaking his head. "Mom was so right! I should have never mentioned Nancy to you. Mom's the one who showed me how stupid I'd been and made me rethink Nancy's importance in my life. I haven't mentioned her since that night because I realized she'd completed her mission, to make me wait for you. The restriction of looking for her in others kept me from making the mistake of taking what was offered by women who took advantage of my loneliness. She kept reminding me that lust was no basis for a lasting relationship."

"When I met you that night something clicked into place. I could spend the rest of my life trying to tell you what it was and never come up with a good explanation. I just knew. Maybe it wasn't a click. It could have been Nancy hitting me over the head with a sledge hammer to stop me in my tracks. All I know is I'm glad I did stop. No, I'm ecstatic!"

Maddie would not be swayed. "You can't just wipe out the memory of someone who's been a major part of your heart and soul for so many years. It's not possible."

"Look, Maddie, you're not comfortable with her around, so I won't mention her again."

Maddie saw the muscle in his jaw tighten as he turned away from her. *This isn't right. Maddie, get yourself out of this.* "Paul, she's a part of you; she's Monika's mother. She can't just disappear. I understand that better than you think I do. David still haunts me too, only his presence is not welcome. What I need is to know Nancy and I are two very separate entities in your mind and heart."

He didn't respond and she decided to go for broke. "Do I make love like her? Am I as good? The little things you've guided me to do, are they what she used to do without being told? What I really want to know is...is it me or Nancy you're making love to?"

Paul walked back to the settee, sat and motioned Maddie to join him. When she got close enough, he grabbed her and sat her on his lap.

"Now hear this, Madelyn Chase! You have just asked a question which could start a major war. Now hear this! You make love like I've only dreamed about. You asked me to tell you what I like and I did. The best part has been that you've done wonderful things on your own that I never knew I'd been missing. Maybe, had we been together longer, Nancy would have picked up some new ideas but that didn't have time to happen. Your instincts are astounding—yours, not Nancy's. You're a wonderful lover. Each time with me you've acted and reacted like it was your first. I never felt a woman, any woman, getting as much pleasure as you and, wonder of wonders, I'm the one giving it to you. You can't imagine how exciting that is!"

His words soothed her doubts and she ran her fingers through his hair, welcoming and then reveling in the heat rising through her body. She rose slowly and extended her hands. "You, dear boy, are in for an active late afternoon! Come on, up and at 'em. You've got me so turned on I can hardly wait to get upstairs."

Paul laughed as she dragged him through the doorway toward the staircase. "After Marina and Boris leave for the night, let's make love by the lighted Christmas tree."

As they walked upstairs she formulated an itinerary. "This afternoon in your room and then in my room. This evening by the tree. A midnight tryst on my balcony and a morning get-together on the beach."

Paul hugged her as they headed for his door. "Good thing the beach is last. It'll be easier for you to bury me in the sand after I die trying but I guarantee I'll go with a smile on my face."

Paul clicked off the cellular phone. "Monika's running Mom and Dad to a frazzle but they're having a great time anyway. Once again she by-passed me and asked immediately about you. I guess you didn't hear me call to you in the kitchen."

Maddie carried in a bread plate and butter dish. "Oh, I missed her call? Shoot!"

"What kind of miracle have you performed now? Marina doesn't let anyone except Monika help her."

"Guess maybe she figures I might be scared off if she gives me enough work to do, but her plan won't work. I love to be in the kitchen. I'd do lots more if she'd let me."

Paul smiled and watched as Maddie sat to his right. "That's not to scare you off. It is the highest accolade the Czarina can bestow! She accepts you as the lady of the house. Too bad I didn't get to ask you first. Well, later is better than not at all."

"What in heaven's name are you going on about?"

Paul had rehearsed a pretty little speech just that morning but lost it when the moment came to deliver it. Instead he blurted out, "I don't want to waste another minute! You love me, I love you. Getting married makes sense."

Maddie stared at him. "Getting married makes sense? For whom?"

It was Paul's turn to stare.

"You could be another David. I mean, how long have I really known you? Maybe this is all a good act. After all, you are a sensational, convincing actor. Maybe I'm being duped..."

Paul stood, knocking his chair over, nearly shouting, "You think I've been acting? Good God, woman, what kind of a person do you think I am?" He stormed out of the room.

Before Maddie could get to her feet, he stormed back in again. "Do you actually think I could fake what's been between us these past days? How could you even think I'd do that to you?"

Maddie felt her control slipping and tears start to form. She clasped her hands in her lap and stared at them.

Paul crouched down in front of her, demanding an answer, "How could you think that?"

Without looking up, she whispered, "Because I was fooled twice before. I told you."

A tear fell onto her hands and he knelt, holding her to him. "Oh, my sweet love, you can trust me. Please, please trust me. I couldn't hurt you...ever. I'd never lie to you. Please, Love, trust me."

"Oh, God, how much I want to!"

"We need time alone together. I mean weeks not days. If we lived together for a while, you would see day after day the truth of what I say. But there's Monika. I don't want her to think that living together is as good as marriage."

Maddie rested her head on his shoulder. "There must be some way."

Marina stuck her head through the open dining room door and pulled back immediately, saying from behind it, "Pavel, Ben is on the phone for you."

He kissed Maddie's forehead and went to the kitchen.

She sat back, eyes closed, wishing her life had been less traumatic. In a way she regretted telling everything to Paul but knew in her heart she'd had to. His reaction had been a positive for her. If only she could lose the nagging unsurety. If only they did have that time together.

"Maddie, Whitney wants to talk to you. It sounds like they're having too good a time!"

Maddie went to the kitchen and took the phone from Paul. He put his arm around her and leaned her against him. She didn't resist.

"Mom, I'm going to move into the Genny dorm. It'll make my life much easier. I've got so much to master before Monday and it looks like it's only going to get tougher from then on. If you don't want to be alone at home why don't you move into Paul's room at the dorm. I'm sure he wouldn't object!"

Maddie sorted out the mixture of news she'd been given. "Better yet, why don't we just eliminate him from that building all together."

Whitney winked at Ben and Tony. "What do you mean, Mom?"

"You move out on me. There will be an empty room. He moves in."

"Yeah, Mom. Like I believe he's going to spend even one second in my room!," Whitney retorted in her best Valley girl voice.

"Okay, okay, comedienne of the year! We'll move his stuff out on our way back. How's that?"

"Great! That means I get the best room in the dorm!"

XVIII

The rain fell in torrents, bouncing like hail off the driveway pavement. Monika ran from the cab to the front door, arriving drenched. She grabbed her father in a bear hug, leaving wet marks on his shirt.

Paul returned the hug and then grabbed an umbrella from the hall closet. He ran out to the car. "Here Mom, I'll take you to the door."

He escorted her to the house and ran back for his father. "Here Dad, you take it."

"You'll get drowned."

"I'm okay. I'll take care of the driver and be right in."

The taxi driver stared open-mouthed at Paul. "Are you

Bret Atkins?," he stammered as Paul handed him $40.00, ten over the amount due. He fumbled for change, still staring at the dripping face outside his window.

"Sorry to disappoint you. A lot of people think I'm him. Frankly, I don't see that much resemblance. Oh, keep the change. Be careful going out. It's really slippery on these roads when it's like this."

Paul trotted back to the house as the cab disappeared around the first turn on the road leading back to the gate.

Maddie wrapped a towel around him after helping him remove his shirt. He'd run out without even a sweater. "You'll catch your death! Come on, we'll get you dried off and something hot in your stomach."

Paul followed her obediently, winking at his father and smiling. He left his soaked shoes on the marble floor in the hall and ran upstairs after Maddie.

Monika, hustled off to her room by Marina, reappeared in time to see Maddie and her Dad enter his bedroom. They left the door open and she ran to it, pausing outside, out of sight. Peeking around the edge of the door, she saw Maddie rubbing his back with a towel. He was rubbing his hair with another.

"Oh, good grief, Paul," Maddie exclaimed. "Your feet are soaked." She knelt down, removed his damp socks and wiped his feet with the towel.

"I could become very used to this kind of thing," Paul sighed, falling back on the bed, spread-eagle.

Monika stood straight again, stifling a giggle.

"Sh, Paul. You left the door open. Go change those wet pants."

"Aren't you going to take them off too?"

"Paul! Monika might hear you! Behave yourself!"

Paul sat up, grabbing Maddie's arm, trying to pull her over on top of him. She wriggled free and snapped the towel at him, hitting him in the stomach. He doubled over and lay still.

"Come on, Paul. Get changed."

He lay still as a stone. Maddie approached him and discovered his face contorted in pain.

Scared, she cried, "Oh, Paul, I didn't mean to hurt you," and touched his arm. He reached up, tackled her around the waist and pinned her to the bed.

Monika forgot to be quiet, thinking something had really gone wrong when Maddie squealed as she was lifted off her feet. She stood in the doorway.

Paul and Maddie froze in their wrestling match, sensing more than seeing they were being watched. Maddie implored, "Help! Save me from this mad man!"

Monika ran across the room and landed on top of them both crying, "He's ticklish, Maddie. You take that side."

Paul roared laughing as he tried to escape from the two of them.

Attracted by the rumpus, Marina had run upstairs in concern. Standing in the doorway, she demanded, "Would the children in this house please stop all this noise. I'll have to send you to your rooms if you can't play nicely together. Come, Monika. Let's give those two time to think about the bad lessons they teach you."

Monika abandoned the battle, ran to Marina and laughed as she looked back at Maddie and Paul. He gasped at Maddie, "If I ever catch my breath again, you'll pay dearly for this, my pretty."

"Oh, I hope so," she sighed, standing, straightening out her skirt and tucking in her blouse. She ran into the hall, catching Marina on the top step. "That difference you mentioned...I think I know what you were talking about. What I feel now is more intense than with anyone before but I'm not being consumed by it like I was then, helpless under its power. Instead, it feels like I'm both producing and consuming this passion, one thing feeding the other. It's much more intense and enjoyable."

Marina smiled and said, "You are exactly right. Aren't we lucky?"

Maddie smiled and nodded agreement. She returned to Paul's room and sat in his chair by the bay window while he changed, reviewing the past few days and their many conversations about the future.

Whitney's phone call opened up all kinds of possibilities for them. The opportunity to spend a month alone together, away from interruptions after work lay before them. Paul had mentioned starting their life together and, despite her nagging doubts about how she could possibly hold onto someone so wonderful, she looked forward to it too.

He brought up the subject of marriage again and this time she ran into a wall she hadn't seen. "When you discover that our being together is fine, it will be easier for you to envision living here as Monika's mom."

Maddie looked at him in confusion. "I don't know what you mean."

"It will be so much better for her at home with you there all the time to do those mom things with her that she's missed out on."

"Mom things? Like what?"

"Oh, you know. You've done it before. All the things moms at home do."

Suddenly she realized what he was talking about. "Are you saying you want me to quit my job, leave Ben and the theater? Be at home all the time?"

"Well, sure. It's obvious you won't have to work."

Maddie studied his face for a moment, trying to fathom how he could know so much about her and yet miss a most important ingredient that made her tick. "Maybe I won't have to but I want to."

Knowing that tone of voice, Paul realized how serious she was. "You have no time to yourself as it is now. You practically live at that theater. How can you be Monika's mom and keep up your current pace?"

"Paul, I won't quit and that's that!"

His fear level was rising and with it his temper. He tried

to control both by speaking softly, "It comes down to a simple statement of expectations, Maddie. Monika needs a full-time mother and I need a full-time wife."

Maddie felt the thin ice she'd walked out on cracking under her feet and her instinct for survival, to give in, shifted into gear. *No, Maddie, don't start making the same mistakes again!* She forced herself to look him in the eye and state defiantly, "And I need a full-time husband. Are you going to stay home, not travel all over God's creation doing films, because that's what I want?"

He was stunned at the thought. "Well...no, of course not. I have to earn a living."

"Am I supposed to believe that is the only reason you act, to make a living?"

Paul felt cornered. "Well, no, but—"

"If you dare say it's different because you're the man, you're the breadwinner, I'll kill you here and now," Maddie almost shouted. "My career is as important to me as yours is to you! Oh, I know if I quit tomorrow the world would go on revolving without a glitch. I'm not known to everybody on the planet. If you called it quits, I think everything might come to a grinding stop. I'm just a small cog in the wheel but Paul, it's my wheel, and I love it. I wouldn't be me without it!"

Paul had paced her bedroom for many minutes following her declaration of independence. Maddie was determined to look composed and sure of herself but inside she was dying a little with each second of silence that passed. Finally, he stopped and turned to her, asking, "How about an assistant?"

"An assis..."

"An assistant for you. You do all the creative and management stuff you do so well and get someone else to do all the extras you've piled onto yourself. After all, my Maddie, you no longer have a reason to work 24 hours a day in order to compensate." He approached the chaise lounge where she sat and knelt beside it, taking her hands into his. "Will you at least think about it?"

She pulled her hands free and he sat back on his heels, fearing she was going to explode at him. Holding back for a few seconds, she slowly put a hand on either side of his face, leaned forward and kissed him tenderly. "I thank God every day for you. I've never felt so cared about. I'll start looking for an assistant the day we go back. If I have to pay him or her out of my own pocket, I will."

He lay on her bed. She joined him and they rested together on top of the spread. She nestled her head against his shoulder as he held her close to him. "That brings up another conundrum—this place. It's too far away for you to commute. And then there are Boris and Marina."

Maddie had been thinking along those lines since Christmas day, trying to figure a way she could be with him after the show closed. The realization of how impossible a night with him would be if a show was running had already struck her.

"Maybe we could find a place between here and there. We could put Monika into a private school where she could get home every day. If I'm tied up, Boris could pick her up. If I was late getting home, she'd have you there or, if you were filming somewhere, she'd have Marina and Boris until I got home. We could spend every free moment up here. If Marina and Boris didn't want to leave here they could have the place to themselves until we arrived. School delivery and pick-up would be the least of our problems."

Paul leaned away from her to see her face. "You're really serious! You've thought about all these things before now! You have been thinking about marrying me!"

"Marrying you? No. Being with you? Yes, but this is getting much more complicated than I thought it would," Maddie observed, sighing. "We've both forgotten something, Lisa!"

Paul groaned. "Oh, God, you're right! Those two will die if we split them up! Maybe we should consider leaving Monika in the school she's in."

Maddie interrupted, "Paul she'd never forgive us if we married and she was left in the same situation. Even if we didn't marry and I was just around here, she'd feel the same."

"And neither of those two are happy so far out in the middle of nowhere," Paul observed.

Maddie turned onto her back and stared at the canopy. "You just said something significant. They both want to change schools! Monika doesn't have to board anymore but Lisa does, right?"

Paul said yes softly, looking at her.

Without changing her focus, she said, "She could live with us, share a room with Monika, if her parents would agree to it. They could pick her up and take her with them on the weekends. Lisa wants to see more of her mother, and there'd be no keeping that woman away if she had even an outside chance of seeing you! Oh yes. That would be perfect. Kill a flock of birds with one stone. Everybody gets what they want!"

"You willing to take that on? After all you'll be the one around them the most."

Maddie turned her head and looked at him.

"Sorry, Hon, you were absolutely right. I can't stop making films now. But...I'm going to be in your life every free minute. I won't spend one second longer than I have to on any set, and I'll come home to you every chance I get, even if it's only for overnight. And I expect to see you on the set whenever things work out that Marina and Boris can watch the girls. By the way, you haven't mentioned Whitney."

"I figured I'd leave the choice up to her. Hopefully someone as wonderful as you is going to come into her life and carry her off to his castle."

Paul stood. "Let's take a walk. It's stopped raining. Look. The sun's peeking through."

She ran to the closet for her Irish knit and joined him in the hall, entwining her fingers with his. She raised his hand to her lips, kissed it, and, looking into his eyes, whispered, "I love you, Paul Davidoff. I will love you until the day I die. Beyond that if it's possible. No matter how I hold back and delay, please don't ever doubt how much I love you. I'm truly scared, unsure, but not of you. Of me. I keep thinking I'm dreaming and I'm going to wake up to the biggest disappointment possible. Please, give me a little time to get accustomed to—"

Paul squeezed her hand and finished her thought, "...being with a man who would die for you but would much rather live with you. I'll take the pressure off, Hon. You never have to marry me if you don't want to. We can live together, and Monika will just have to understand. We'll explain everything to her."

Maddie kissed his cheek.

He added, "I'm afraid someone's going to come along and steal you away from me if I don't have that vow holding you to me. I know how much that promise means to you by how long you stuck it out with David."

Maddie countered, "I'll try very hard not to think about your love scenes and all those beautiful actresses around you. Do you have any idea how that thought feels to this insecure person?"

They started down the steps together and Paul said, "How would you feel about previewing my scripts?"

Maddie wondered if she'd heard right. "Previewing your scripts?"

"Sure. If you think it's too torrid, I'll demand a rewrite."

"Paul, please don't be silly!"

He paused at the bottom step and turned her towards him. "Are you beginning to get any idea of how very serious I am about you and me? I'd even let you dictate those scenes."

Maddie looked deeply into his eyes and said, "I was a fool to even mention it. Forget I ever brought it up. You have more women in love with you than I can think about, and it just plain scares me. I beg you to give me time to gain some self-confidence and to heal. Please?"

He put his arm around her as they headed towards the terrace. "Time you want? Time you've got—as long as all that time is spent with me."

Marina, Boris, and Monika sat at the kitchen table devouring butter pecan ice cream from a half-gallon container. Marina commented that it seemed too quiet upstairs.

Monika speculated, "You don't think they're...you know...," looking ingenuously at the housekeeper.

Marina coughed, sputtering, "Don't finish that sentence."

"God heavens, Marina. I know all about what a man and woman do together."

Boris blushed and laughed at the stricken look on his wife's face. "It's the end of the twentieth century, Marina. Kids know everything about everything."

"They call it health class at school. We know it's just because they're too chicken to tell the parents they're teaching us about sex. Have I ever asked you about anything, Marina?"

She shook her head, glancing quickly at Boris, mortified that a child of twelve would mention things out loud she, as an adult, was loathe to say.

"Don't you think if I didn't already know I would have asked you by now?"

Marina answered helplessly, "I thought you might have asked your father instead of me."

Monika laughed. "I've known for ages, long before that class started this year! When I was ten I saw one of Dad's movies that I wasn't supposed to see before I was seventeen."

Her hand covering her pounding heart, Marina demanded, "Where in Heaven's name did you see such a film! Who would show it to you?"

"I showed it to myself. I found it on the ledge in the screening room and put it into the VCR on my TV upstairs. I can't remember the name of it but there's a scene where the girl starts to take off her clothes and then they're in bed. I couldn't figure out what all the gasping and moaning was about. I thought when you go to bed you go to sleep...until then."

Marina put her spoon down and looked pleadingly at Boris to interrupt but he was too fascinated to catch Marina's signal.

"Well, I went to the gym teacher. She's the only nice, young teacher at that school, and I asked her what was going on in the scene. She told me all about it."

Marina whispered, "When you were...ten?!"

"What else could she do but tell me the truth. It was my own father who had made me curious. She first told me to ask him but then thought better of it. He would have just about died if I'd asked him that!"

Boris laughed heartily and got up to put the half-full ice cream container back into the freezer. Movement outside attracted his attention and he walked to the window to check, turned, took Monika by the hand and asked Marina to follow them.

Once they were on the patio, the cliff below was entirely visible, and so were Maddie and Paul, standing together, holding hands on the point where he'd spent so many hours alone.

Monika ran to the far edge of the patio and stared as if to confirm what she saw. She turned to Boris and Marina and ran back to them, "He's never taken me there! I always thought it was where he felt closest to Mom and he didn't want to share it. Do you think Maddie will be my new mom?"

Marina hugged Monika to her. "Have patience, little one. Some things cannot and will not be rushed but they are well worth waiting for."

Monika returned Marina's hug and bestowed one on Boris. "Come on, you two. There's at least another dish of ice cream for each of us left in that carton."

"Shouldn't we leave some for Maddie and your father?" Marina asked, remembering there was no more in the freezer.

"What do they need sweets for? They've got each other and plenty better things to do than sit and eat ice cream...unless, of course, they want to lick it off each other's—"

Marina gasped.

"Well, he did that in that movie!"

Marina clutched Boris's hand, whispering, "What happened to our little Monika? What kind of movies has he been making, licking ice cream off a woman's body.

"Off her body?" Monika exclaimed, hearing every word. "Ugh, how gross! You're so silly, Marina! They were at a fair and she was eating an ice cream cone. Some got on her chin and he licked it off, then they kissed!"

Marina looked in desperation at Boris. "Did I say body? I meant face. Sometimes my English doesn't come out right."

"I didn't think you meant body!" Monika declared. "The chin was bad enough! They must have paid him a whole lot to do that scene. I don't think I could force myself to lick someone else's chin. Could you do that Boris?"

He shrugged, looking more negative than positive for Monika. Changing the subject, he stated, "Marina and I will drive you back to school tomorrow and then we go off on our trip to Lake Tahoe. Your Dad and Maddie are planning to leave before us. I've got to make sure everything around the property is set for all of us to leave. I'll head to our house after that. I need my eight hour beauty sleep."

Monika giggled at the word beauty and turned away to look at the cliff.

Boris leaned close to Marina and whispered, "When you're through up here, I'll be waiting in the bedroom, in bed. Don't forget to bring the ice cream!"

ISBN 0-9664483-5-9

5 1 1 0 0 >